ANNA J SKYE

Out of the
RED

spanked for profit & pleasure

ANNA J SKYE

Out of the
RED

spanked for profit & pleasure

MEREO
Cirencester

Mereo Books

1A The Wool Market Dyer Street Cirencester Gloucestershire GL7 2PR
An imprint of Memoirs Publishing www.mereobooks.com

Out of the Red: 978-1-86151-316-8

First published in Great Britain in 2015
by Mereo Books, an imprint of Memoirs Publishing

The address for Memoirs Publishing Group Limited can be found at
www.memoirspublishing.com

The Memoirs Publishing Group Ltd Reg. No. 7834348

The Memoirs Publishing Group supports both The Forest Stewardship Council® (FSC®) and
the PEFC® leading international forest-certification organisations. Our books carrying both the
FSC label and the PEFC® and are printed on FSC®-certified paper. FSC® is the only
forest-certification scheme supported by the leading environmental organisations including
Greenpeace. Our paper procurement policy can be found at
www.memoirspublishing.com/environment

Typeset in 10/16pt Bembo
by Wiltshire Associates Publisher Services Ltd. Printed and bound in Great Britain by
Printondemand-Worldwide, Peterborough PE2 6XD

CONTENTS

Acknowledgements

Dedication

Prologue

Acknowledgements

I am very grateful to Robin, Blue, Jeremy, Mr Spanker-at-Heathrow and other spankers for allowing their secret spanking stories to come to print, and for easing me gently (and sometimes not so gently) into the spanking scene during my debut year.

I would also like to thank all the guys from the dating sites who liked my profile enough to spend their time with me. You brought me back to normality.

I am indebted to Peter Joshua, who gave me helpful editorial advice and made me realise my rules on commas might not be quite what the rest of the reading public expect.

I am sincerely grateful to Chris Newton from Memoirs Publishing for his sense of humour, patience and editorial expertise in producing this book.

Most names and locations referred to have been changed to protect the privacy of individuals.

Dedicated to all the brave spankers and spankees out there who have dared to follow their fetish dreams. Have fun!

Prologue

Room 132, he had said. Go past reception and turn right down the corridor. I arrived at the door and took a minute to compose myself before knocking.

The door opened and a very tall, well-dressed man in his early sixties stood back, smiling and holding the door open for me.

'I'm hoping it's you,' he said.

'And I'm hoping it's you,' I said, smiling back.

I walked into the room, feeling a growing sense of excitement. How hard would the spanking be this time? When would we start? How naked would I be? What position would he put me in? What implements would he use?

I sat on the bed, he on the chair opposite me. After some small chit-chat, he suddenly said 'I'm going to spank you now - come here,' and he beckoned to me. 'You were 45 minutes late last time and I never punished you for it. Stand there.' He pointed to the floor just by his left leg.

I walked over to him and he pulled me over his knee and started caressing my bottom over my yellow dress. He gave me a few initial firm slaps to warm up my bottom and his hand. Then he pulled up my dress, then my petticoat, and then he started feeling my buttocks over my yellow knickers. He pulled down my knickers to my knees, paused a moment to look at my reddening bottom, as if surveying his handiwork, and started spanking me again, harder this time.

It was an engineered excuse to discipline me; I had been late the previous time. Of course in most social circles an apology would have been accepted. When you're a spankee, however, it doesn't quite work like that.

After about five minutes' continuous spanking he suddenly stopped. 'Right,' he said. 'Shall we go and have a drink, or would you like something to eat?'

I found this interaction rather strange, being as yet unaccustomed to the spankee's life. Some of the spankers would even ask me mid-spanking, 'How are you, by the way?' They would come out of spanker-spankee mode for a few minutes, and then just as suddenly tell me, 'You're a naughty girl, and you deserve a good thrashing,' and then their 'normal' personality would be gone, to be replaced by the not-so-nice, dominant spanker personality.

I didn't expect guys to be nice to me, of course. I assumed they would treat me like a prostitute and look down on me, bully me or patronise me. In fact, apart from one man, the first as it happens, all the 30 or so spankers I've met so far have been friendly, polite and gentlemanly. Quite a few have wanted to date me. I have been totally naked with some, bent over chairs and beds, red bottom raised, my lips on display, but I've had nothing but humour, respect, friendship, and gratitude for having such a nice, spankable bottom. Some have admired me for daring to enter the world of spanking so late; I was 57.

We went down into the lounge at Heathrow Airport, where we had arranged to meet as a midway point between our two homes. As I sat down, I could feel, with some satisfaction, that my bottom was smarting slightly. We chatted like old friends about our families, work and our previous spanking experiences.

I looked around the lounge at other customers, wondering if they could tell we were a spankee and her client. I was wearing a knee-length yellow summer dress, under a coat; not a bra and thong with a label saying 'Spank me,' but I still felt the thrill of slight guilt and deception.

After one gin and tonic for myself and a half of lager for him, which I paid for, to his great surprise (he told me most spankees expect their spankers to pay for all expenses), he suggested continuing the session.

As soon as we were in the room again, he pushed me over the bed, raised my dress, pulled my knickers down again, and standing beside the bed, spanked me hard for about 10 minutes. Then he sat down on the chair and ordered me to change into my short silk nightie and place myself on all fours on the bed. Then he got up and came round the bed and stood beside me. He caressed me between my legs for a few minutes under the nightie. Then he pulled the nightie up to expose my bottom and asked me if I was OK.

'Sure,' I answered, waiting expectantly for the oncoming punishment. With that, he took off his belt and proceeded to thrash me about 20 times across my bare buttocks.

CHAPTER ONE

Secure Beginnings

I was brought up, by well-off, white upper-middle-class parents, to be a nice young lady. For the first eighteen years of my life, I lived in a fairly large four-bedroomed detached house with a big, sloping garden, surrounded by other large (some very large) houses with even bigger gardens, at the top of a quiet hill on the edge of a quiet country town. I was educated from the age of seven to eighteen in a 'High School for Girls' grammar school. I was obedient and repressed and I wanted above all to be accepted by friends, and to do well in school and sports. I didn't want to be captain at anything, or be put in any position of responsibility. I was once made form vice-captain and, although secretly proud, I was constantly fearful of having to speak in front of the class or tell any of my classmates what to do. Luckily I never had to.

I don't remember ever feeling worried that I wouldn't make the grade in school, either on a popularity front or on an academic level. I was good enough at all subjects to pass the exams if I worked hard. I wasn't a brilliant pupil, just a fairly intelligent, hard-working pupil who wanted to pass everything, be accepted, not stand out but be quietly admired by people. I was fairly quiet in class. It took some courage to put up my hand to ask or answer questions. I wanted to be successful at everything I did.

When I was four I came back from kindergarten with a small marked test. The teacher had written on it 'Very Good'.

'Well done!' my mother said in encouragement, perplexed at my scowling face.

'I don't want 'Very Good' – I want 'Excellent',' I proclaimed. 'Excellent' was the top mark.

School in general though was a relatively easy experience for me. Because I had been there from the age of seven I already had my established circle of five friends, and the all-important best friend, Helen. At the age of eleven we were joined by many other girls from other primary schools who had passed the eleven-plus exam and managed free places to our school. With the arrogance of youth, it never occurred to me to try and make friends with them. I never thought about it from their point of view, nor did the teachers point this out to us. It must have been very scary at the age of eleven to join a posh, rather grand-looking 'big school', leaving all your friends in the primary school behind.

However, one of them, Cara, did become the sixth member of our group within a few weeks. Not because we thought it would be kind of us – she just seemed to fit in well, and made the third set of 'best friends'. She was intelligent, funny, friendly, sporty and very soon became my second best friend. After a year or two we even decided to promote each other to best friend, as I had started to have less and less in common with my other best friend. I even had the audacity and the dreadful unkindness to go and tell my original best friend that I'd decided to take Cara in her place. I shudder to think of that today. How cruel and hurtful. And Helen had no choice but to remain in our group, even after that happened. You can't just join another group of girls. They would almost certainly shun you. And about this time, I had another offer of a best friend from a girl outside the group.

In the end I spent time outside school and summers with all three of them, as well as two of the other girls in the group. I thought this was normal. People often liked me and wanted to be in my company. Little did I know that sometimes friends are hard to find, and you can be left to your own devices for days or even weeks at a time. My world back then was a very safe middle-class life. I never heard my parents argue (apart from the odd slight disagreement) and it didn't enter my head that my life at the top of the hill would ever need to end. Helen's parents divorced when she was about thirteen. We didn't really talk about it, as it was all rather taboo back then. But that was her, not me. That wouldn't happen to me.

My mother was a pretty, petite, cheerful, sociable, gregarious, God-fearing lady who doted on her husband and three daughters. She believed a wife should obey her husband, that he was the head of the household and his opinion should be respected, even when she disagreed with him. She even arranged the milk bottles in the fridge according to the motto 'Take the bottles from the right, because George is always right', which she would say to us if we tried taking unopened milk bottles from the middle or left of the line of bottles. I found this incredible, I have to say, since I didn't agree at all with the principle that my father was always correct.

Family life was all both my parents had ever wanted. Their

system worked. Mum did the cooking, cleaning, washing and ironing and looked after the needs of three growing girls. Dad went out to work in his office about a mile away, where he was director of his own building contracting firm. He worked 48 weeks of the year, from 9-5 pm Monday to Friday and from 9 am to 1 pm on Saturdays. He would walk back home most lunchtimes, and Mum would have prepared a lunch for him. He would then walk back to the office. On Saturday afternoons, when Mum took us riding, Dad would play tennis at the local tennis club.

On Sundays, we were made to go to church. I hated going to church. It was all a waste of time in my opinion, even as a fairly young girl. I found people too sycophantic towards the pompous (in my view) vicar, and I would wonder exactly who all the prayers and hymns were aimed at. That is still my view today. I was brought up a Protestant Christian to believe in God, Jesus Christ, the nativity story and the crucifixion, although I found it all a bit far-fetched and unlikely. How did Mary come to be pregnant if she was a virgin? Didn't Joseph mind? Why was Mary a virgin if she was married? Didn't that annul the marriage? If God were that powerful, why didn't he just manifest himself? Why was it God's will to let children die? Assuming he was a good god, and wouldn't have wanted that to happen, the fact that he didn't do anything to stop it must have meant that he had no power to stop it. So what was ever the point of praying to him, I wondered? How did we know he was male? Wasn't it all a story invented by men years ago to subjugate the local population, especially the women?

On Sunday afternoons, if I wasn't doing homework, we would be made to go on a walk in the area near our home. I never enjoyed these walks, and to this day still don't enjoy going on long walks.

Which is a shame, because on the dating sites which I have tried for a couple of years now many people say walking is one of their main interests.

My parents never made any reference to what they hoped would be our futures, apart from my mother sometimes saying she hoped she would have many grandchildren. I took it as read that I would provide her with some of those grandchildren. I grew up with the same simple ambition - to get married and be a stay-at-home mum of two children. That was it. I never wanted to go out to work or have a career. Not for one single day. And that seemingly simple goal has never changed, throughout my life.

CHAPTER TWO

Sexual awakening

Not that everything was rosy and straightforward during my educational years. My older sister, Grace, born two and a half years before me, was quite happy having her parents' adoring attention – and then I came along. I was a lovely baby, with ash-blond hair and grey-blue eyes. It started a life-long difficult relationship between my sister and me which continues to this day. As I grew up I just seemed to be better than her at everything, which was admittedly unfair and nobody's fault. I was much prettier – being blonde probably helped. I had more friends at school. I was better at sports and music. I got better grades. I had a tall, dark, good-looking boyfriend for three years, from the age of fifteen. In her first eighteen years, she had only one boyfriend, who lasted two weeks.

As the oldest of three, Grace thought she had the right to boss people around and let them know her opinion about everything they said, did, wore, thought and stood for. It might well be a symptom of being the oldest. Second children are often more competitive, since they have to compete with the older child for their parents' attention. Grace definitely bullied me with words, and I assume much of it was out of jealousy. She would make some cutting remark about what I looked like, or my clothes, or what I said. I would always try and fight back, but it did affect me. When we were in the same room, I felt she was watching and judging me, ready with some damning verdict of my behaviour.

Nowadays we've reached a truce. I, along with the rest of our family, often tease her for overly 'helpful' comments, and she is able to laugh at herself and her wish to give often unsolicited advice, which she knows now people take with a pinch of salt.

I was also being bullied by a girl who lived down the road from us. Amanda was only a year older, but she constantly put me down as we played together. Many times I would march home to Mum declaring that I would never speak to Amanda again. Mum would say wisely 'oh right,' knowing full well that in a few days Amanda would come knocking on the door, asking to play again. Now, years later, Amanda is still trying to remain friends, and I am doing my utmost to hint that I will no longer put up with her.

She came once for a visit to my home, about fifteen years ago, and I drove to the station to pick her up. I pulled into my drive, with Amanda in the passenger seat, parking in my normal spot next to the wall. Amanda opened the passenger door and by mistake banged it against the wall with enough force to damage the paint. I unwittingly took a sharp breath in, and before I could stop myself said 'ooh, careful'. She was furious. 'You'll never make a good mother,' she snarled. And to my utter amazement, she grabbed the door and banged it against the wall again, with the same amount of force. I guess she hadn't liked the criticism. Anyone else in the world might have apologised and offered to pay for the damage. I chose not to say anything, as I was still tied down by the fact that she could just turn up at the family home at any moment. But I didn't forget it.

The final straw came about two years ago. She had been trying to come and stay for about three years. I had been 'busy', but she wore me down by saying 'When are you available this year?' and I gave in. I suggested a date, but said I didn't have much money so couldn't afford to do much. She said she would pay for everything.

She came up and we drove to the nearest birds of prey centre, a common interest of ours. At the entrance she decided to go to the ladies', so to save time, since we wanted to see the next public display of the birds of prey and time was getting on, I decided to go in and get two tickets, thinking that she would probably insist on paying me back. I was going to let her pay me back, but wouldn't have minded if she hadn't offered.

I came back out with the two tickets and met her coming back from the ladies. 'I got the tickets to save time,' I said in explanation, when I saw her questioning face.

She was enraged. 'You're such a silly girl!' she spat. 'I told you I was going to pay for everything.' That was it, as far as I was concerned. That was about three years ago. She's rung up a few times to ask when I'm available in the year, but I'm not having any of it. When she turns up at our family home for the occasional social visit I am polite, but not enthusiastic. Basically, life's too short. I'm 59 now. I could be diagnosed with a terminal illness next week and have only months to live. *Carpe diem.*

And then there was my father. He didn't possess my mother's sunny disposition. He was very quiet, reserved and conservative – a quintessentially upper class, English gentleman - and although he tried hard to be a good father, he didn't really know how to treat three girls. If we ever found ourselves alone in the same room as him, we would strike up an awkward conversation, in which he wouldn't listen to our point of view. After a short while, one or other of us would make up some excuse and leave the room. On the rare occasions when I decided to tell him about something that had just happened to me, he would feel he had to give advice about it, so I tended to avoid telling him anything, for fear of getting his seeming disapproval and more advice. I told him once that I didn't do very well in a Geography test, and he just said 'You probably didn't listen'. I was crushed. Later I realised he was trying to tell me I was intelligent enough to have done better in the test, if only I had tried. He was a man of extremely high integrity, honest to the letter. We knew that if he praised us, he meant every word. He didn't agree with giving children false praise – or letting them win at games like 'snakes and ladders' if the dice dictated otherwise, unlike Mum who would conveniently forget to go up the ladders sometimes, especially when we were very young, or ill.

Bullying or disapproval can have an unforeseen and paradoxical effect on the person being bullied. I found that I wanted to have Dad's approval more than Mum's. Mum's was freely given. Dad's was hard to come by, so it was all the more treasured when it was bestowed. Likewise, I secretly cherished Grace's very rare compliments, even though my younger sister was far more forgiving, and more amenable to my ideas and activities. It left me with a character trait that I try and fight - too often trying to please all the people all the time.

Dad never hit us, was never drunk, was always home by supper time, and always generously provided for us. He was also a talented musician and sportsman, but remained very understated. He played club-level tennis, county-level badminton and could play almost any tune (with both hands) on the piano by ear – he couldn't read a single note of music.

Mum used to tell us that he was very proud of us, and loved us dearly, knowing that it would have been far too embarrassing for him to say so himself. He simply hadn't been brought up to show his feelings, or be physically demonstrative. We loved him back in our own way, knowing he utterly adored our mother, and realising he was doing the very best he could for her and us. When we said goodnight, it was an awkward peck on both cheeks. He almost never lost his temper, and never swore in front of us. I remember him raising his voice to me about three times in my whole life. But unfortunately, instead of being alarmed by it, because of its rarity, I was actually annoyed by it. As a rather self-righteous teenager I found I didn't take him seriously as a parent. He was too distant, socially awkward and patronising towards me for me to want to accept discipline from him.

Of course I never let these feelings be known, and complied with his and my mother's discipline and rules if they felt the need to enforce them on me, which was very rare. Normally if any of us girls said anything approaching rudeness or impertinence, Mum and Dad would only have to say a quiet 'Steady!' and we would know we had gone too far.

When Grace was six and I was four, she decided it would be a good idea to start hitting me with a metal clothes hanger, so I picked up one and started hitting her back. Mum heard the commotion, marched into the bedroom and put Grace over her knee for a spanking. I had to watch, knowing that the same fate awaited me. And it duly came, while I protested my innocence. I was outraged at the miscarriage of justice. It was self-defence!

That was the only spanking I received from either of my parents. When I was about eight Mum slapped my hand for being cheeky, and another time she gave me one slap on the bottom for the same reason. At school there was no corporal punishment whatsoever, so physical discipline really played no part in my young life.

★ ★ ★

Looking back now, I wish it had been a bit more free and easy at home. I wish my parents had been able to discuss things more openly with us, especially sex. Once, when I was eleven, I had a strange sickness that would mean I would take to my bed for days. I only felt OK if I was prostrate. My mother arranged a doctor's appointment for me, and for some reason I went alone to it. The doctor did a test and asked for a urine sample. When the results came through a few minutes later, he declared 'Well you're not pregnant, anyway!'

I was secretly annoyed that my mother hadn't told me she had arranged a pregnancy test for me. I thought she should have let me in on the reason I was going to the doctor's. I felt it was secretive and going behind my back not to tell me. She was obviously too embarrassed to tell me why and how I might have got pregnant. Yes, it was sensible to have the test, but it was the first time I was aware of her deceiving me. I never told her I knew it was a pregnancy test. She must have found out the results straight from the doctor, who was probably not supposed to have told me what the test was for.

Sex remained a taboo subject in our house. When I was twelve, Mum gave us all a little leaflet called 'Where do babies come from?' I was in my bedroom when she knocked on the door. She looked extremely embarrassed as she handed me the leaflet. 'You might like to read this,' she said quietly, and left quickly. I started reading the very short leaflet, and was disgusted at what I found out. It said a man and a woman have to lie very close to each other, and often they are completely naked. I remember thinking 'Well I'm never going to do that with a man'.

Mum knocked on the door about 20 minutes later. 'Was that all right?' she asked tentatively.

'Yes thanks. I knew it all anyway,' I lied.

I bet she didn't believe me for a moment, but the whole idea of sex was just so awkward in our family that I wanted to drop the subject.

Another time, I was reading the Bible for a school essay when I came across the word 'circumcision'. I opened my bedroom door and went to the top of the banisters. I could hear Mum moving around in the kitchen downstairs.

'Mum' I yelled, 'what does 'circumcision' mean?'

There was a silence, and then I heard Mum walking quickly through the hall and up the stairs towards me. She ushered me into my bedroom and, looking very embarrassed, proceeded to describe a penis to me, showing me how the foreskin is peeled back and snipped for health reasons. It made me feel rather stupid for not knowing, yelling it all over the house and causing her such embarrassment. But why should I feel embarrassed for asking a normal question about a man's anatomy?

My own ventures into sexual discovery started with a rope.

Amanda and I would play in another neighbour's garden, where there was a thick rope tied to a tree, originally for swinging on. We discovered the most delicious feeling would spread from our groins if we climbed the rope and hung on for a few minutes, clenching it with our upper thighs. We called it the 'botty feeling', never having heard of an orgasm at the age of 11. We never equated it to sex or men.

When I was sixteen, I had been out with my boyfriend, Alan, in his car. He drove me back to the house and parked on the drive, where we proceeded to have a snog in the passenger seat. His hands went very quickly down to lift up my blouse and find my breasts. We had split up for six months because I hadn't wanted sex, but he had missed me despite the lack of sex, and asked to get back together. He said he wanted to marry me one day, and that perhaps we could experiment gradually with sex, without having penetration, since I was only sixteen. I agreed to this. So that night in the car, breasts were the only thing on the agenda.

After a few minutes, I suddenly became aware that my bare tummy was being lit up by a strange light coming from outside the car. I looked up to see my mother leaning out through the dining room window and shining a torch through the car window in order to see the antics of her wayward middle daughter.

I gasped. Alan was horrified and immediately withdrew his hand. I rearranged my clothes, got out of the car and prepared to face my mother's reprimand. As soon as I was inside the door she said 'I suppose you've been there for 30 minutes'. I replied that it was a few minutes. That's all that was said, and we went to bed in stony, awkward silence. I didn't look at her for three days.

Eventually she brought it up in a very vague and roundabout

way, though it was soon 'forgotten' in that life resumed as before. But I didn't want to ever talk about that side of my life to her. My generation had such different attitudes from hers. This was the early 1970s. The Beatles and free love had changed society forever, and the older post-war generation of parents were finding it hard to keep up and accept it. It seemed so unfair. She should have been glad that I wasn't gay (since life is harder for gay people, I believe), that I had a very nice boyfriend, and that I was doing what normal teenagers do, rather than being a recluse, with no confidence with the opposite sex. We could have laughed about it and had some mother-daughter bonding time. Instead, she made me feel guilty and slutty for a perfectly normal, healthy activity that wasn't harming anyone.

As a Christian, she believed sex should only take place within a loving marriage. She wanted to stop me becoming a slut, or getting pregnant too early. Understandable, but executed in the wrong way, in my opinion. Most teenagers are going to have sex. Their parents might as well embrace it, let them get on with it, and make sure they take precautions. To treat it as a disgusting, dirty activity is to drive it into secrecy.

And that's exactly what happened. I never told her anything about what Alan and I got up to. We had penetrative sex two weeks before my seventeenth birthday, as I didn't want to be 'sixteen and never been fucked'.

It was at a party of a friend of Alan's. We sneaked upstairs and used his bedroom without asking, specifically to lose our virginities together. I was amazed at the size of an erect penis, never having seen one before, and wondered how on earth all that was going to get inside me. It took several attempts and was quite painful, and I left a lot of blood all over the sheets. We didn't clear it up, own up or apologize. About 40 years later, I happened to meet the same guy at a mutual friend's dinner party, and was able to apologize for my wayward behaviour. He was generous enough to accept my apology, and even chuckled at the memory.

Sometimes we used condoms and sometimes we didn't, which was crazy and irresponsible, but I never became pregnant by him.

I wish there had been more male figures in my life. I was extremely shy of men and didn't know how to talk to them, or behave with them. I had only sisters at home, with a distant and undemonstrative father, only girls as friends and neighbours and there were only girls at school. I grew up in a female world which didn't prepare me for men's sometimes unthinking, focused, ambitious, uncompromising attitudes. Nowadays, I love and like many men. I understand where they are coming from, and I have many men friends. They are often much more straightforward than women, don't hold grudges, and are therefore much easier to work with. But if you are not used to their ways, it can be hard at first to adapt to them.

So despite my young world being a bit staid and repressed, all in all it was a wonderful, privileged, innocent childhood. I came through with flying colours, head held high, with realistic expectations that life would continue on its designated path of finding happiness in the shape of marriage and two children.

But sometimes, often in fact, we take things for granted. I was about to be shocked at what life would throw at me.

CHAPTER THREE

Fun and games with men

After 'O' levels (GCSE equivalent) and 'A' levels, I didn't know what I wanted to do. I had split up with my boyfriend of three years by then. He was a lovely chap, but unfortunately familiarity breeds contempt, and he had just started to irritate me to the point where I didn't want to see him any more. He was heartbroken when I told him, but within three years he was married to someone else.

Years later I wondered if I had made the right decision, and just out of curiosity I got back in touch with him. We met up and had a brief affair, but very soon he began to annoy me again, so yup, at the tender age of eighteen I had made the right decision.

The only real agenda for me was to meet someone else and get married. That was basically the only thing I was interested in. I didn't want to go to university; I was sick of academic life and exams.

I decided to take a six-month secretarial course at the local college. Not that I wanted to be a secretary, but I thought it might be a useful back-up when I had my children and needed a part-time job. It consisted of shorthand and touch-typing. After the novelty of shorthand had worn off within the first week or so, I grew to hate it. The only way to learn shorthand on that course was to practise, practise, practise the same few paragraphs time and again, until you knew the symbols inside out. It was utterly, mind-bogglingly boring, and I became quite depressed during the six months, wondering how I was going to get through another day. It was a sharp contrast to having to use my brain for 'A' levels.

It never occurred to me to give it up. It wasn't in my mind-set to abandon anything I had started, even if I thought it wasn't right for me. I had to see it through. I had to do my best. I had to pass the exams. I had to be successful.

I liked the typing. I remember the teacher playing some musical notes to which we would have to strike certain keys with certain fingers. 'L, L, L' – change of note – 'S, S, S' – making us use the ring fingers on either hand. I became quite proficient at it, I thought. I passed Stage I. Then we all went onto Stage II, but only certain people were allowed to take the exam – I was one.

Finally the day of the results came through. 'You've all passed except Anna Skye,' announced the teacher to the whole class, with astonishing insensitivity. I was so embarrassed, and so annoyed at her. That was probably the first public failure of my life. Everyone else was better than me. And everyone knew it. Or so it seemed to me, as soon as I heard the 'awful' news. I had forgotten that most people in the class had not been put forward to take the exam in the first place.

I somehow managed to move on from this 'dreadful' setback, and went on to take and pass Stages II and III of RSA Typing. I will always be glad I learnt to touch-type. I ended up being able to type at 55 words a minute, a decidedly acceptable speed. I've used it for many different situations and jobs, all my life. If you can't type fast nowadays, you often risk annoying people, rightly or wrongly, for example on chat lines like Skype, or emails.

During the six months of the course, my father made one of his rare appearances in my bedroom. He asked me gently if I had considered going to university the following year. He knew I was struggling with the course. To begin with I said no, as I didn't see the point. I was thinking privately that I would soon be meeting the man who would become my husband. He would have a good job, and I would have children and stay at home. But ring-proffering, solvent gentlemen weren't exactly queueing at the front door, flowers in hand. So I agreed, thinking it would delay the decision of what to do as a career, if my knight-in-shining armour hadn't had the good character to show himself by then.

I applied to a university to do French and Italian. It was close to my family home, and had good sports facilities. My 'A' levels had been French, German and Latin, with two B grades and a C, fairly average today, but a satisfactory standard back then. I got an interview and was accepted straight away. Most of the candidates had yet to take their 'A' levels.

The secretarial course ended in March 1974, and I was going to university the following October. What should I do until then? I needed some stimulation. I know, I thought – I'll go and work on a kibbutz in Israel!

I remember asking my father if I could have the £86 airfare. With typical generosity, he agreed straight away, and everything was fixed in two months. I asked the organizing agency to station me in a kibbutz near a national border, for the buzz, and that's precisely where I ended up - five hundred yards from the Lebanese border in northern Israel. This would be dangerous and exciting, and to my eighteen-year-old mind just what I needed after six months of shorthand drudgery.

On the day I was to travel, much to my annoyance, my mother accompanied me on the train to the airport in London. I felt that this was my new adventure and wanted to be alone from the beginning. I would soon have to make my way in a strange country for goodness sake, so I thought I could manage a train journey to London. She left me at last to go through security - alone at last, probably for the first time in my life, apart from attending three university interviews by myself.

When I started going through security, a security man stopped me and asked me to open my case. He started rifling through my things and came across my wellingtons. He looked inside them, saw that they were full of tampons, lifted them to chest height above the table, and turned both upside down. Out fell all the tampons all over the table, some falling on the floor.

I went crimson. He just said 'Don't get embarrassed, love,' which of course made it worse. He helped me put them all back, and waved me on. I made a mental note: when someone gets embarrassed in front of you, don't tell them not to be embarrassed. It draws attention to it.

★ ★ ★

The five months in Kibbutz Shav Lod in the Golan Heights, so close to war-torn Lebanon, was a slight culture shock to a naive, inexperienced English girl, but human beings are nothing if not adaptable. I picked pears for six weeks, six days a week, six hours a day. I learned to use a crane that would crank me up to 20 feet or so to get to the highest pears. I worked in the dining room, doing the washing up alone for 80 people at a time; in the laundry, where I learned to fold clothes; in the gardens, where I learned to grow a lawn, using grass seedlings, and dig a hole with a pickaxe when it was 110 degrees Fahrenheit; and in an apple factory for three weeks, getting up at 4 am. We would work until 8 am, when we would stop for breakfast in the huge communal dining room, and go back to work until 11 am. Then we were free for the day.

Most of us chose to go back to sleep for a few hours, and then the fun started. A 25-metre swimming pool was available for everyone to use, and most afternoons the volunteers would spend hours swimming, diving, flirting and sunbathing. On my kibbutz there were about 30 volunteers, mostly of college age, from all round the world. We were sharing very basic concrete accommodation, where boys and girls were in the same room, and we got to know each other very quickly. In the evenings, we would walk through the kibbutz in groups and have dinner together in the communal dining room. After dinner they would clear the tables, and once a week Israeli dancing would be taught, or a film would be shown on a huge makeshift screen.

After that, the water fights would start. We would end up completely drenched, and helpless with laughter. It was the first time I had interacted with men on a regular basis, and I had them round me throughout the day. They seemed to like me. I was really quite cute then; five foot three, eight stone, blond hair naturally bleached by the Israeli sun. I was athletic, and becoming increasingly flirtatious.

After we all went our separate ways, I kept in touch with several of them for a year or so. Admittedly I had had a boyfriend for three years, but that was just one guy, and I had got used to him. I never got used to being out with his friends in a group. Israel afforded me the first opportunity to live, play and work with the alien male species, not as one of their girlfriends but as an equal. And I loved it.

There was a good-looking volunteer there called Jim. I discovered he was British and about to go to the same university as myself in the autumn. My husband-finding antennae shot up, and I immediately went on flirt-alert. Sadly, it was obvious that he wasn't interested, so I quickly gave up.

There was also a shortish guy called Mark from Belfast there. I didn't really have that much interest in him as a potential boyfriend, but I enjoyed flirting with him in the swimming pool. Gradually though I started finding him attractive, and our flirting became more serious. Nothing happened in Israel, but it was obvious that something could or would do in the future, if we chose.

We took each other's home addresses. Email was unknown back then, and we didn't possess mobiles. How much easier dating is nowadays with these technical advances.

After four months at my northern kibbutz, I decided to go travelling by myself. It was easy back then, as soldiers regularly hitch-hiked everywhere. I would see a group of soldiers, or just one by himself, on the side of the road, pointing to the road (the sign for hitching), and stand beside them. Good god, I wouldn't dream of doing that now. What was I thinking? But nothing ever serious happened to me while hitching.

I even got into Palestinians' cars by myself, if there were no soldiers around. One Palestinian guy indicated what he wanted to do to me by putting his finger through a circle made from his first finger and thumb on his other hand and thrusting it in and out. I got the picture, and declined politely. He accepted this, and we carried on with our journey.

Another encounter, with a Palestinian hotel manager in Jerusalem, didn't turn out quite as I had planned. He started showing me the room and then suddenly he came over to me and stuck his hand down the front of my trousers. I moved back immediately and he stopped, but it was a wake-up call. Arabs see women differently, especially European women travelling by themselves. I couldn't blame him for his actions. It was just a cultural difference. But I didn't take the room.

When you travel by yourself, you tend to meet more people more easily. I teamed up with quite a few European men who were also travelling alone round Israel. It made me feel safer being seen with a white man. Israeli lorry drivers also gave me a few lifts. They were charming and fun, and never tried anything, just grateful for the company.

I spent one night trying to sleep with my head jammed up against the windscreen of a moving lorry and my body on the passenger seat. Needless to say, I hardly slept. But the lorry driver kept on driving through the night, and never touched me.

I talked to quite a few of the Israelis on my kibbutz about the political situation. None of them could see a solution to the area's problem, and most hated the Palestinians. I saw many Palestinians on my travels and most seem to have the poorer jobs such as sheep herders, manual labourers or waiters in run-down cafés or hotels. But I didn't get embroiled in political discussions. I was nineteen, out to find a husband and increasingly to have fun, before having to knuckle down and study again.

★ ★ ★

I went to university at the age of nineteen, in 1974. It was nothing like doing 'A' levels. I had very few lectures a week, and not much homework. The sports were all free and on my doorstep, so I spent many hours in the sports hall, trying as many sports as possible. I was even nominated as Sportswoman of the Year. Back then the university was only ten years old, and was very much a technical institution, attracting largely young men. Only about 10% of the students were women, so I was in with a good chance of finding a man, I thought.

I saw Jim in the corridors sometimes, but he just said hello and obviously didn't want to chat. I was still in touch with Mark from Belfast, whom I had met on the kibbutz. We were writing roughly one letter a week to each other by this time. He had started to hint at coming over to see me, and I was hinting back at him along the same lines.

I was already into my second term by the time he eventually came over. Our letters had become more and more explicit about the idea of meeting up and seeing what transpired. I had decided I was in love with him. We had had great fun in Israel together, so why not in normal life?

Beware the holiday romances that turn sour as soon as normal life resumes. We met up a couple of times and had been home twice to meet my parents before he finally popped the question in a college disco. I declared to my family that we were engaged. My mother's reaction was 'No you're not!' My father just said 'Well, he'll have to speak up,' since Mark did have a very soft Irish voice. Grace just asked why I was doing this.

I then went to meet his family, and it was just embarrassing. They were working-class Catholics from Belfast, and I was a middle-class English Protestant. We had nothing in common, and I was beginning to realise I had made a mistake. His mother made a few rude personal comments about me, including saying I had a rather large bottom (I didn't), which brought a rebuke from Mark. But it wasn't a good sign. He came over one more time to stay with my family, but when I met him at the railway station I realised I no longer loved him.

As we walked up the hill to my house, I knew I was being unfriendly and cold, but I couldn't help it. 'I think it will take longer to get to know you this time,' he remarked a little sadly, trying to hold my hand. During the three days it was obvious that there was no chemistry left, at least for me.

My last memory of Mark is of him asking if I wanted to go cycling with him on my last morning before I had to go back to university. He was going to leave that afternoon, and he wanted some last moments with me away from my family. I said no, I didn't have time. He asked if he could borrow my bike. He said he hoped to see me again, but then said quietly that he didn't know if I wanted to. He was hoping for a positive response, which never came. I watched his forlorn figure cycle off alone down my hill and knew I would never see him again.

Back to being single, and on the search. I had learned an important lesson. Similar backgrounds are fairly important for a long-lasting relationship – they are more likely to engender similar life attitudes and goals. And holiday romances are a minefield.

There was one romance in the second year at uni. He was also called Mark, was great fun but hadn't quite based his career ideas in reality. He told me he was going to be a fireman and have a Batmobile-type car with a green lightning symbol on the side that everyone would recognize as he drove around Birmingham. He was the third guy I had sex with. I went out with him for one summer term, but as soon as I left for the holidays I didn't contact him again. I found out years later that he was quite hurt by it. I wonder where he is now. He's probably a nice, normal, unpretentious guy, leading a happy married life.

I wonder how many guys I dated and let go for seeming immature or false when they would have become 'normal' if only I had waited for maturity to arrive, or even waited a few more weeks for them to be themselves. And how many guys would have not let me go if only I had not tried so hard to impress them or be funny. If only they had allowed me to relax and be the nice person I can be. How many of us can say that, looking back and wishing we hadn't behaved in such an embarrassing way? It seems such a cruel quirk of nature that falling in love can make you behave like an irritating fool, driving away the one person in your life you want to hang on to.

★ ★ ★

My other language at university was Italian, which we were expected to learn from scratch to degree level in the four years of the course. At the end of the second year we were to spend a month in the city of Perugia, to give our language skills a boost. We were supposed to attend lectures in Italian at the local university. I sat in on two lectures, couldn't understand a word, and decided I would just meet the local people instead and learn that way.

I met two English girls in the university canteen, and we decided to go out to the local bars in the evening, walk up and down the streets, as so many other young people were doing in the warm summer air, and sit on the steps of the church, to chat to anyone there, especially any boys. I noticed one guy often sitting by himself on the steps, night after night, and he started noticing me. He was good-looking, about 20, with dark Mediterranean features. One evening he came over to us, sat down on our step and started chatting in Italian to us. It was obvious that he was more interested in me than the other two. I was flattered.

We chatted, and he invited us all to go for a walk. During the walk he managed to extricate me from the other two and asked me if I would meet him the next night on the steps by myself. He was friendly and charming, and I thought it would be a good opportunity to practise my Italian.

The next night I walked to the steps and there he was, already waiting. He immediately walked down the steps, took my hand, and said we could just take a stroll and talk. We walked along the main street of Perugia as far as the end of the shops. He asked if I wanted to see his room, which was just around the corner. No antennae went up; I suspected nothing. I knew we might kiss but I was fine with that.

I followed him to a narrow back street, and in through a door in a building, then up some marble steps into his room. As soon as I was in the room, he shut the door, grabbed me and started kissing me fervently on the mouth. I responded to the kiss, but was beginning to wonder if this was what I wanted. He pushed me down on the bed and lay on top of me, kissing me all the while. Then he started caressing my breasts and trying to undo my jeans.

I put my hand on his, and told him to stop, that I didn't want to go any further.

He stared at me, and a strange look came over his face. He got up and turned the key in the lock. Then he came over and stood by the bed, staring down at me.

'I am Algerian,' he said. 'I will keep you here until we have sex. I cannot face my friends until we have sex. I am not a proper man if we do not have sex. You will not leave this room until you give in to me. I will keep you here all night until we have sex.'

I froze. He was an Arab. This was tantamount to kidnapping. He was going to rape me! Would he let me go in the morning? What an idiot I had been.

I went quiet, not wanting to enrage him. He left the bed and sat on the chair, watching me, while I continued to lie on the bed, not daring to breathe, wondering if I would be in the papers the next day, or whenever my body was found. If I let him have his way, and stayed calm and acquiescent, he might let me go. I thought I had heard of girls surviving similar ordeals by talking to their kidnappers, and almost forging a friendship with them.

After a few minutes of silence I told him OK, he could have sex. He got up and came over to the bed. His face was less menacing now. He bent down and gently pulled off my jeans and took down my knickers. He climbed on top of me, fully clothed, and started to kiss me again, and caress my breasts through my top. After a minute or so, he pulled out his penis and slowly inserted it into me. There had been no foreplay whatsoever, so I was amazed it didn't hurt, and even more so, that he managed to insert it so easily. I can remember his face even now, moving up and down two inches from mine, unsmiling, just focused on the task in hand.

He suddenly said: 'You don't want me to do this, do you.' It was more a statement than a question, but I assumed that he wanted an answer. If I lied and said I did, he would be sure to see through it, which might annoy him. I decided honesty was the best policy and said 'No,' waiting for a possible enraged reaction. But none came. He just carried on pleasuring himself with my body, staring at me while he pinned me down.

He climaxed and without more ado, pulled himself roughly from my body. It was over, and I was still alive. I had been date-raped.

'You will stay with me tonight, and tomorrow I will let you go,' he said in a matter-of-fact way. oh god, no! I wondered how many more times he would want sex, or if he might change his mind in the morning.

And then he added, almost as a casual afterthought: 'And if I see you walking around the streets with another man I will get a razor and cut your cheeks so no other man will want you.'

I didn't answer. I couldn't believe that I had got myself into a mess from which I might well not emerge alive. I started to think of my family and how lovely it would be to see Mum and Dad again. At that moment my only wish was to be back home, in the safety of English suburbia, with people who knew and loved me. Mum would be asking me if I wanted a cup of tea and a piece of cake. What a waste of a life! I had done all that studying, all that monotonous shorthand and typing, only to have my life cut short by some Arab. I hadn't really experienced life yet.

I also thought about this man who had cruelly taken what he wanted from me, without my permission. It wasn't his fault that he viewed Western women like that. I knew that from my experience in Jerusalem and the hotel manager. It was his culture.

He lay down on the bed behind me and put his arms around me. It was most bizarre. It was as if his behaviour was normal, and kidnapping, raping and threatening someone with disfigurement was completely acceptable. We exchanged few words after that. I didn't initiate a conversation, thinking it better to leave him to start one if he so wished.

I didn't sleep a wink that night. He stayed behind me the whole night, with one arm round me. I didn't dare try to remove it or bolt for the door. The key wasn't in the lock anyway by that time, so I would have had to look for it, and the resulting noise would probably have woken him up. I was desperate to go to the loo, but didn't dare ask.

Dawn came at last. Around 6 am he got up off the bed, fetched the key, went over to the door, unlocked it, stood aside and said I was free to go. I could hardly believe that he was in fact going to just let me go, after committing such crimes. Maybe in his eyes they weren't crimes, just a man having sex with his woman.

I got up, walked towards the door, holding my breath, and without looking at him, walked through the door, adjusting my clothes, then down the marble steps to freedom and the rest of my life. He didn't say anything as I left. I expected to hear his steps on the stairs behind me. I thought he would warn me not to go to the police. But there was just a strange silence from him.

I ran home, not least because I desperately needed the loo. Surprisingly, although I was relieved to have been released, I didn't feel as elated as I thought I would. My overwhelming sentiment was embarrassment – that I had let that happen to me. I wasn't even angry with the guy. He was in the past now. Amazingly it hadn't put me off sex either. I certainly had no intention of going to the police. It would be his word against mine. I didn't want any probing questions into my past, which might reach the papers and England and my parents. I was just going to leave Italy as soon as possible and put it all behind me. As I look back now at my reaction, although I was a naive young woman, I think I showed remarkable mental resilience.

The next day I booked the first flight back to England. That night I met up with the other two girls for a drink and actually sat outside with them on the street again, watching the world go by. I didn't tell them what happened. And amazingly enough, the Algerian suddenly appeared with two other guys and asked to join our table. Most bizarrely, he had permed his hair into tight curls, and his eyes were shining extremely brightly, from some drug, I speculated, but didn't ask. He clearly thought he had done nothing wrong and that we were going to continue where we had left off from last night. I felt I had had a lucky escape from such a character.

We stayed a few minutes making awkward conversation with these three guys, with the two other girls giving me questioning glances. My eyes never met his. I quietly motioned to the others under the table that I wanted to leave and they got the message. We stood up, politely said goodbye, and slowly started walking down the street together. When we were about 50 yards away, I glanced over my shoulder. To my great relief, all three guys were still sitting at the café.

I decided to have an early night, and keep out of harm's way. The next day, I flew home to England a few days ahead of schedule, and to safety.

★ ★ ★

The following year I spent in France, teaching English to kindergarten children as part of the university course. I had two French boyfriends, both of whom I fell in love with, but I never contemplated continuing either relationship once my year was complete. One of them did come over for a visit but we had little in common, and the old holiday romance scenario reared its ugly head. No, I wasn't interested in dark, swarthy, chauvinistic men any more. I wanted a nice, kind, polite, personable Englishman to love. A friend first, who would become a lover and a soulmate.

During the fourth year I had no boyfriends at all. I tried out volleyball, which quickly became a passion. It took over my search for a man, at least for that year. Perhaps I was growing up at last. I remember feeling good about being free from relationship complications for once, enabling me to concentrate on my finals.

My interest in the university course had somewhat dwindled during the last year as well. I still didn't know what I was going to do afterwards, so a degree didn't seem to be leading anywhere. I knew though that I didn't want to fail. For one thing, my parents had helped fund me through the last four years, and I couldn't contemplate letting them down. How embarrassing to come away without a degree certificate. I knew though that I was borderline third. In contrast to the 'A' levels, I hadn't worked very hard at all. I had really gone to university hoping to find a husband and one had not materialised.

On the day the results were posted on the languages department noticeboard, I couldn't bear to join everyone else to find out the results, in case mine were bad. I took a train to the next city and sat in the station for about six hours, drinking endless cups of tea and reading newspapers. At about 10 pm, I crept back onto the university campus, hoping no one would recognize me and come up to discuss my results. I managed to get to my room unseen. Pinned to the outside of my student room's door was a piece of A4 paper with the words 'Congratulations! 2:2' written on it.

I danced up and down the corridor in delight. I hadn't failed. I could ring up my parents with the good news and hold my head up high. I always wondered how close I came to a third.

CHAPTER FOUR

Pedro and pregnancy

My sister had gone to London after she had finished her 'A' levels and loved it, so I thought I would do the same. But I didn't love it. I found it big, unfriendly, dirty, expensive and noisy. There were people everywhere, and travelling anywhere seemed to take at least an hour. But I knew there were job opportunities there like nowhere else in Britain, so I was determined to stay for at least a year. In the event, I stayed for ten.

A girl I had met in France was living with her boyfriend in Peckham on the Old Kent Road, in one of those large apartment blocks with dark brown bricks and long white balconies that stretched the width of the building. Horrible, depressing constructions, but cheap to rent. The rest of the Old Kent Road was not much better. She said I could stay with her in her spare room until I found somewhere of my own.

It was freezing. I would lie in bed and watch my breath condense in the air. When the alarm went off in the morning, I would nip out of bed, turn the fan heater on, and rush back under the covers to wait while the room heated up.

I registered with an agency for secretarial work, and very soon got a job in a local export firm. I was like a fish out of water. Everyone else had East End accents, and with my rather posh BBC accent I didn't fit in. Having to work in an office environment is quite a knack anyway. I didn't know what I was doing there and left after a few weeks.

I found another job as secretary to an export manager in a large international company. Within three months I had been fired for being disorganized, not taking the job seriously, flirting with the boss inappropriately and having insufficient shorthand skills. I had been rumbled – I didn't want to work at all; I wanted to be a housewife and mother.

In the flat things were not going that smoothly either. The friend from France was becoming jealous of my interaction with her boyfriend, even though I had no designs on him at all. For his part he had started complaining about my use of the fan heater in the morning.

Within three weeks I had decided to look for another job and different accommodation. Going home to Mummy and Daddy though, after so little time, was not an option. There were quite a few young working people and students in the apartment block, and one or two of them invited me for cups of tea. Through them I learned that a Portuguese guy named Pedro, who lived in Peckham Rye, was looking for a flatmate to help pay the bills. We were soon introduced. Unfortunately he was rather good-looking, five foot eleven, with long black hair, huge brown eyes and olive skin. I wondered if the move was a good idea, as I could see that he was taking quite an interest in me too, but I was fairly desperate to move out. I also gave up my job and went on the dole.

So I moved in to Pedro's spare room. Soon after this he bought a lovely mongrel puppy with long, silky, black hair and called him Mush (to rhyme with 'push'). Mush was a rescue dog, and had been found abandoned on the side of a motorway. He had the sweetest personality and I wondered how anyone could treat any animal with such cruelty, let alone one so gentle-natured. Pedro was a chemistry student and a part-time chef. Since I was on the dole, I would take Mush for walks to the nearby park, and sometimes Pedro would accompany us. I felt as if I had a mini family and knew that Pedro and I were becoming closer.

One morning, while I was still in bed, there was a knock on the door and Pedro walked in in his underpants, looking strange. He said he was cold. I nearly laughed at this atrocious chat-up line, but contained myself and asked if he wanted to get into bed with me. He didn't hesitate, and we became lovers.

It was lovely at first, as with all relationships. Mush was adorable, and it was cosy to have supper or watch a film with all three of us on the sofa. But it bothered me that Mush was being left alone for hours at a time while Pedro and I were out. On one occasion when he was left alone, Mush chewed off the end of my brand new squash racket (thirty-five years later I still have that racket and I still play with it with the end missing).

But gradually I realised that I wasn't myself with Pedro. He was a useless listener and we didn't have the same sense of humour. I had been on the dole for about four months and although it was nice for a while to be able to sleep in until 11 am if I wanted, and read the paper till 1 pm after a long walk with Mush, it was not achieving anything. Moreover, most of my school friends seem to have found good jobs and were moving on with their lives.

Then one day I realised that my period was a few days' late. I was often slightly off the regular four weeks, so I waited a few more days - nothing. Another two weeks passed and no sign. So I went to the doctor's and asked for a pregnancy test. It was confirmed. I was about eight weeks' pregnant.

Pedro was ecstatic. I was not. I didn't want to stay in this relationship. I certainly didn't want a hybrid baby with olive skin, born out of wedlock. What would my parents say when I brought their first grandchild home, with big brown eyes and shiny black hair, looking decidedly non-white? My father was the biggest racist I knew. He had even said, half as a joke, in his clipped English accent, that 'we can't let the nignogs get their hands on England,' when there was talk about letting migrants into the UK.

But it wasn't only my parents' likely reaction that stopped me wanting the baby. I didn't love Pedro, I didn't have a job, I didn't have a clue what I wanted to do (apart from finding the elusive husband) and I didn't want to bring a child into such a situation.

Now I wish I had. I wish with every fibre of my body that I could go back in time. Foresight would be such a useful addition to the human species. It didn't occur to me then that conception would be a problem in the future.

I discussed an abortion with Pedro, and he reluctantly agreed. He knew I wasn't happy in the relationship and that a baby would only complicate things. I have to say that I didn't really consider the fact that it was his baby too. It was my body, my pregnancy and my choice. I wonder if he ever thinks of that child now. I hope he has children of his own, so that he doesn't have to regret allowing me that decision.

An abortion was arranged for a month's time at a hospital in East Dulwich. My breasts had become enormous and painful, and

I was feeling very sick. I couldn't wait to get the baby out of my body and get on with my life.

By this time the foetus was 12 weeks old. Years later I saw an image of a 12-week-old foetus – it had a head and arms and legs, and although it looked like a little orange alien with bulgy eyes, it was nevertheless very obviously a small human being in the making. I burst into tears at the sight. Luckily I was watching TV by myself at the time.

They put me in a ward with about 10 other pregnant girls, all having abortions except one. The girl next to me was trying to get pregnant and couldn't. She told me it was very difficult for her to be surrounded by mothers-to-be who were all choosing to get rid of their babies, while she longed for her own. She said her ovaries were going to be stimulated by the hospital, that they had to shave off all her pubic hair, and that she was dreading having to spread her legs in front of nurses and doctors. I said they had probably seen it all before, but understandably that doesn't make it any less embarrassing for the individual concerned. She said if this didn't work, that she was going to try using donated eggs from other women. I made a mental note that once I'd had my two children, I would donate my eggs to poor women like her.

I stayed in overnight. The next morning I was taken away in a wheelchair and put to sleep, and when I woke up I had a huge sanitary towel between my legs. I had period pains, but the sickness had gone. Obviously the baby had gone too. Just like that. A little human life stubbed out. I don't even know if it was a boy or girl. The lining of my womb had been gently sucked out with a small tube, and with it my child. They told me doctors in the future would never be able to tell that I had had an abortion.

Awful to say, but the fact that it was a potential baby was not at the forefront of my mind. It had just been an unplanned pregnancy. I was so relieved not to feel sick any more. I wanted to move on, leave this depraved area of London behind and forget about this somewhat disastrous start to life in the big city.

There was nothing now binding me to Pedro, though he was much more affected by my imminent departure than I had anticipated. That had been partly the trouble with our relationship. As a proud, rather shy man, he had been unable to show me much affection, or reveal his true inner self. I needed a soulmate, one with whom I could share my innermost thoughts and secrets, and he with me.

★ ★ ★

I moved out into a small room with eight other friends of friends in a large house in Golders Green, an area which was much more middle-class, I felt. A few weeks later, Pedro rang me. He said he'd been to the doctor, who had put him on anti-depressants. I was very sad to hear this. Being jilted can be horrendous, but jilting someone who's a decent person because you can't love them is not much better. Then he suddenly blurted out down the phone 'Will you marry me?'

I ached for him. He must have really loved me, but never told me. For him to ask me like that over the phone to marry him, after I had just left, knowing the likelihood of my agreeing was zero, must have been desperately difficult. But sometimes it's better to ask and be rejected, than to always wonder what would have happened. I said 'ah no, sorry' as gently as I could.

How ironic that by the time I was 24, I had had three proposals and one pregnancy, all of which I had rejected. They constituted two of the things on my must-do list. But it had to be right. I didn't hear from Pedro again or see him again for about three years. Then our paths crossed unexpectedly at a party given by a mutual friend. He was married and looked very happy with his new wife, a pretty, quietly-spoken Irish girl — in fact I knew her from university. She and I laughed at the situation, since we had both been after the same guy at university as well, another Mediterranean type. She had ended up with the man that time as well.

Pedro and I spoke briefly but amicably at the party. I wasn't jealous in any way and it in no way made me regret my decision. I was very happy to find out that he had decided to give Mush away to a retired lady who lived in the country. Now I could think of Mush with a constant companion, going on lovely long walks with his new owner and no longer having to chew squash rackets in his boredom and loneliness in a flat in the big city.

* * *

I had great fun in this large house with young professionals. I was paying £13 a week for a tiny room, but I had the run of the house. About this time I landed a job as secretary for a conservation society whose offices were inside London Zoo. I loved the fact that my commute to work would sometimes cross paths with a baby elephant being taken for a walk by his keeper, and that my office was between the lions and the wolves!

I had always loved animals, so it seemed a perfect combination for my interest in conservation and my secretarial qualifications.

No shorthand required, just touch-typing on large, slow electric typewriters. No computers back then, no internet, no email. If you made a typo, you used good old Tippex liquid or paper strips.

Within six months, I was assisting with the administration and fund-raising of one of their high-profile missions, the Mountain Gorilla Project. The gorillas were in Rwanda, Zaire and Uganda while I was located in London Zoo, thanking people endlessly for their donations and designing information leaflets, posters and other publicity material depicting the plight of the magnificent mountain gorilla. A mere 500 remained in the wild, mainly due to a devastating reduction in their mountain habitat from the ever-increasing human population on their doorstep. There was also at the time a sickening tourist trade in gorilla hands for ashtrays, and gorilla heads as trophies.

I started giving talks to schools, using a set of slides so I could hide in the darkness. I heard some of the kids referring to me as the 'gorilla girl', a fabulous title in my eyes. But although I enjoyed the sense of achievement after a talk, I was still very fearful of public speaking. When I was confronted with having to give a talk to Dulwich College (all boys and masters at that time) and discovered it was going to be during assembly with the whole school watching, I very nearly ran away five minutes before it was due to start, but then decided to brave it out. After the 15-minute talk, I gave them a quiz and was amazed to be met by a sea of little hands raised in eagerness to give the answers.

I went out twice to Rwanda to stay with field personnel and see the gorilla groups at close hand. I shall never forget crawling on hands and knees to view a gorilla family as they peacefully chewed on vegetation and took their midday siestas only yards away. They shared so many mannerisms with humans.

I had one rather uncomfortable encounter. On this particular day no tourists turned up, so the Rwandan guide and I set off by ourselves for the trek into the forest. When we caught up with a group of gorillas, the guide signalled to me that something was wrong. The silverback, the dominant male of the group, seemed to be agitated. He was chest-beating, grunting and moving fast through the vegetation, so fast that some of the females were finding it hard to keep up. Poachers frequently set traps in the forest for other animals such as antelope and duiker, but sometimes gorillas got caught in them, losing hands or feet in the process. The guide whispered that an encounter with a poacher might have unnerved the male.

Suddenly he dropped to his knees and motioned me to do the same and stay still and very quiet behind him. The silverback had just appeared in front of us, about five yards away, and was sitting up on all fours, looking at us. I stared at the vegetation I was kneeling on, as I had been taught. Don't eyeball the male, as it's seen as threatening. Act humble. I've never felt so humble in all my life.

Suddenly he let out a tremendous roar, lurched towards us and gave the guide a huge shove so that he fell backwards onto me. I actually thought I was going to die there and then, in the Virunga Volcanoes of Rwanda. The guide didn't move from where he was kneeling, bravely presenting a human barrier between me and the silverback. I heard the gorilla breathing about six feet from us, but didn't dare look up. Then I heard the vegetation rustling and this enormous animal disappeared back into the forest as quickly as he had appeared. As with most charges from gorillas, it had all been a bluff, a mock threat to make him seem big and bold and warn us that this was his part of the forest. We got the message. To my great relief the guide, whispering that it was 'pas bon', led me quickly away from the area and back down the mountain.

★ ★ ★

I wondered if I would meet a nice (but probably poor) conservationist who would need me as his assistant to travel the world saving endangered species. In fact I did meet a man, one who on paper seemed to fit the bill – a biologist who was giving lectures round Britain on conservation. He would drop by the office occasionally to pick up gorilla information to sell after his lectures. We had a brief affair, but our senses of humour didn't gel, and when he left to do field work in Rwanda I wasn't sure what I wanted. I did write him a letter to say I was coming out to Rwanda but he didn't reply, so I assumed he had come to the same conclusion about our potential as a couple.

As if to prove our incompatibility, he had the lack of good grace to actually mention my letter in a formal letter to the office: 'Please thank Anna for her letter, and tell her I look forward to seeing her on her trip out here'. How dare he! That was a private letter. I did not want the whole office knowing I had written to him, and even worse, the office thinking he had chosen not to write back privately. But I decided I didn't care enough about the situation to pursue it.

CHAPTER FIVE

Thrills and spills

Three things happened while I lived in Golders Green which had a lasting effect on my life. One was being possibly responsible for saving a child's life. I was cycling down the hill on my way to work when a little girl aged about 18 months crawled out onto the road between two parked cars, about 10 yards in front of my bike. If I had set off only five seconds earlier from the house I would have been past her by the time she emerged. I stopped and picked her up and took her to a house nearby. An elderly lady came flying out of the house, saw me with the child and cried 'Oh thank God!'

'She was on the road.' I told her, as I handed over the child. She stared at me with a look of horror. Then she just kept saying 'Thank you. Thank you!'

I felt absolutely elated that I had very likely saved that little girl's life. I still think of her occasionally. I wonder if she grew up, got married and had children of her own. I've even thought of going back to the house to see if I could meet her again, but what would that achieve? Did I want her eternal gratitude? What if she had died? Would that have lessened my 'heroic' act?

I thought of that elderly lady, who was probably the grandmother, babysitting her daughter's or son's baby. How unspeakably devastating for her if she had had to tell the child's parents that she had been run over on the road under her care. It would have ruined that family's life. I hadn't done anything that anyone else wouldn't have done, but you don't know how precious another life is until you are touched by it in such circumstances. How ironic that two years earlier, I had extinguished the life of my own child without much thought.

The second thing that happened was far less dramatic. At about the time my relationship with the biologist was coming to an end, I had started going out with one of the guys in the house, called Charles. Within about a year we had started to argue. One of our frequent arguments ended with him sitting on top of me on the landing, bending my ring finger back until I cried out with pain, which brought two of our flatmates racing up the stairs to help me. I knew that yet again I had to move out from my accommodation and look elsewhere, especially when my finger hurt for weeks afterwards, and he just laughed and said I was being a wimp. In fact, of course, it constituted an assault, or domestic abuse. But our sex life had been exciting and interesting. He had expressed an interest in spanking me, as part of sex. I was too embarrassed to admit that I liked the idea so we didn't make it a regular thing.

Then on one occasion, I crossed the line, in his eyes, and he decided to punish me. I had become very drunk at a party on Martini, cider and wine, carefully mixed together in the same glass – all very funny until I came home and got into his double bed. The room spun and I proceeded to vomit all over myself and all over my side of the bed. I then turned over and vomited all over the other side of the bed – his side. He came into the room, turned on the light, saw me lying in a large pool of sick, promptly turned off the light and went downstairs to spend an irritated, uncomfortable, sleepless night on the sofa.

The next day I was very ill. I wanted to die. When I finally dragged myself out of his bed at about 3 pm, he demanded that I wash his sheets, but I refused as I felt too awful. He was utterly furious, and as he took the stinking sheets from the bed, he warned me that I hadn't heard the last of it. I was too ill to care.

About three days later, when I had recovered and we were back in his bed after a normal night's sleep, he suddenly got up and swept the sheet back, leaving me lying in my nightie and feeling rather vulnerable and perplexed. I hadn't cottoned on to the fact that he was still simmering about the sheets. 'Turn over onto your front,' he ordered, 'I'm going to spank you for getting so drunk, and not helping me with the sheets.'

I knew I had deserved his anger in a way, and that it would probably make him feel better if he did carry out some sort of punishment. I assumed it wouldn't be very hard. I also thought I might secretly enjoy it. So I turned over onto my front and watched him walk over to the wardrobe and take out one of his slippers. It had a shiny, hard, smooth base. That wasn't quite what I expected.

He came back to the bed and knelt beside me. I turned away, waiting for the onslaught. Then he belted me hard across the bottom through my nightie. Thwack! It stung. He waited a second or two, then raised the slipper and brought it down on my upturned bottom again, harder this time. I remained silent. Again he waited a few seconds. I heard his arm go up again – and thwack! He belted me about 10 times in succession with the slipper. My buttocks were stinging but I didn't move or make a sound. I just waited for him to finish.

When I realised it was over, I turned over and looked at him. 'Naughty girl' he said, standing up, with a slight smirk, 'Let that be a lesson to you.' It had been a huge turn-on for both of us, and had peaked my interest in spanking as part of a prelude to sexual activity. After that he spanked me three more times on separate occasions, while I was fully clothed, and in front of the other flatmates, which drew clapping and cheers, and which I found equally erotic.

★ ★ ★

While I was in the Golders Green house I got involved in another activity which had an effect on my life - skydiving. I loved the whole concept and was fascinated by the idea of flying through the air. Charles and I and a few friends booked ourselves on a day course at Brenton Parachute Club in Kent. We spent the day in the classroom, taught by tough, no-nonsense instructors, who had heard all the smart-arse quips from students a thousand times before.

'What happens if both your parachutes fail?' asked one cocky guy. 'Well,' answered the instructor, 'You think about it for a while, then you tuck your head in between your legs and kiss your arse goodbye'. Laughter all round. The guy didn't ask any more questions.

The next day, we waited for our names to be read out over the manifest. On hearing my name, my heart rate leapt dramatically. As I put on my gear and was checked out by a little Irish guy named Paddy, I could feel my heart pounding in my chest. Paddy was unbearably cheerful as he went through the checks of my harness. How could he be so cheerful when I was about to die?

About five of us first-timers were finally ready and checked out. We walked rather gingerly in line towards the tiny little Cessna, which looked as if it was made of paper. I was the last in line, so I had to sit right by the door. As the plane climbed to altitude, I decided that this was the last place in the whole world I wanted to be right then, and that this was the worst decision in the whole world that I could ever have made.

The plane started its slow circle towards the point of exit. Although I was utterly petrified, refusing to jump was not an option. How embarrassing to have to face fellow first-timers on the ground and admit that you wimped out! No, I had to see it through. It was definitely one of those OMG moments. If you ever want to live in the now, try a parachute jump. Most people will never feel terror as I experienced as I sat on the lip of that small, rickety plane, looking down at the earth about 2,500 feet below.

I was aware of Paddy reaching over me and pressing a button above the door. Then he looked intently at me.

'Ready?' he said, smiling. I stared back and didn't answer. 'In the door,' he shouted, above the noise of the plane. I swung my legs over the side of the plane, and felt the slipstream push my feet backwards.

'Look up!' Paddy yelled. I looked up into his face. 'And GO!'

I pushed off like a zombie, making the biggest arch I could muster, as taught in the previous day's training... into sudden silence. The relief to be out of the plane, even though in a potentially more dangerous situation, was immense. It was too late to feel fear. The event was happening and I had to deal with it. 'One thousand, two thousand, three thousand, four thousand, five thousand, six thousand...' I said aloud to myself. There was a huge jerk, and I was bolted upright in mid-air like a string puppet.

I looked up and the most beautiful sight in the world greeted my eyes. A little, round, green parachute had almost fully opened up like a flower above me. I had been trained to count to four thousand, not six thousand, and then yell in perfect control 'Check canopy!' All that had gone out the window in the moment of exiting the plane and the threat of imminent death.

Once I knew I was not going to die, I strangely and suddenly became very brave. I loved the ride down to the ground under canopy. I felt utterly fearless and safe, strapped in and soaring through the air like Superwoman.

Paddy signed my little logbook, 'Very good all the way'. I didn't tell him I had counted to six thousand and forgotten to check my canopy during the designated safety slot. He could only see my arch as I left the plane.

I was completely hooked, and couldn't wait to do it again. Charles didn't like it that much. I didn't care. It became my passion. I spent my weekends on the drop zone, getting to know everyone, and sleeping in the rough bunk-bed accommodation available to jumpers. I went quickly through the parachuting category system that trains you slowly from static line to freefall by yourself and then on to freefall with other jumpers (called relative work, or RW).

During the jumps with other skydivers from around 14,000 feet, which allows you about one minute 10 seconds of freefall, you attempt to join together in as many pre-determined formations as the altitude will allow while falling at 124 miles an hour, before having to deploy your parachute at around 2,500 feet. It's an incredible buzz. The amazing thing is that you can often forget that you are hurtling towards the earth, because you are having so much fun trying to link up with your fellow skydivers. Because you are not passing anything, you have no point of reference for your downward speed, and it's just as if you are floating on a stable cushion of air. It's only your sense of elapsed time from the time you left the plane and an occasional glance at your altimeter that alert you to the approaching earth. As I heard said often enough, 'It's not the jump that kills you, it's the sudden collision with the planet.'

During one of my first RW jumps with an instructor, I forgot the altitude completely. I watched with surprise as the instructor moved away from me in freefall and suddenly started flapping his arms wildly, but I didn't cotton on. It was only when he turned away from me and opened his parachute that I realised I myself might need a parachute above me, sooner rather than later. I immediately opened my main parachute, and was finally under a full canopy at 1500 feet - eight seconds from hitting the ground and almost certain death. The recommended minimum height is 2500 feet. On the ground, the instructor was very relieved to see me alive. There was nothing else he could have done to try and save me.

I had two near-fatal malfunctions while skydiving. One was on my first jump under a 'square' parachute, the large oblong canopies which can be flared to allow tiptoe landings. I couldn't get it open and was 10 seconds from hitting the ground when I decided to get my reserve open. Unfortunately I didn't know how to steer this little round parachute, and I crashed into the ground at about 25 miles an hour, crushing two vertebrae, and damaging my hip joint. My back still aches today when I stand still for more than a few minutes, and I need constant back support when seated.

The other malfunction was when one of the steering lines got caught up as the canopy opened. I could only reach the left-hand steering line, a situation that would put me into a permanent spiral and corkscrew me into the ground at a dangerous speed. I should have released myself from this, gone back into freefall and opened my reserve, but I just couldn't bring myself to leave an almost fully operational canopy, so I mustered more strength than I ever have in my life, pulled the stricken half of the parachute towards me and grabbed the steering line, which righted the canopy.

While quite shaken by both these incidents, I still loved skydiving too much to give it up. I took part in local competitions, where four-man teams would try and create as many aerial formations between exiting the plane and deploying their parachutes as possible. I was once asked to take part in a parachuting display onto a village green with five guys who had smoke canisters tied to their feet. I have a snapshot memory of seeing the guys in freefall spread out around me, all grinning, with bright pink smoke billowing upwards from their boots. The village was only a few miles from my parents' house so I had rung them proudly to tell them about my 'parachuting demonstration'. Unfortunately, my father was rather deaf by then, didn't hear the word 'parachuting', and thought I was telling them I was going to take part in a street demonstration, so they decided not to attend my moment of swooping fame.

But one thing I was not hooked on was my relationship with Charles. Although our sex life was pretty good and part of me loved him, his arrogance and lack of respect for my opinions stopped me feeling close to him. We knew our relationship was too volatile to continue in the same house. It was difficult being a couple in a house with seven other young people. Our frequent arguments sometimes made for an awkward atmosphere for the other flatmates, especially when we didn't speak to each other for days. We were both in fact quite upset at my departure, but it was not what I was looking for. I wanted a *nice* guy, for goodness sake. Was that too much to ask?

After the finger-bending episode, it was time to move on. I left the house in Golders Green and found a rather dismal, run-down flat-share in Hendon a few miles up the road. Charles rang once to talk to me, but as soon as we began the conversation, I felt an argument brewing. I think he was just lonely as well, but we knew it wouldn't work.

I didn't see him for three years, and then he suddenly rang up and asked if I wanted to meet up. I wasn't seeing anyone at the time, so I agreed.

Within an hour I knew I never wanted to see him again. He was as arrogant as ever, and I realised that I was still scared of his temper and potential violent nature. When we'd had our quick drink he asked if I wanted to see him again. I was scared to say 'no' to his face in case he became angry, so I said 'Yes' and very quickly turned on my heel and walked away in the other direction. He took the hint. I never saw or spoke to him again.

★ ★ ★

My three years in Hendon were fairly uneventful. I continued my work in London Zoo for the Mountain Gorilla Project, and I continued to skydive. I actually combined the two once during a daring jump by six army guys dressed in gorilla suits. They were to jump out in quick succession, at low altitude so the TV cameras could catch them, and form what's known as a stack. This entailed all their canopies being fully open and one parachutist linking with his ankles to the top of the parachute of the next guy underneath him, who then linked in turn to the next guy under him, until eventually all six parachutes flew together. They would all separate near the ground, just in time to be able to land safely. They were then going to surround me, while I was interviewed by the TV presenter about the gorillas.

At least, that was the plan. The execution was somewhat different, but it created much more publicity. During the morning of the appointed jump, the cloud base was lower than they had wanted, but they decided to go for it anyway. This would leave them less time to form the stack. The first link was just about complete when one of the canopies started to collapse. They hadn't allowed for the fact that they couldn't see very well because of the gorilla suits, and they misjudged the docking distance.

I looked up in horror to see a bundle of canopies all entangled, swirling round each other. Suddenly a small black-suited figure could be seen freefalling away from the tangle. About two seconds later, a little round reserve shot out and bolted him upright. That one would survive. The rest of the canopies continued to spiral out of control towards the ground. One guy, Steve, remained in the centre of this mess. He had pulled his reserve open and it shot up into his own parachute as well as becoming entangled with the main parachute of the guy who had cut away. He was hanging head down, with one line round his foot and the others attached to three partly-inflated parachutes, spiralling down towards the ground, with the TV cameras recording every moment.

'I don't want to die!' he kept screaming, as the ground came ever closer. One of the army guys near me called Duncan suddenly started to sprint towards the potential landing point of his mate. 'Keep your head up, keep your head up!' he yelled. A few seconds before Steve hit the ground, Duncan's instructions filtered through, and he lifted his head up enough to stop him breaking his neck. He landed on his chest with a heavy thud.

Of course, this unscheduled excitement was exactly what the TV channels wanted. The cameras captured it all and it made the national news. I was never surrounded by gorilla-suited army parachutists or interviewed about the beleaguered mountain gorilla (I was secretly relieved) but I had managed to make the headlines.

Steve was carted off to hospital but declared fit and well, apart from a bruised chest. In subsequent press interviews the gorillas were hardly given a mention. The reporters were more interested in how dangerous a stack was, how close Steve thought he was to dying, and if he would carry on jumping (he did).

CHAPTER SIX

Not-so-great expectations

Having reached my 30th birthday unmarried with no children, earning £6000 a year and living in a dump of a house in Hendon, I decided I needed to get a 'proper' job, one where I would be using my brain. I was passionate about the mountain gorillas, but not being a biologist I could only really do admin work, which had ceased to be a challenge. Moreover, my boss and I did not get on. He was very impatient. I think it would be fair to say that we disliked each other immensely, with no respect on either side. Time to move on into the adult working world. But to do what?

One Saturday in October 1985, I decided to go windsurfing on the Isle of Dogs, in West London. I'd just finished a sail and climbed back onto the bank when I noticed a chap I recognized from university. I hadn't found him attractive then as he was very shy and boyish. Now he had matured into a man and had broadened out. He seemed more confident. I went up and said hello, and he immediately recognized me and smiled broadly. We chatted for a while and then we swapped telephone numbers. His name was Clive. He was also 30 and was training to be an architect. He also liked to windsurf. That would do nicely, I thought. On the down side, he was from Bolton – but someone's got to come from there, I reasoned.

We went out for four months, but I became too keen too early. He started making comments about the fact that I was 30, didn't have a proper job, had no career prospects and still wanted to go dancing in clubs. In short, he accused me of being immature. 'You're still a student,' he said. He was probably right. I tried to say that I *was* looking for another career but I wasn't quite sure what yet. I wasn't going to tell him that in my hopes *he* would be my career, because I would be a stay-at-home mum looking after our two children while he went out to work as an architect.

One day I opened the door of my flatshare to find a tall, slim young man standing there. He asked if one of my flatmates was in. I said she wasn't, but that he could come in and wait for her if he liked. He hesitated, and then said he would.

While I made him a cup of coffee, I asked him what he did. 'I'm a computer programmer,' he said, absent-mindedly. I didn't know that this conversation was to change the rest of my life. How often do chance conversations change the course of people's lives?

'What sort of person do you have to be to do that?' I asked.

'Well, we have people with all sorts of backgrounds, but the ones that seem to do best are good at maths, music or languages.'

I started to take note. I had a talent for languages, but I wasn't good at maths, and I found reading music difficult enough that I had decided not to pursue it. Perhaps I should have taken more notice of these early signs.

I looked into it. The government was offering an incentive of

£42 a week for people to receive training on TOPS courses. I went for an interview and an aptitude test; I got 21%. An out and out failure. I was devastated. But I hadn't given up. I rang them and said it was the first time I had ever taken a computer aptitude test, and could I retake it, because I was really keen.

'One second. I'll just go and ask,' said the lady on the other end of the phone. A minute later she returned: 'They said that was fine. You can retake it.'

I was ecstatic. A few days later I went in and sat another aptitude test. I was the only candidate. I handed it in and sat waiting forlornly for the results. I stared out of the window and down onto the streets, thinking that the next few minutes were going to affect the rest of my life. If they didn't accept me, I would have to think of some other career. What would Clive think? I tried not to think that I minded what he thought. This was MY career, dammit.

The door opened and the woman who had allowed me to come back to take the second test entered. 'You got 28%,' she began. 'The pass mark is 30% I'm afraid.' I went numb. I didn't know what to say or where to look. 'But' she continued, smiling, 'they are so impressed with your attitude, your determination to have come in again, the fact that you've never done this before, that you did improve from 21%, and that it's only 2% off a pass mark, the fact that you are a graduate, and the fact that they do need to fill the places, that they are prepared to let you on the course.'

Reprieved! I fairly floated out of the room and onto the London Underground.

★ ★ ★

I could see the signs. Clive rang me less and less. He had been getting more and more irritated by things I did or said. I wasn't confident enough with men back then to talk to him about it; I just noticed his reactions and made a mental note to try and correct them. Then after a silence of a week or so, I received a letter. He told me he no longer wanted to see me. His letter ended with three words 'Sorry – no buzz'. The last two words were underlined three times.

I was completely devastated. My future with him had suddenly been cancelled, and I could see only emptiness ahead of me. The pain of being rejected when you think you are in love with someone goes very deep and can be utterly devastating. It can destroy your confidence and stop you from wanting to take part in life for some time. Unless you've been through it, you cannot know the dreadful feelings of sadness, loneliness and hurt pride that haunt you night and day. You may have to face other people's questions when you are obliged to tell them it's all over, when so recently you had been extolling your ex-partner's wonderful qualities and your wonderful relationship, little suspecting he was plotting his escape all along. You feel an idiot for making your feelings so public, and you feel an idiot for not knowing what your partner was really thinking behind your back.

You go back over many of the times you had with your ex-partner and wonder if it was at such-and-such a party that he decided to get rid of you. Was it your behaviour? The way you looked? Did you smell? Were you hopeless in bed, but he never told you? Were you irritating? Not confident enough in front of other people? A thousand questions circle in your mind, and there's no escape for weeks and often months. Only time heals, or meeting someone else. Sometimes people never recover.

But in fact I knew the main reason. He didn't respect me because my life was not on a sensible track. I was living at the time in a run-down flatshare in Finsbury Park. Most people he knew were already on the property ladder, had partners with good careers and were well on their way to furthering their own well-paid careers. I was indeed rather stuck in Peter Pan world, seemingly not wishing to take on 'grown-up' responsibilities. Sometimes I had also acted childishly with him, in the first throes of love. Both those reasons, I told myself, were correctable. The next time I fell in love I would deliberately *not* act stupidly. And I *was* looking for a suitable career – it just hadn't quite got off the ground yet.

The phrase 'It never rains but it pours' comes to mind to describe this period of my life. More disastrous events were to follow in quick succession. About two weeks after the letter from Clive, I discovered I was pregnant again. I stared at the pregnancy test result in the bathroom. I couldn't believe it. We had used condoms. They were supposed to be 98% safe, weren't they? Yet again I resolved immediately to get rid of it. I wasn't going to raise a child with an absent father who had rejected me moreover, when I didn't even have an income.

I told Clive about it by phone. I secretly hoped it might lead to his seeing a more serious, mature side of my nature.

'Hi,' I started, knowing he wouldn't want to hear my voice anyway. 'Er – I'm just ringing to say that I'm pregnant.' Silence. 'And it's yours.'

'Oh god' he managed to whisper.

'Don't worry – I will get rid of it, and I'll pay. It's about £150.'

He was relieved, but he didn't offer to help, or suggest meeting up to discuss it. Not that there was really anything to discuss. The abortion was arranged for about four weeks after that. I was beginning to feel very sick from dawn until dusk, and would take to my bed for hours at a time. The computer course was due to start in two weeks' time, but the task of sitting up all day at a desk and concentrating on a brand-new subject for eight hours a day seemed insurmountable.

On the first day of the course, I got up, dressed in a smart suit and started walking towards the tube station. Halfway there, I knew I wouldn't make it. I felt so terribly sick and ill that it was pointless. So I turned round and went home. I rang them to tell them that I wouldn't make the course. They said they would keep the course open for two days, to see if I could recover in time, but that after that I would have missed too much important base information to be able to catch up. I didn't tell them it wasn't likely that the baby would have magically emerged by the third day.

On the third day, I rang them and said I wouldn't recover in time to join the course. I took to my bed for hours, crying incessantly, because of Clive, the missed opportunity of the computer course, and because my chances of having children within a loving relationship were receding with every passing year.

My second abortion took place shortly afterwards. Again my thoughts were on getting back to my life, not the fact that it was a baby. I just wanted the sickness to stop. Clive sent a message of support via the hospital, which I received when I woke up. He didn't phone or visit, but then I didn't really expect him to. I never heard from him again.

More bad news was to come. During the four weeks leading up to the abortion, I discovered a lump in my breast. I thought at first it was because I was pregnant. My breasts had become tender and had begun to inflate like balloons, as before. Nevertheless I thought I had better have it checked by a doctor as soon as possible after the abortion, when everything had settled down.

Four weeks later I made the appointment. The doctor confirmed that it should be looked at by a specialist. Within a few days another appointment was made for me – the speed with which it was made was in itself slightly alarming. We are talking the NHS here, after all.

A cheerful young bearded doctor examined my breasts. After a while he said: 'Well you're 31, single and unemployed. What are you going to do?' How strangely unkind that sounded, and yet I think he didn't mean it to be unkind, just concerned. But being summed up like that just emphasised to me that my life really wasn't going according to plan. Not any plan. And now I might have cancer.

'We will have to take this out and have a look at it,' he went on, 'but I'm about 99% sure that it's benign. It's moving around quite nicely in here.' He demonstrated by pinching the lump gently and moving it backwards and forwards inside the breast.

'I don't want to lose the nipple,' I managed to say, since the lump was a few millimetres away from the pink of the nipple. You'd think the thought of having cancer would have far outweighed any embarrassment at having to talk about nipples and breasts with a stranger, but I felt myself turning red, especially with an unknown young male feeling my naked breasts.

'No, you won't lose it. They will make the scar coincide with the outside line of the nipple and you will hardly see it,' he assured me.

On the day of the operation I remember walking by myself to St Mary's Hospital near Paddington. I hadn't decided who I would confide in about my cancer, if that's what it turned out to be, so I hadn't asked anyone to accompany me. It was a lovely sunny day and I noticed the trees that were lining the street. They suddenly seemed magnificent. Life was magnificent. This strange little planet whizzing around the sun was extraordinary. What if I had cancer? I could lose my life – at the age of 31. The doctor had said he was almost sure the lump was benign, but doctors can be wrong.

I was put to sleep and the lump was removed. When the nurse replaced the dressing for the first time, I saw that my entire right breast was deeply bruised all over. She saw my reaction and by way of explanation remarked: 'You should have seen what he was doing with your breast.' I supposed he had been digging deeper, looking for further lumps, but I was too scared to ask.

A few days later the doctor rang me. The lump was benign. No other lumps had been found. I didn't have cancer after all. I was now free to live for possibly another 50 years. The difference between dismay, and exuberant joy and hope, delivered in one short phone call.

Now I had to get myself onto another computer course. I hoped I didn't have to take another aptitude test. I found one, rang them up and explained what happened to the first course. They asked for the details and said they would contact me in a few days. Amazingly, within 30 minutes they had booked me onto the course. Perhaps they too were struggling to find enough candidates to merit the funding they needed; that was certainly one of the main reasons the first course had accepted me.

★ ★ ★

The three months of the computer programming course that

followed were probably the hardest of my life. I worked about 60 hours a week. I wasn't a brilliant programmer, but I did pass everything. Some people fell by the wayside. It's definitely not for everyone.

We had a project at the end of the course and only by staying awake for about 72 hours did I finish it, and even then I gave it in late. I got 78% for the whole course, but 5% had been deducted for giving in my project late. I refused to acknowledge this deduction in writing my CV, and stuck doggedly to 83%. I felt I deserved it.

At my end-of-course review my delightful teacher made a reference to the fact that I was already 31, 'of which we will say nothing,' he added, smirking. He was at least 50. It's true that many people starting a career in IT are considerably younger than 31, but it's not exactly senile.

For the second time in my life, I went on the dole. I had moved to Mile End by this time, to another flatshare. I applied to every advertisement I could see in London, and every computer agency. After four months there was still nothing, but I was determined. I finally answered an advert and went for an interview. They said they would accept me if I took an aptitude test. My heart sank, and I didn't expect to pass it. I found it very hard and was almost certain that I'd failed, but I got 78% - and they gave me the job.

So began my IT career. That was 28 years ago now and as I write, I'm still a computer programmer. I've been made redundant three times, but I've always found another job straight away. I'm not a natural, as was probably borne out by the aptitude tests. People with maths or music degrees are probably the most talented at this sort of logical thinking. Most of my fellow programmers have been men, and I've frequently been the only woman in meetings, offices and business lunches.

Ironically, because I'm not naturally brilliant at my job, I've had to work harder at it, and this very struggle has brought immense satisfaction when I've managed to produce a complicated piece of work which someone else with a maths degree might have sailed through, and even found boring. I can't think of anything else I would have done as a career, apart from being a full-time mother. I do have an eye for detail, as linguists tend to, and a stubborn determination to see things through.

So that was the career taken care of. I could hold my head up high when people asked what I did for a living. It was good for references, good for potential boyfriends, since now they could see I was part of the real, sensible, responsible, adult working world. It was also good for paying bills, and allowing a bit more freedom to go on holidays, buy a car etc. Now I just needed to meet that man, and have those two children…

★ ★ ★

While I was living in Mile End, we had a burglary. I was the only one in, and I was asleep at the time and didn't hear a thing. I came down into the sitting room of the flatshare the next morning, to find the hi-fi had gone. The wires had been slashed. I called the police, who said if I had been awake and heard them, I could have just turned my bedroom light on and the burglars would probably have fled.

'You're fucking joking,' I thought. 'If I had woken up and heard intruders, knowing I was by myself, the last thing I would have done would have been to alert them to the fact. I would have crawled underneath my bedclothes and lain there as silently as possible.'

A few days after this, I was sitting talking to someone on the phone in the kitchen. The kitchen was a strange L shape, and the phone was positioned at the end of one of the ends. All of a sudden there was an almighty crash of glass. It came from just around the corner at the other end of the L, just yards from where I was sitting.

The door to the kitchen was glass, and it led to the little back garden. Anyone could have climbed over the wall into the garden and smashed their way into the kitchen. I immediately assumed the burglar had returned, and was standing in the kitchen, yards from me, but just out of sight round the corner of the L shape.

I gasped and quietly put down the phone without explanation. I just had to face the intruder. He would see me soon enough anyway.

I stood up and took a step. Then another. It seemed the longest four yards of my life. I took another two steps and turned the corner. My heart was pounding in my chest at this point. There was glass all over the floor, but no burglar and the kitchen door was intact. Then I noticed a stone in one corner of the kitchen. It had been thrown through the side window, presumably from the street.

The police came again, and asked if I had any enemies I could think of. I couldn't. My landlady was slightly weird, and I didn't think had many friends, but I didn't know if she actually had people who hated her. Perhaps it was just kids throwing stones, and coincidence that it followed so soon after the burglary.

I felt uneasy in the house after that. I would jump whenever people put anything through the letterbox or made an unexpected entry into the room I was in, or if I heard an unexplained sound somewhere in the house. (Actually to this day I still jump slightly at the post being pushed through my letterbox, viewing it as a little threatening, as if someone is attempting to invade my territory, however crazy that sounds.)

Bad things had happened while I was in that flat. I had split up with Clive, had become pregnant, had had a lump in my breast, there was the burglary and then the stone through the kitchen window. All right up there on the stressometer. And I didn't really like my landlady. It was time to move on – again.

* * *

I moved to Leyton, East London, to yet another flatshare. For the next few months things settled down on the boyfriend front. I was working as a computer programmer in a stockbroking company in Chelmsford. I was not very good at all, and found it extremely stressful, but I managed to keep going for about a year. Then one of the flatmates had to leave suddenly, admitting that he owed £35,000 on the Stock Exchange and had to 'disappear', asking us to deny any knowledge of his whereabouts to callers. This left a spare room.

Within a few days, we were interviewing candidates. One of them was a very good-looking Irish guy called Aidan, and although I had a few misgivings about having such a sexy man at close quarters, I felt we had found our man for the flatshare. He moved in straight away. Aidan and I started flirting from day one, although it transpired he did have a girlfriend, Joyce, living in Florida. He never seemed that keen to hear from her though, so I never felt guilty about my flirtatious behaviour.

One day I was invited to a party the other side of London, and asked Aidan if he wanted to come along. He seemed to jump at the chance. I said I would drive, as the party host said we could stay overnight at the house so I could sleep off any over-the-limit drunkenness during the night. It was his parents' house and he was just borrowing it for the weekend. So we grabbed our sleeping bags and off we went.

The party was not that brilliant. There were only a few guests, so I poured myself a large glass of wine, to help my part of the party go with more of a swing. I was quite happy just chatting to Aidan. Three full glasses later the party seemed to be going with great aplomb. Then suddenly everything changed. The host's parents arrived home unannounced, and switched all the lights on. People stood around awkwardly, making polite conversation with the parents. To be fair to them, they knew their son was throwing the party and didn't object to guests staying overnight, but turning on the lights ruined any atmosphere that might have been brewing. Guests started making their excuses, and leaving.

I thought I would just fetch our sleeping bags from the car and quietly find a corner of a room somewhere, to try and doze off for a few hours before driving home in the morning. I went outside, got the sleeping bags, and went back to the house – with my car keys still in my hand. 'You're in no fit state to drive, young lady,' stated the father, with concern in his voice, when he saw the car keys dangling from my hand.

In my drunken state of mind, I felt suddenly defiant. Hadn't he seen the sleeping bags? I hadn't had any intention of driving – but now I had. 'I'll show you,' I thought. 'I AM capable of driving.' 'We're going' I declared to Aidan. Without saying goodbye, we stuffed the sleeping bags in the back of the car and drove off. I was secretly pleased that Aidan wouldn't be able to see me looking awful in the morning.

We soon came to a small roundabout. Aidan was navigating. 'Er... take the next turning. Ooooh no... can you go round again, I'm not sure'. So I drove round once more. 'OK, take this exit... oh fockin' hell... no, go round again.'

I drove round the roundabout about four times before eventually taking one of the exits. A blue light suddenly appeared behind us, but I didn't pay much attention. Then I noticed it was flashing, and I realised with horror, even in my drunk state, that it was a police car.

I pulled over. The police car stopped behind me, blue light continuing to flash. A young policewoman got out and walked towards me. I wound down the window to speak to her. I don't remember the question she asked me, but within a few seconds of my answer she had asked me to 'step outside the vehicle' and take a breathalyser test. Good thing I was so drunk, or I would have been horrified at this turn of events.

I breathed into a little bag. The 'too drunk to drive' light obviously shone like a beacon from this little contraption. She took back the object that had sealed my fate, and then said words I never want to hear again, which were more or less, 'I'm arresting you on suspicion of being drunk while driving. I have to inform you that anything you say will be taken down and may be used against you in a court of law.' Blimey! They really say that! She continued: 'I must ask you to accompany us to the police station, where your breathalyser test will be confirmed, and you may be charged.'

Oh good god. I got into the police car. I have no idea what happened to Aidan but somehow he made his way home.

In the police car, the policewoman bizarrely became quite chatty. 'Well was the party good?' 'Not really,' I confessed. 'If you hadn't been going round the roundabout that many times, we wouldn't have been able to arrest you,' she said cheerfully.

Great. Thanks for telling me. Back then, they had to have a reason for stopping people. Nowadays, I think they only need to suspect someone of being drunk while driving.

The second breathalyser test confirmed that I was more than double the limit. Strangely, the police treated me very nicely. They took me to a police cell, which I remember being yellow. I lay on the bench and fell asleep in a drunken stupor. At one point during the night the little hatch in the door opened and a man looked in, smiled, and closed it again.

I was aware, even in my state, that this was the second time in my life that my freedom had been taken away. I was not free to do as I liked. I could not walk out of that cell, just like when the Arab had turned the key in the lock in Italy.

At about 4.30 am, they came to fetch me. A surly man gave me back my things and told me that my insurance would shoot up now. He said I was free to go. I had no car, no money, no phone, no Aidan – and was still drunk. It was five o'clock on a February morning and outside it was very cold and still dark. It seems quite an odd thing for the police to do – to let a young woman out into the night, in that state.

I found a phone box and asked the operator if I could reverse the charges to a taxi firm. Amazingly they took the call, and a taxi appeared within minutes. The taxi driver spent most of the journey back to Leyton telling me how I could get round the problem of losing my licence. According to him, you just have to tell the DVLA that you've lost your licence before they take it off you at the court hearing. The replacement licence arrives, and then you can carry on driving after your ban. If you're stopped by the police during the year's ban, you produce the replacement licence. Nowadays, that would never work. Instant technology would reveal in seconds that you had been banned.

Back in Leyton, I got a telling off from my flatmates. They said the police had arrived at the house, complete with blue flashing lights, in the early hours and woken them up, demanding to know if Anna Skye lived there. They couldn't tell my flatmates what had happened to me, so they were very concerned. One of the guys remarked how stupid I was – that really hurt. All the more so, because he was right. How irresponsible and dangerous for me to be on the road like that. I deserved everything that was coming to me.

The day of the trial was set for two weeks later and a solicitor was appointed for me. He was a small, rotund man, who sweated profusely the whole time I was with him, and smoked like a chimney. But he was absolutely charming, and seemed to be on my side.

'I'll do my utmost to get you off. Can you think of anything that might lessen your sentence?'

'Well the parents came back early and put the lights on and everyone stood around awkwardly, so we thought it best to leave, even though we had brought our sleeping bags to sleep the night,' I offered, as my only, extremely weak, defence. (It was only weeks later that I remembered the father accusing me of not being able to drive in that state, although I hardly think that childish defiance in the face of sensible advice would have been accepted as mitigating circumstances.)

'Hmm. Pity,' he said. 'But I still reckon I can get you twelve months instead of eighteen months. At over double the limit, you should be getting eighteen months'.

Eighteen months without a car! It was unthinkable. Even though in London public transport was pretty good. What would I say to friends and colleagues? The shame of it.

I was ushered into the court and stood in the dock. I had deliberately worn a shabby-looking jacket to try and appear penniless – as if the court would have fallen for that old trick.

'How do you plead?'

'Guilty,' I said in a small voice, the only word I've ever said in a court. And then the solicitor started to give his defence, complete with details that were a complete lie.

'My client was at a party. The parents of the host came back early unannounced and turned on all the lights. A huge row ensued and a fight broke out and my client thought it prudent to leave the party.'

I was amazed that a man of the law could lie blatantly like that in court. I was standing beside him, and could have blurted out that there was no row or fight. Unlikely, but possible! I received only a 12-month ban, thanks to my dear, sweaty, smoking solicitor. He could have chosen not to make the effort since he was being paid anyway, but I could see that he felt sorry for me. Rightly or wrongly (mostly wrongly), I did feel very sorry for myself as well. Maybe it was just a personal goal to see how far he could get a client's sentence reduced. But I shall always be grateful to him for this small act of kindness.

Life without a car was in fact not too bad in London. By this time I had given up on Aidan, who had proved to be arrogant, negative and critical of everyone, and I had started going out with a tall, handsome Geordie called Dan. He was laid back and kind, and didn't mind ferrying me around. So the year's ban went quickly, without too much interruption of my normal way of life. The shame of it was the worst consequence, and the fact that my insurance increased. What if I had killed someone? A child, maybe. That could have ruined an entire family's life. It would have affected me forever. The police did me a big favour.

Dan and I lasted four months, which I always think is a critical point in most relationships. After three or four months the first-love rush has subsided. The 'real' people have revealed themselves and the irritating characteristics or incompatible traits which have been bubbling under the surface all along and have been ignored for the good of the relationship have become intolerable. We didn't have the same background. He was working class, and worked in construction. I was middle-class and worked with computers. He left school at 16, I went to university. After a while we had nothing in common and I started getting bored.

During the four months I made an impromptu visit to the doctor's as I happened to be passing the surgery one day. I had suddenly decided that I needed a cervical smear and asked if it would be possible to have it there and then, a very unusual request. The nurse was called, checked my records and said I wouldn't need one for another three years, given my age and the date of my last smear. But I insisted, which was very unlike my normal, fairly docile, polite self, and in the end she relented. She carried out the smear and I went home.

Some time later I received a letter informing me that the test had revealed I had abnormal cells on my cervix that could turn cancerous if not treated. They arranged for me to have an operation within the next few weeks, in which they used a laser to remove the cells. I was given the all-clear some time later, but ever after, penetrative sex hurt for the first few attempts after a period of abstention.

This turn of events hadn't helped my sex life with Dan. To take my mind off this souring relationship, I decided to go skiing with the badminton club for a week. As Dan was a non-sporty person, and one with few interests or hobbies, he was not invited. At the end of the week, I arrived back into London and took the tube to Vauxhall. I remember standing on the station platform and looking around – it was dirty, noisy and depressing. I'd just spent a week in the beautiful, clean, fresh air of the Alps. I thought that at 34 I could do better. I needed a more suitable boyfriend, and a better life. I resolved to leave London and Dan immediately.

The following Monday, I gave my notice in. I had just finished a piece of work, and my boss agreed that it would be pointless for me to start another project. So I left at the end of the week.

That weekend I packed up and moved back to my parents' house in the West Country. I had spent 10 years in London. I had lived in 13 different flatshares. I had slept with five guys. I had been pregnant twice and had had two abortions. I had been arrested and incarcerated. I had been made redundant three times. That was the bad stuff. But I had played a lot of volleyball, tennis and badminton. I had been to a lot of parties. My friendship with Cara, my second best friend from school, who was also in London, had continued. I'd helped the survival of the mountain gorillas in Rwanda. I'd forged a career in computing, even if I did strain my head with every program I wrote. I'd just about saved the life of a little girl. At 34, I was still very fit and healthy. And I'd learnt a lot about myself and men. I guess I had just grown up in the big city, albeit not the way I would have chosen. I was free of emotional baggage, solvent, available and still fertile, and ready to start the next phase of my life.

CHAPTER SEVEN

Pen

After four weeks at my parents' house being pampered and made to feel very welcome, I was ready to move on. You forget how restricting it is, living with your parents, however kind or nice they are. I had for some time now considered living in Bristol. It was a good-size city, with plenty of young people, amenities, jobs, shops, sports facilities and culture. And of course, it would be harbouring my future husband.

I had had enough of flat sharing. I reckoned that at 34 it was time to buy my own house. With typical generosity, my father helped me with a vast sum of money towards the cost of a mortgage. Cara's parents, who lived in Bristol and had known me from the age of 11, offered to put me up temporarily while I looked for a house. Within three days I had found a modern, two-bed, semi-detached house in north Bristol. I had also found a computer job with a local Bristol financial company. It all fell into place quickly, as if the gods were wanting me to move out of London (not that I believe in that nonsense).

★ ★ ★

For the next three years I lived quite happily in my little two-up, two-down in Bristol, though my job at Sun Alliance was a disaster. I wasn't interested in the subject matter, and found it hard to motivate myself. I started looking around for another job (just as they were thinking of getting rid of me, I found out later), and very quickly secured a programmer's job at British Aerospace at Filton, just up the road from my house. Now I was interested in the subject matter. Aviation! Airbus wings! Wonderful.

I joined the local volleyball club. That could have been a potential source of boyfriend/husband material, I thought, but apart from a fleeting crush on one of the men's team members, who made it very obvious that he was after a much younger member of the girls' team, there was no romance in sight. In a way, this made things easier. I adored playing volleyball. At one point I was playing five times a week, and still couldn't get enough of it. It became quite an insular way of life. The other team members were becoming my friends. I would go round to their houses for meals and parties, and pretty soon volleyball was simply the life I led outside work.

And then as in most clubs, I found there were divisions. There were two girls' teams, the good and the not-so-good. At 34 I was still young enough to jump high, but at five foot three I couldn't 'block' (jump up at the net to stop the opponents' smashes). Even so, I was in the first team for the first two years. Then gradually new, younger, taller girls started to join and I was soon relegated to the also-rans second team. We all trained together, but cliques were forming among the better girls, from which we second-teamers were excluded. Bitchiness and rumblings abounded between the two teams, to the point where we wouldn't contemplate going to parties or meals 'if SHE's going'.

By the time I was 37 a few creaks and joint pains were making themselves felt, but I still loved the game and wanted to keep going as long as possible. Our club had done very well. We had won the Avon League and the South West League. I loved the thrill of playing in competitions and even qualified as a referee. Although I played for the first team occasionally, gradually I was being relegated to the benches more and more, and I found that on some of the away matches I would come home, having spent the entire day travelling to the match and back, with about 10 minutes' court time to my name. Not only was this becoming embarrassing, and demotivating, but I wasn't getting any exercise.

I also felt I was a slight drain on the team's resources. The coach was only putting me on court out of social etiquette. Volleyball is a young person's game, and players are very accident-prone. I've seen many people get injured in the 20 years I played this amazing game: broken ribs, ankles, and fingers; strained tendons and ligaments; damaged knees were not unusual.

In the end, I couldn't even smash the ball over the net. I had damaged my right shoulder trying to serve in a frozen sports hall without warming up properly. It's a horrible feeling knowing you are a pain to play with, when you still love the game, and when your social life is so bound up with the sport. This damaged shoulder still affects me today, as I try and play tennis as much as I can.

So before I was pushed, I decided to look around for another sport. I couldn't live without a sport. It was my second passion in life – my first being to find a husband. I also seemed to choose group sports, although I was quite shy in group situations. I guess that as I liked competitive sports, I needed other people to make up the competition.

I had been skydiving on and off during my years in London, and had always meant to go back to it one day, even though I had often been terrified. I decided to take it up again, and looked on the map for the nearest drop zone. Netheravon on Salisbury Plain fitted the bill. I drove down and found myself excited to be starting another activity, another phase of my life. It's a mistake to take up a sport only to meet other people, and I knew I loved skydiving for its own sake, but at the back of my mind, or maybe the front, I wondered what hunky man, or even ordinary man, might be just waiting to jump at that very moment.

I arrived at the car park, and sat in the car. And continued to sit in the car. I couldn't see the main area for jumpers from there as it was just out of sight round the corner of a big hangar. Thoughts of a malfunction I had had a few years before whirled in my mind. Memories of people who had died, or been brain-damaged, or injured through skydiving accidents came flooding back.

I turned on the ignition again, and decided the whole thing was too risky. Then another thought: 'What if my husband-to-be is round the corner?' This wasn't a psychic moment. I often thought this before going to parties, new clubs, anywhere in fact where I knew I would meet new people.

I switched off the ignition, got out of the car and walked round the corner to where I knew people were often standing around, waiting to be called to jump, packing their canopies or just watching the action. There was little wind, but the cloud base was at about 1000 ft, too low for jumping. You need at least 3000 ft for a safe jump, to ensure you can see the ground from the aircraft when exiting.

Unsurprisingly, there were few people around, so I assumed most people were inside the hangars, or in the nearby café. I saw three guys hanging around the benches outside the hangar, and thought I would ask them if any imminent jumping had been announced. It was obvious there wouldn't be, but my confidence was waning, and I needed to talk to someone.

Two of the guys were actually sitting on top of the bench, and one was standing a few yards away by himself. I approached the man who was on his own. He was about 45, short and stocky with a grey beard.

'Hi. Is there any jumping going on soon?' I ventured, knowing this would make me seem like a beginner.

'Not at the moment. Clouds are too low, apparently.'

I assumed from the 'apparently' that he was probably a first-timer, and that he was quoting his instructor's explanation for the lack of jumping.

'You here to jump?' he asked.

'Yes, hopefully. I used to jump at another DZ [drop zone]. I've had a break and now I'm going to try again'.

'Oh right. What category are you?'

His voice had changed, to one of slight awe, as if I was a 'real' jumper.

'Cat nine' I said, feeling rather proud, even though this is way down the experience ladder for the vast majority of jumpers who jump hundreds, sometimes thousands, of times each year. But this guy probably didn't know that, so I enjoyed my little moment of glory.

'Look out, she's an expert,' said someone. I looked round and saw that one of the guys on the nearby bench had approached us. He had obviously overheard the conversation. He was about five foot nine, early 30s and broad-chested, with dark brown thick, wavy hair, brown eyes, a strong masculine face, a moustache and a broken nose. He was very handsome, and I instantly felt an attraction.

He was smoking a cigarette, but held it away from me. So that's why they were outside when everyone else was inside. This guy needed a fag.

I laughed at his remark, knowing it was a self-deprecating comment to make me feel good, and we started chatting. It turned out that the first man I had talked to was totally blind, but I hadn't noticed, since he'd turned towards me and his eyes were open and seemed to be looking straight at me.

Pen, the second guy, told me he had been roped into doing a parachute jump during a chance conversation in a local pub with John, the blind guy. Pen had said he would have a go at almost anything once, just to try it. John then stated that he had always wanted to try a parachute jump and intended signing up for one, so Pen felt that if a blind man could do it, he could hardly not go for it himself, after his recent claim.

So there they were, the pair of them, waiting for the clouds to lift before doing their first static line jump. If they hadn't had that conversation in the pub, or if it had been sunny that day, or if he hadn't wanted a cigarette, they wouldn't have been standing there. They would probably have completed their first jump and gone home.

Someone suggested going inside for a tea, so I went in with them. I sat two chairs away from Pen round a table, with about 10 other people already sitting at it. We wouldn't be able to chat any more. At one point I looked at him and he was looking straight at me. We both looked away quickly, but I was pleased that he had been looking at me, with an intent, interested look.

The others started to get up from the table, which left me, Pen, John and another guy at the table. I wondered how we were going to engineer this situation so that Pen and I could carry on chatting. I needn't have worried. Pen was suddenly sitting next to me. John had miraculously disappeared. Pen told me later that he had told him to beat it, in no uncertain terms, because he was rather keen on talking to me. So Pen and I were free to talk.

And talk we did. For hours. We found out all about each other. He was 33 (he told me) and taking his law degree at Southampton University as a mature student. He was also working on the Isle of Wight ferry to pay for his studies. He lived near Bournemouth with his elderly mother and slightly crazy sister, who didn't work, and her hen-pecked husband, who worked all the hours god sends. All that sounded just fine, I thought to myself.

He asked for my number and we went our separate ways. He told me later that had he not got my number that day he would have asked to look through the car registration numbers at the drop zone's security gate, hoping to find a Bristol-based owner.

He rang up the next day and we continued to chat. He was a great listener, and made me laugh. He was also articulate and chatty, without hogging the conversation. Very soon we arranged to meet at a pub with a room half way between us. It was called the White Swan, in Salisbury.

I was very nervous when I drove into the car park. I really felt as if the next few hours could seal the next 50 years of my life. Pen was there waiting for me, smiling broadly. We sat outside drinking wine. I felt instantly at ease with him, and all my nerves vanished. He was holding my hands across the table, and when at one point he said I needed a good spanking as a flirty joke, I felt myself going red, with nowhere to hide.

He said he wanted to go upstairs to the room, and I readily agreed. If it was too early, and I seemed slutty, I didn't care. We went to bed and it just felt right. Our hands were all over each other's bodies, while we kissed and laughed together.

I reached down to help his erection – but there wasn't one. I was slightly surprised, but just thought I could help him along with it. I felt further down and found it, small and limp, and seemingly uninterested. I started to massage it, but there was no change.

After a few minutes, a slight change came over Pen. 'I'll do it' he said, embarrassed, 'You don't need to.'

'OK,' I said, trying to sound nonchalant. But try as he might, he couldn't get much of a reaction and in the end we gave up, and just cuddled each other.

'I'm a bit nervous' he said, quietly, after a while.

'Sure' I replied. I thought nerves probably were the problem. In a way, it was nice that he was so nervous. Having sex with me obviously meant quite a lot to him, I decided. Perhaps I should have taken more notice of this sign of a potential circulation problem.

We got dressed and decided to go for a drive in the car. I sat in the passenger seat while he drove. Without thinking I opened the glove compartment. I spotted his passport, so I took it out and opened it. The photo was awful, as usual, and I laughed at it. But just as I was about to look at other details on the page, he suddenly snatched the passport out of my hands.

'You don't need to look at that,' he said, slightly flustered. But

I had already seen it – 'Date of Birth: 31st July 1958'. Hang on – that made him a year older than he had told me.

'Er – you're 34. You said 33.'

'Yes. Well it's only one year. I thought you were much younger than you are, so I was trying to make out I was more your age'.

Hmmm. It was only one year, and didn't really make any difference, so why lie? And why try and hide it now, when he knows I'm three years older than him anyway?

I felt slightly disappointed. Honesty in a relationship is so important. I know that people do fib about their age to begin with, hoping their partners-to-be will get to know them first, and like them for their personalities, before finding out their real age, by which time hopefully they would be hooked. I decided to move on from it. But I didn't forget it. But we got on so well. We could chat to each other so naturally and make each other laugh so easily.

Pen asked to see me again and despite my slight misgivings, I readily agreed. We arranged for him to come up to Bristol for the weekend, and that started a pattern that would last for five years. His mother was becoming quite frail, and although her manic daughter also lived in the house with them, Pen felt his mother needed him as the voice of reason. He didn't want to move in with me, unless we were married, and he didn't want to marry me unless he had a good job. So he would leave Bournemouth Friday evening, and return Sunday evening, or Monday morning, so that he could spend the week with his mother, and the weekends with me.

We continued to parachute at weekends. Pen was trying to get his category 8, which would allow him to do relative work with me. I heard of a drop zone in France called Gap where you could stay for days and they had many planes, many instructors, and accommodation on site. We looked into it, but the only week I could make, Pen could not. So we decided to go separately.

By coincidence Pen was climbing Mont Blanc, no less, with three friends the week I was free so he would actually be in the same area of France. He said he would try and join me if the weather was bad and he couldn't climb. So I went off to Gap for a week, and achieved Category 10, which meant I could jump with any number of other skydivers at any level. The weather was perfect, so Pen set off up the mountain. He phoned me when we were both back in the UK. We had both had successful trips but couldn't wait to see each other again.

The next weekend he started to discuss going to Gap again so that we could jump together soon.

'But you've got your finals coming up,' I remarked, thinking he'd forgotten.

'Nah, it'll be OK. I'll be back in time to take it.'

Hmmm. That didn't sound very responsible to me, but there was no talking to him. Although he'd enjoyed his climb to Mont Blanc, he'd decided that skydiving was a whole lot more fun. 'We can spend the summer jumping together,' he said, so off he went. A week before his finals.

We spoke on the phone on and off throughout the week. He was loving it and making good headway up the category system. Then I spoke to him two days before his exams, when I assumed he'd be talking about packing for his journey home.

'Er – there's been a change of plan,' he said. 'I'm so close to getting my cat 8 that I've decided to change my flight to the day after tomorrow.'

'What? That's the day of your finals. You'll be knackered. You won't have slept for 24 hours by the time you take your exam!'

'It'll be fine. I'm used to not sleeping.'

'Oh no, please give yourself more time. You can get your cat 8 at any point in the summer. Your finals are much more important. You need to make sure you've had at least some sleep before you take them.'

'Nah. It'll be fine. Anyway, I've changed my flight now.'

So that was that. I'd only been going out with him for six weeks, so I didn't feel I had the right to tell him what to do, other than to try and put forward my argument. But this didn't bode well. He was being really irresponsible. I should have told him that I wouldn't carry on going out with him if he carried on with his plan. But I was in love with him, and wanted to marry him and have his children. I couldn't get rid of him and couldn't even contemplate threatening to do so.

Pen got his category 8, which meant he could now jump with me in the same freefall groups. He took the later flight home and took his finals the same day, having not slept for 24 hours. I was frustrated and enraged by the short-sightedness and selfishness of it, but it was too late now. We could only wait for the result.

Six weeks later the result came through: he'd got a 2:2. He told me over the phone from Bournemouth. He sounded sheepish and deflated. His university tutors had predicted a 2:1. What a complete waste of all that hard work. We will of course never know if he would have attained a 2:1 had he slept the previous night, but it was his duty to try and give himself the best chance. There was no point my saying 'well, if you'd only come back from Gap earlier...'

Many times throughout our life together when money was tight, I came back to this moment and the telephone conversation where he had told me he was changing his flight, wondering if I could have done more to prevent it. I felt he had begun to rely on me already as his support system. Before he met me, he had been working hard for his degree, while getting up at 5 am every day to work on the ferry. Now it almost seemed as if he felt he had found a meal ticket and his own earning capabilities were less important. I didn't want to resent him for anything, but unfortunately I found myself doing just that for this episode. But I told myself he might find a good job anyway, and then the Gap decision would be irrelevant.

I managed to move on from it, and concentrate on our growing relationship. We became lovers and soulmates and friends. I was supremely happy during those four months. We had hinted at marriage and children long-term, after planning to take some skydiving and diving holidays together. Pen was an excellent PADI diver, and I felt safe with him in the water. He had even been an assistant diving instructor on Majorca for three years.

He didn't want children at that point. It was too soon for him, he said. He was only 34 and wanted to live a bit more first. I was 37 and watching the biological clock. By 40 I knew a woman's egg quality dramatically decreased. But I told myself that many, many women have children in their forties. My monthly cycle was fine. I hadn't noticed anything changing in that regard. I didn't want to rock the boat and start making him feel trapped into marriage and a family so soon after we had met. All mention of such things was kept very light. Rightly so, I feel. After four months you might think you know someone, but you probably don't. It would be crazy to rush into anything.

CHAPTER EIGHT

Change of life

Pen's erections, although not always as stiff as a board, returned quite soon after he started travelling up to Bristol. Our sexual activities were fun and intimate, and brought us closer.

'I think I might go on the pill,' I said to him one day, about four months after we had met. 'Then you won't need to use condoms.'

'Great,' Pen agreed. 'When?' he added, with a chuckle.

So I went to the doctor, and was given six months' supply of the contraceptive pill, with few questions asked about my medical history. They never found out, for example, that when I had come off the pill at the age of 24, it had taken about another four months for my monthly cycle to return.

For the next few weeks sex was lovely – no condoms to faff around with. Then one day I realised that I hadn't had a period since I'd taken the pill. I wasn't concerned because of what had happened when I was younger, so I thought at 37 this was still normal behaviour for my body. But this time I noticed gradually that my libido was ebbing away. I was becoming drier and drier. Pen found it increasingly hard to penetrate me.

After four months on the pill, I decided to come off it. Our sex life had virtually died, since I had just lost interest, along with my libido. Two or three months went by, with no change. Pen couldn't penetrate me because it was too painful for me. My periods hadn't returned, but I assumed again that this was normal. So we stopped trying to have sex and decided to wait until my body had resumed its cycles.

Months went by, and still nothing, yet we were still getting along fine. The lack of sex didn't seem to be dampening our love for each other. Pen continued to travel up from Bournemouth every weekend. He had his degree (albeit only a 2:2) and was looking for solicitors' jobs within the Bristol area. Unfortunately a recession was just hitting Britain and law firms were cutting back on hiring staff. But Pen wasn't worried. The Crown Prosecution Service had made him what seemed almost tantamount to the promise of a job on finishing his degree. They had interviewed him at some point during his degree years, and had been impressed enough to make him a virtual offer. When the recession ended, Pen declared, the CPS job would be there again for the taking. But at the time of the offer, Pen was heading for a 2:1. A 2:1 is viewed as a 'good' degree, while a 2:2 is viewed as only 'average'.

He started sending off CVs to law firms. He received many replies, all rejecting him even for an interview. We'll never know of course if it was the recession or the 2:2, but the lower qualification cannot have helped.

'There's no point sending out any more CVs,' said Pen, sounding resigned after one more rejection, 'I'll wait for the CPS job to come up.'

'You could still try and apply for jobs now,' I pleaded.

'No point – I'll wait'.

So he went on the dole, but continued to travel up from Bournemouth each weekend. His mother helped him with petrol money. Without a job, there would be no wedding. Pen was adamant that he didn't want to marry me if he wasn't working.

Although we had continued to get along in our relationship, our sex life had died a death. My periods hadn't returned and it was coming up to 18 months since I had taken the pill. I had actually got used to not having them, but at the back of my mind, I still assumed they would come back one day. My libido had dropped away and even when we did try on the odd occasion to have sex, it proved impossible to achieve penetration. So after a while, we gave up, but continued to kiss and cuddle and hold hands on walks or in cinemas, etc. On the outside, we looked like the perfect couple.

One day as I was doing my teeth over the sink, I felt a sudden hot flush. It seemed to start around my chest, and then flushed up over my face. I felt very hot, but when I looked in the mirror, my face appeared only slightly warm. Within a minute, it had vanished, so I dismissed it, but a few days later, I had another one, and then another a few hours after that. Over the next few months the hot flushes came more and more frequently.

I actually mentioned it to my mother one day on the phone. 'No, you're too young for the menopause,' she said with a chuckle. I was 39. But Pen suggested I go and see a doctor, just to check it out. I agreed, although I thought it was a waste of time. The nurse took a sample of my blood and I went home. I would have to wait a few days for the results.

About a week later I was at home, and decided that I might as well ring up for the results. I didn't see the point of going all the way into the surgery again.

'Hi. My name's Anna Skye. I had a blood test recently, and I'm wondering if the results are in yet.'

'OK' said the surgery receptionist on the other end of the phone. 'I'll just go and check.' A few minutes later, she returned.

'Yes. The results are in. You're post-menopausal,' she stated matter-of-factly.

Pardon? I remember staring at the Wi-Fi near the phone. I couldn't believe the words. This couldn't be happening. This was my life we were talking about here. My happiness. My world came down.

'But I'm only 39 and I wanted children,' I said very quietly.

'Oooohhh' answered the receptionist, now realising the enormity of what she had done. 'I'm sure the doctor would like to talk to you about this.' I think she had assumed that I was the normal age for the menopause, and that I was expecting this news.

Everything was different after that. Everything seemed irrelevant. I couldn't have my own children. I would never have my own grandchildren. I would never breastfeed my own child. People wouldn't be able to congratulate me on the birth of my child. I would never be a successful woman. I would never be able to join pre-school mother-and-toddler groups. I would never build sandcastles on the beach with my child.

I rang Pen in Bournemouth and cried down the phone. He didn't know what to say, but sounded shocked. He assured me it didn't change his feelings towards me. Luckily children hadn't been something he felt he had to produce to feel whole. But it's different for men. They can go on having children into their 80s. It's always something they can call on, if required. Women are so restricted by their fertile window, never knowing when it might close.

Pen said that we could discuss options when he arrived in Bristol that weekend. I was devastated. The only real goal I had had for my life had just been destroyed. It was so final. I couldn't go back and untake the pill. It left me with a sadness that wouldn't go away.

As far as I was concerned, the pill had caused my menopause. I had had normal periods from the age of 13 right up until the very month I had taken the pill, when they had stopped abruptly forever, with no warning. My two sisters went on to have their menopauses in their early fifties, and my mother had hers at 47. But the doctors were adamant that my menopause couldn't have been caused by the pill. Sorry – the pill *must* have at least indirectly had some bearing on this. The pill does affect your monthly cycle, and your hormones, so it must be at least possible for it to affect your monthly cycle long-term.

I contacted *The Guardian* and they put me through to the reporter in charge of health issues. I explained what had happened. She listened sympathetically, but then replied that while it was very sad for me, she couldn't print something that might make many women panic and stop taking the pill.

Pen and I discussed our options. We talked about adoption, but when you've been looking forward to having your own child, adoption seems a sad substitute. I didn't want someone else's child – I wanted my own. We talked about IVF, using another woman's eggs with Pen's sperm. At least then it would be Pen's child, and maybe look like Pen, so we wouldn't even have to tell people it wasn't mine. Then we realised that we would have to tell the child

OUT OF THE RED

anyway who his/her parents were, so we would just have to come clean and tell everybody.

'But it would look like you as well, wouldn't it?' said Pen, hopefully. 'It would have grown inside your body.'

'No,' I said sadly, slightly surprised at his lack of knowledge. 'It wouldn't have any of my genes, or characteristics. I would just be carrying it for nine months. It would have the biological mother's genes, and yours.'

We couldn't believe we were even needing to have this conversation. Why had it happened to us? Well why not, came back the answer. Women go through this every day. And worse. People are told they have cancer, or are losing their sight, every day. At least we both had our health. It was cold comfort to me.

I went to the doctor's and he apologised profusely for the way I had found out the news. He had intended to go through it gently with me. But the end result would have been the same. Then he offered me some hope. 'I wonder if it's a mistake. You are so young to be having the menopause. I think I will take a second opinion.' He arranged for me to see a fertility specialist – a Dr Hillman at Bristol University.

The first thing I noticed when I walked into Dr Hillman's surgery was a family photo on his desk. It showed him, his wife and their five children happily posing at a family gathering. I was disproportionately affronted. I felt he was turning the knife in my wound, showing off his lovely children while I couldn't even have one. The second thing I noticed, apart from Dr Hillman himself sitting behind the desk, was another man sitting on a chair, a little way away from us, writing notes.

'I hope you don't mind,' Dr Hillman began, 'your case is quite unusual, so we have a student with us to observe.'

Yes I did mind, actually. I minded a whole lot being a 'case', being observed like some strange object in a scientific experiment. I just wanted a child. I wanted to be able to be pregnant. I didn't want to be here, being stared at.

'No, that's fine,' I said, smiling.

He asked me about my medical history, about when my periods had begun, when I had taken the pill before, about my two abortions, and the dates of taking the pill recently. He then said he would examine me, take a sonar test and take a blood test. I would then have to return for the results a week later.

I arrived a week later, heart pumping in my chest. The results confirmed that I was post-menopausal - but there was more.

'Your ovaries are not that small,' Dr Hillman commented, giving me a fleeting window of hope. 'There was a developed egg in each of them. You have an auto-immune disease which is affecting your entire endocrine system. And your thyroid is not producing nearly as much thyroxine as it should. Your TSH (thyroid stimulating hormone) is 36. It's supposed to be between 0.5 and 4.5 or 5.0. You must be put on thyroxine straight away, since your body has been working overtime to compensate for the lack of thyroxine. Tell me, are you still getting hot flushes at the moment?'

I thought for a moment. 'Actually no. I haven't had them for a few days now.'

'That's because of the two developed eggs that have been produced, which are emitting oestrogen. This may be your last chance to conceive. Go home and make love. Also, it's just possible that your fertility will come back at certain periods, but it's impossible to say when, and for how long.'

I was utterly jubilant. Maybe I was a normal woman after all.

Maybe I could conceive and people wouldn't have to treat me as someone to pity after all.

I went home and told Pen that we would have to have sex NOW. He didn't seem that pleased. 'But it's too soon. I don't have a job. We're not married. I wanted to do some more skydiving, and diving with you. I don't feel ready to have a kid.'

'It may be my very last chance. The doctor said so. PLEASE can we do this? I need this baby. I'm actually begging you.'

So we went to bed. Pen found it very difficult to perform to order and couldn't get an erection for the first 20 minutes or so. But eventually, seeing how desperate I was, and knowing that it might be our last chance to conceive naturally, we managed to achieve penetration and he climaxed. That was the first time we had had sex in months, and his entry hurt me, but I couldn't care less.

After he withdrew and went downstairs, fairly unhappy with the situation, I turned around in the bed and put my feet on the wall above the bedstead, lifting my pelvis at a 45 degree angle, trying to do ANYTHING that might help the sperm on their little journeys up through the cervix into my womb and on into the fallopian tube, where I hoped one of my developed eggs was making its way down, and where fertilisation normally takes place.

We waited about two weeks. No period and no hot flush. Then I felt a familiar damp feeling. I rushed upstairs into the loo. My period had come. I was not pregnant. I was numb with grief. I couldn't even cry. Pen was sad for me, but I could tell that he was relieved.

I went back to the doctor and asked if they could stimulate my ovaries somehow, since they were 'not too small'. He thought the chances were very slight indeed, but since I was so desperate he made an appointment for me at a fertility clinic, and I went along on the appointed day.

A nurse came in with a little bowl and two enormous syringes. I was shocked at their size. The needles were about two inches long and about a millimetre thick. After polite chit-chat, she told me to turn around and drop my trousers and knickers. She then stuck both needles into my buttocks. It was very painful, but I was prepared to put up with any pain if it meant I could have a child.

I went back to the clinic four or five times to have the needles stuck into me again. Each time after that, I stood with my trousers and knickers down, visibly shaking in anticipation of the pain to come. On the fifth and last time, the nurse said sheepishly: 'I'm really sorry, but I've been using the wrong length needle. I should have been using this length and this type.' She produced a syringe with a needle of tiny diameter and about half an inch in length.

'Oh, OK,' I said, annoyed, but what could I say?

She then sighed and said, with staggering insensitivity: 'This isn't going to work, you know.' Thanks, just what I needed to hear! I asked to keep the original needles and the current one, so that I could show Pen what I had been going through. I kept them in a drawer for many years, and then somehow they got lost in a house move.

Well, the charming nurse was right. It didn't work. My hot flushes resumed as before. I found it increasingly difficult to sleep. I would wake up sweating buckets and throwing my blankets off. Five minutes later I would be shivering, and pulling them all back over me again. By that time I would be awake, and annoyed, and then I couldn't get back to sleep for hours, being prone to insomnia since childhood anyway.

I went back to my doctor to ask if there was anything he could do. 'We could try you on HRT,' he said. 'It will replenish the oestrogen and progesterone and stop the hot flushes. It should also help your libido.'

Oh really? What wonderful stuff that sounded. Within two weeks or so, my hot flushes disappeared and my libido returned. Vive la HRT!

OK, so ovary stimulation hadn't worked. Now I wanted to try IVF (in vitro fertilisation, literally 'in glass fertilisation', or test tube fertilisation, where a developed egg is injected with sperm to try and create a fertilised embryo).

At the back of my mind was the fact that Dr Hillman had said that my fertility might return at any moment. Since my libido had also returned, we started having sex again. One thing we never checked out, however: the HRT was replacing the oestrogen that a developing egg would have produced itself normally, on its journey through the fallopian tube to the womb, so presumably eggs did not now have to be stimulated by the endocrine system to develop and break out of the ovaries, since there was enough oestrogen in the blood stream. At that rate my fertility, in the shape of my own eggs, would never return, it seemed.

We found an IVF clinic in Plymouth and made an appointment. We were very apprehensive about the whole thing. Pen was a Catholic and wasn't at all sure he agreed with the concept anyway, but he went along with it for my sake. Whilst acknowledging our gratitude for the existence of such procedures, we were still very angry at having to use them.

In the waiting room, there were other couples. Their grim faces all told the same story. No one spoke. No one swapped infertility anecdotes. The staff were lovely. They said what a strong couple we seemed. They took our medical history, and then Pen had to produce a sample of sperm to test its motility. If the sperm proved healthy and normal, the next step was to find a woman who was donating her eggs. They already had a list of women who had volunteered, but they would try and match her up with my characteristics. They added that I would be expected to send her flowers on the day, as the procedure was pretty invasive and painful. For some reason I was quite surprised by this. And I'm ashamed to say that when I was first told this I felt quite indignant. These women had their children. They didn't need their eggs. But very quickly I realised something else. They were donating their own future children to be looked after by unknown parents. For all they knew, we could be bad parents, cold, reserved people who wouldn't give their children a safe, loving home. We might be violent, bad-tempered or worse, paedophiles. These women were making a huge sacrifice for me, and they hadn't even met me. They were also not being paid a penny. I felt chastened, but couldn't help feeling jealous of them nevertheless.

Pen's sperm was normal enough, and its motility was high enough for fertilisation. He was given an appointment about three days before mine. A woman had been found. She was 24, fair-haired and weighed nine stone. Eggs were collected from her and Pen's sperm was injected into them. We had to wait three days to see if any fertilised embryos were created. We had a phone call three days later. Two eggs had developed into embryos, and I should go down to have them implanted.

But Pen was adamant. 'We can't have two babies. We wouldn't cope. How would we afford them?'

'It just gives us more chance of conceiving with two embryos instead of one,' I pleaded.

'On no account are you to have two implanted. You often hear of people having multiple births.'

I rang the clinic and explained the situation. I was put through straight away to the consultant. 'I've been working in IVF for 15 years,' she said, 'and I've only seen one multiple birth. It's MUCH rarer than people think.' I told Pen this piece of information, but he wouldn't budge.

As I drove down for the implantation, I realised that I could still have two 'put back,' as they called it. I too only wanted one baby, but it seemed crazy not to use the two that had been created. The staff had emphasized that quite often no embryos are created, and we should treasure any that were available. The treatment was also expensive, at £3000, which I was paying. Pen didn't have any money to contribute.

I was laid out on the bed and my feet put into stirrups. The nurse looked at me and asked me again, 'Are you going to have one or two put back?' It was one of those moments. I wanted to say two with all my heart, but how could I face Pen if two babies were produced? He would resent me for years probably. He would hate the deception. I wanted a relationship built on trust and honesty. I would have to look him in the face for years to come, if twins were produced, knowing he would know I had betrayed him. But then would I hate him for years if no baby emerged. We would never know if two embryos would have produced at least one baby.

I had only a few seconds to answer. The nurse wasn't going to wait forever, as they had two or three other procedures to get through that morning.

'Just the one,' I said, with huge regret. After the procedure was over, I burst into tears. This wasn't how I had wanted to conceive my first child. It was humiliating lying on my back, with my legs strapped apart, and a metal opener inserted into my vagina to keep it open during the procedure. I wanted to have conceived him/her on a warm Caribbean Island, on the beach at night, or in a four-poster bed in a beautiful little cottage in Scotland.

'Why are you crying?' they asked me, concerned. I didn't want to tell them the real reason, as it seemed so ungrateful. I should have been thankful this procedure was available at all. Well I was, but I didn't want to be the one using it. So I just replied that I was just so happy, knowing that I might now be pregnant.

We would have to wait two weeks before it would be known if the embryo had implanted itself into the lining of my womb and during this time I felt happy and excited. I felt like a proper woman, who could be pregnant at last. Thoughts of not telling the world that it wasn't mine again resurged. No one would know. The baby could look like Pen at least, or it might even have some of my characteristics, since they had tried to choose a woman who looked something like me. Some children don't resemble either of their parents anyway, or only look like one of them. Perhaps those children were in fact also adopted or also the result of IVF, but the parents were not letting on! I had read somewhere that a staggeringly high percentage of children are not the biological offspring of the male in the home, with or without his knowledge.

Pen, surprisingly, also seemed to be quite excited about a possible son or daughter, who would, after all, be his biological child. I no longer looked at other pregnant women with jealousy. I no longer minded when people at work talked about their children. I was going to be one of them soon.

Two weeks crawled by and I bought two pregnancy tests in preparation. The day finally came, and I took the pregnancy tests in with me to work. I didn't want to take the tests at home, with Pen in the near vicinity. I wanted some time to prepare myself, should the worst happen.

About 10.30 am, I disappeared into the ladies' loo. I took out the first test, and peed onto the little stick. 'Leave for 4 minutes.' the instructions said. Four minutes became four hours as far as I was concerned.

I picked up the test. Negative. I was not pregnant. I took out the second test, and peed again on the stick. Four minutes, same result. I was not pregnant. No baby.

I had to somehow get through the rest of the day at work. I had to face Pen and tell him the news. He had decided to stay late in Bournemouth, so I had to tell him by phone. 'What? Noooooo!' He couldn't believe the result. I started to cry down the phone. I knew he felt extremely guilty as well, for his stubborn refusal to let me have two embryos inserted. But for him, I might be pregnant now. But I didn't say anything about that, because it was pointless to bring it up at this moment. We had to pull together, not fall apart.

When he arrived in Bristol that weekend, I was adamant. 'I want to do it again, and this time they are going to insert two,' I wailed. Pen was silent. 'Even if you say no, I am going to do it this time. I'm the one who's paying, and you stopped me having two last time. We should have listened to the experts. They said multiple births were very unlikely, but you wouldn't listen, as usual.'

What was that about resolving not to mention his dreadful, awful, life-changing, selfish decision? I was determined, and furious, and heartbroken – and there was not much he could do or say anyway. If he didn't want to donate his sperm, I decided secretly, I would find embryos that had already been fertilised by some unknown donor.

* * *

We had two more IVF cycles, using Pen's sperm and donated eggs, the first time with two fertilised eggs, and the second time with three. Each time we felt great excitement and hope. Each time our hopes and dreams were dashed to smithereens.

Then the clinic suggested another procedure that had been hitting the newspapers in recent months. I would be paired up with another anonymous woman who was also having problems conceiving. This woman couldn't afford the IVF fee, but she did have her own eggs. Her ovaries would be stimulated so that several eggs, even as many as 20 or more, would be collected. Half would be given to me, in return for my paying for both our procedures, and she would keep the other half. The ones she kept would be fertilised by her husband's sperm, and my half would be fertilised by Pen.

The reason it was so controversial was that sometimes the second woman's embryos developed into babies, while the biological mother's embryos did not. She had then to live with the awful reality that her only biological children were being born and raised by strangers, and she wouldn't even get to meet them. I don't know if this procedure is still practised today. It seems a terrible burden for the biological mother to carry with her through life.

We went ahead and tried this method. Twelve eggs were given to me, and the other woman kept 12 of her own. I was never told if her eggs developed into embryos, or whether those embryos turned into babies.

Five of mine didn't survive. That left seven. I was allowed three more IVF cycles using these seven at a cheaper rate, since the collection stage had been completed.

During the first procedure, three were inserted. No pregnancy. During the second procedure, two were inserted. No pregnancy. That left one little embryo. I had to try it - but there was no pregnancy.

We were emotionally exhausted. It had been a rollercoaster of hopes and crushing disappointment. Over the weeks of the IVF cycles Pen had completely come to terms with the idea of a child to the extent that he felt devastated with each failure, and even cried with me.

We decided to give it a break, not least because of the cost. Even though I had become a software contractor during those years and had about four times my salary as a permanent employee, £3000 on average a time was becoming prohibitive. I even cashed in some of my pension to pay for some of it.

★ ★ ★

Pen and I decided to go for a holiday to Florida to ease the pain and have some respite. We took our jumping and diving gear - there's nothing like the prospect of imminent death to take your mind off your problems.

We did a few jumps and could already feel our spirits lifting. We decided to do one last jump of the day, and were waiting around to be called up by the manifest, so we started putting on our gear. I noticed that Pen was suddenly unusually quiet, but I put it down to nerves. We climbed into the plane alongside the other 10 or so skydivers, who were jumping in their own groups.

During the ride up to altitude, I wanted to go over one more time with Pen the jump pattern he and I were about to attempt in freefall, and particularly the exit, but he didn't seem to want to discuss it. During freefall where there are several jumpers together trying to create aerial patterns, the whole group must leave the plane as one unit, as far as is possible given the constraints of the aircraft door. The 'tighter' the exit, the better chance of linking up in the air. To achieve this, half the jumpers need to climb outside the aircraft and hang on to special handles, ready to let go when the rest of the group is in the doorway. Even though there were only the two of us, Pen and I decided to have Pen outside the plane and myself inside.

We reached the correct altitude and the plane started the jump run. The first group of jumpers arranged themselves in the door, and were gone. Then it was our turn. Pen crawled outside the plane and hung on. I stood in the door, leaned out onto him and took grips and waited for his shout of 'Ready' – which never came.

He was looking intently at me as I clung on to him, wondering what was going on, my face three inches from his. Then he shouted above the aircraft noise: 'Will you marry me?'

Although we had joked about doing this at some point, I was still taken by surprise. There were jumping groups still in the plane, waiting to jump. They must have wondered what was going on. I had half a second to think about it. I screamed out through the rushing air 'YES!'

And then we left the plane, in a rushed, topsy-turvy exit. I wrote in my log book for that day: 'Tried a 180 [turn]. Can't remember if Pen pinned [caught me]. Who cares. Yippee!' I was engaged!

CHAPTER NINE

Married, single income, no kids

The wedding took place 18 months later. It was a big white wedding in the nearby church which we had been made to attend as children, just as I had always imagined. Yes – I know we weren't religious. Yes – I know I thought religion was a load of dangerous nonsense, but we both felt a marriage in a registry office would have been less than perfect.

The night before the wedding I was still putting finishing touches to the dress when my big sister Grace came into my room. I wondered what she wanted. I thought it was probably a difficult time for her. This was the second time a younger sister had got married, and she didn't even have a boyfriend.

She held up my dress on its hanger to look at it and asked with typical sarcasm, 'Which is the front and which is the back?' (as if to declare that my dress had been so badly designed that you couldn't even tell the difference, and wasn't I going to look awful in a dress whose front looked like the back.)

ANNA SKYE

'That's the front,' I said, a bit deflated. 'I'm still putting finishing touches to it.'

'I see you're obsessed,' she retorted, with staggering unkindness.

'No Grace. I'm just trying to make it look nice,' I answered calmly.

'Yes' was all she could think of saying, and left the bedroom. I could see she realised I wasn't rising to the bait. I was happy and she was the loser. She was jealous and was trying to find any way she could to take even a tiny modicum of happiness away from me. It didn't work – I just felt sorry for her and rather smug.

I will always remember walking down the aisle on my father's arm and seeing Pen standing at the front, looking so handsome in his tuxedo and bow tie. 'You look beautiful,' he whispered, as I reached him. With my heart pounding in my chest as hard as I can ever remember, I swore to stay faithful to Pen 'until death us do part' and to share all my worldly goods with him. I sincerely meant these words at the time. How those words came back to haunt me during the years that followed.

'I now pronounce you husband and wife.' I had done it! I was a married woman, and had fulfilled the first part of my dreams.

* * *

We liked being married. It made us feel accepted in society. I liked the notion of being a 'Mrs'. For the first week I tried using my new married name, O'Neam. The reaction rather disappointed me. 'To be sure, to be sure,' said one friend. 'Blimey O'Reilly,' said another. 'So what have you done with the IRA?' said a security guard. 'What's an apostrophe?' said a girl over the phone, when I tried to spell my new name for her.

Within a week, I had decided this was too much hassle to face each time I said my name, so I made the decision to stay with my maiden name, which was a nice, straightforward, easy-to-spell English name. Pen accepted this, albeit rather sadly. He was still holding out for the CPS vacancy which was going to come good when the recession ended, he said. In the meantime I urged him to apply for any type of job, to help with our finances and to keep his hand in an employment mindset. I refrained from mentioning the fact that, had he got a 2:1, he might be sitting in an interview for a solicitor's job at this very moment. But it was at the forefront of my mind as I commuted to work every day, leaving him in bed, to idle the day away. At least when I arrived home each night, he had prepared the evening meal.

* * *

Two years passed, and Pen had got into the habit of being a house-husband. He had virtually given up applying for any sort of job, let alone a solicitor's job. It was true that I was earning enough for both of us, but that wasn't the point. I hadn't married him so that he could lounge around at home.

It was during the first two years of married life that I began to question whether I still loved him. He was a nice guy. We would still talk very easily to each other and he was a very good listener, so rare in men, but I started to realise that I was taking everything he said with a pinch of salt. He would tell me a small anecdote about something that had happened to him recently and if he mentioned the story again later, I would notice that the details were different. Maybe only slightly, but it meant that one or other of the stories contained a fib. He once told me he had been stuck in a motorway queue for four hours. The next time he told me about the same event it was two hours. Only minor details, but they seemed to be appearing with increasing frequency. I remembered the first fib that he told me about his being 33 instead of 34. Perhaps I should have taken more notice. Even his mother confided in me one day as a warning 'Don't take any notice of what he says. It doesn't mean anything.' I mentioned this to him, but he just laughed it off.

I started pointing out the differences to him, and he would shrug and say 'What does it matter? You're so pedantic'. Lying to me was bad enough, but I found it hard to know what to do when he lied to my friends and even his friends. He would tell my friends he was running a properly business from home, or that we were going to go on an expensive holiday, purely because he couldn't bear people to know the truth about his lack of prowess as the household's main breadwinner.

To begin with I would support him, but after about five years I gave up and started openly disagreeing with him in front of people, hoping it would make him stop. I didn't see why I should lie to my own friends because of Pen's self-doubts. 'Just be yourself and be honest with people. It will be so much easier for you and you'll find people will like you even more,' I would plead with him. He was a very personable chap, but just couldn't see that to admit to lack of earnings was anything but a weakness. 'You don't know men. They WILL judge me.' he would insist. But I liked him as a person too much to just give up on him for the sake of a few little fibs. Most men lied, didn't they? Maybe most women lie, but men don't care enough to take notice. I also wanted my marriage to be a success, and hoped that with the passing years he wouldn't feel the need to lie. I also wanted to try again for a baby, when we (or I) had saved up for it, and our emotions had healed.

The UK came gradually out of recession, and one day Pen said he was going to contact the CPS. A very short phone call ensued. There was no job vacancy any more. The department that had been interested in hiring him had been restructured and no longer needed him. He tried to make light of it, saying he wasn't that interested in law anyway. I think that was true, but the fact remained that he now had to rethink his career.

He decided on car sales. He rewrote his CV and I typed it up for him. I noticed that he said he was in the navy for a good period. 'But you weren't! What if they find out?'

'All employers like it when you've been in the armed forces,' was his explanation, and he insisted I keep it in the CV.

Amazingly, within about a week, he had gone for an interview as a car salesman and got the job. Pen claimed he had never gone for an interview and failed. I had to admit that he was very charming when he wanted to be. He would say exactly what he knew the listener wanted to hear, whether he himself believed it or not. Recipe for a good salesman I suppose.

So life continued for us as dinkys (Dual Income No Kids Yet). Our sex life had become a bit sporadic. I was still taking HRT, so my libido had returned, but I didn't know how much I fancied him now. Pen would hint and start coming onto me but after a while I would find I had no appetite for it. We even tried spanking each other on occasions to see if that would spice up the sex life. To begin with, it worked, but after a while we got bored. We weren't familiar with the erotic role plays or implements that I was to experience in later years.

So most of the time we avoided both having sex and talking about it. The fibbing and the lack of employment for two years had taken its toll on my feelings for him. If we wanted to go for a meal, or a day out, or a holiday, it was I who had to pay, and it galled with me. I had been brought up to think the man would be the bread-winner, however unfair that premise is nowadays. It also meant that I was paying for both of our jump bills, and that was something I resented. This was my hobby. Why should I pay for his hobby? But this was also our common interest. If I wanted us to be able to pursue it together, which would undoubtedly engender harmony within our relationship, I had to keep paying.

About this time, I found out that he had taken out several credit cards and the balances were in their thousands on each one.

'We mustn't get into debt,' I kept saying, with increasing alarm.

'No, some debt is good debt,' he would reply. 'You can't get by these days without some debt. And anyway, how else am I going to pay for food and household goods, and my car expenses?'

'By asking me for money, and not putting it on credit cards!' I would say, exasperated.

'I'm not coming to you to ask for money,' he declared.

I was very worried about his attitude. 'Look - Mum and Dad have given us some money,' I said. 'I will pay off all your credit cards if you promise not to use them any more. Then we can start from scratch, with a clean slate.'

He reluctantly agreed, but within six months, he'd started using credit cards again. I asked him why, and he just said he couldn't manage on his salary, and having to run a car. He refused to talk further on the subject, and I felt helpless and very concerned that he would lead us into spiralling debt that would eventually mean we would lose the house.

★ ★ ★

The subject of children was still at the back of my mind, but we had fallen into a routine of married life that was quite comfortable, and we didn't want to rock the boat, along with our increasing age. Our financial situation was hardly ideal for children anyway, although that wouldn't have stopped me per se. Despite my concern for Pen's attitude towards debt, I still felt I wanted him to be the father of my children one day, whenever we felt we could face the ordeal again.

My feelings for him came and went. Whenever he did something nice or sweet, I felt I loved him still. Whenever he came asking for more money, I resented him and felt I could do better. Perhaps that's normal for married life.

We had been married about nine years before I broached the subject of trying for a baby again. I was 51 and the idea of having a child much after that seemed a bad idea. The child would only be 30 if I died at 81, a not unreasonable age to reach. Pen, three and a quarter years younger than me, agreed quite readily. We both felt emotionally ready.

I went to the same IVF clinic as before. They said I was at the upper end of the age limit allowed and that the price had gone up to £5000 per cycle. That was too much. I had stopped contracting by that time, and my salary wouldn't stretch that far.

I had heard that it was cheaper abroad, and decided to google it. Several European countries offered IVF at half the price of Britain. We would need fully-fertilised embryos. I couldn't afford to send Pen to Europe to donate a sperm sample, and then if this was deemed suitable and fertilised embryos resulted, travel separately to the clinic to have them inserted. Fertilised embryos had to be ready and waiting for me on my arrival.

I chose Cyprus. One IVF cycle with two embryos would cost

£2000. The clinic would choose sperm donated by British men. Not surprisingly, Pen was unhappy about the fact that the embryos wouldn't have any of his DNA, but he knew that this would be the only way I would feel happy, so he didn't stand in my way.

I rang the clinic, and it was all arranged over the phone for about three months' time. I had to order drugs to enhance my womb lining, and have scans to check if it was reaching the correct thickness at the appointed date. I also had to coordinate buying a plane ticket with the agreed embryo insertion date. An English girl at the clinic said she would arrange for me to be picked up at the airport.

I landed at Nicosia airport in the darkness at one in the morning. A surly-looking man was holding up a placard with my name on it and as soon as he saw me approach him he turned and walked out of the airport to his car, leaving me to follow him. On the 15-minute journey I began to wonder if this was all one big hoax. What if I was going to be kidnapped by gangs publishing bogus web sites on the internet for desperate foreign women? I hadn't researched it very well. I had just been assured by talking to the English woman at the clinic. But she could have been a plant.

We reached the outskirts of Nicosia and carried on into the centre. When we turned down a small back alley with no street lighting, I became extremely concerned. How naive I had been!

The driver stopped the car, got my case out of the boot and pointed to a small white building nearby. I tried to pay him but he waved the money away, which sent a huge sigh of relief through me. He must be from the clinic – or maybe from a very rich gang.

I went up to the building and knocked on the door. No reply. I turned round to ask the driver what I should do, but he had driven off. I was left in almost total darkness - in a back street of Nicosia in the middle of the night, and no one around. For some reason, I found the situation funny. It seemed so bad. I could only think of a phrase from Laurel and Hardy: 'Well, here's another fine mess you've gotten me into'.

I pushed on the door – and it opened. I entered gingerly and found myself in a white hall, full of photos of babies on the walls! It wasn't a hoax after all.

'Hello?' I said loudly. I heard a noise from somewhere down the corridor, and a woman came bustling into view and said with a broad Yorkshire accent: 'Hello. You must be Anna. I'm Aisha. Welcome to Cyprus. I'll show you to your room.'

She left me to settle into the room, and then came back in and said they would be defrosting the three embryos the next morning. They would take the two that looked the best quality and insert them into me. They weren't allowed to insert any more than two, according to Turkish law, even if all three survived the thawing. So I would have the rest of the night and the next morning to wait before knowing if I was to receive any embryos at all. I had a restless night, partly because of mosquito-like gnats that whined round me for hours, leaving itchy bites all over my face.

In the morning Aisha came into my room at about 11 am. 'Two embryos have survived, so they will be inserting both. Be ready in 30 minutes,' she said. She left a blue gown, a plastic elastic hat and shoes for me to wear, and two cups of water for me to drink, explaining that the water made it easier for the surgeon to see my womb on the scan screen.

A nurse who spoke no English whatsoever (why should she?) came to fetch me. I followed her into a dark room, with a spotlit operating table in the middle. A Turkish-looking man said 'Please' and indicated to me to climb up onto the table. Two nurses either side put one foot each into stirrups. They inserted a metal opener into my vagina, and quite roughly opened me up. I winced.

Then Aisha was at my side, translating for them. I felt very relieved to have an English speaker near me. She explained the procedure. She said they were about to bring the embryos out, and would use a tube to insert them into me. It was all over in about 10 minutes, and I was wheeled back to the room on the operating table. They told me not to urinate for as long as I could possibly bear. I held on for about two hours, but then it was so painful that I had to go.

I stayed that night, along with the singing gnats, and went home the next day, looking as if I had contracted chicken pox. Again we had to wait a fortnight before I could take a pregnancy test. I disappeared into the same toilet at work as before, peed onto the stick and waited the four minutes.

The result made its dreadful statement – no baby. I was almost resigned to the disappointment by then; Pen was more crushed than I was. He had really looked forward to having a child and had decided that the fact that it wouldn't have been the biological offspring of either of us would make it fairer.

We didn't think we could cope with another IVF cycle, either emotionally or financially, so we started discussing alternatives. We talked of adoption, although my heart wasn't really into having an older child who through no fault of its own might have behaviour issues. I googled adoption from abroad. This seemed to be fraught with problems, was very expensive and could take two years.

A guy at my work had recently successfully adopted three little brothers through their local council. 'At least it's free,' he told me. I rang the local council. A helpful lady informed me that, though not set in stone, the minimum age for a child would be 45 years younger than the younger of the parents. That would be Pen at 48. So the child would be at least three years old.

'How much experience do you have with children?' she continued.

'Well, I taught kindergarten for a year about thirty years ago, and I've got a niece and nephew,' I ventured.

'I'm afraid that won't be enough. We need you to have recent experience. You will need at least six months' experience with children before we can consider you. We need to know that you know what you are letting yourselves in for. Some people come back to us after their six months' experience and say they've changed their minds.'

I understood this, but I had also heard parents saying they weren't particularly bothered with children per se until they had their own, and then they were completely bowled over by the experience. With a heavy heart I started ringing local schools to see if I could volunteer for anything with their children within the confines of the school for one or two hours a week. Amazingly the second school I rang said they were looking for adults to listen to children reading. Perfect! I went for an interview with the headmistress, who thought I was suitable. She said the process used was called 'Better Reading'. I would be sent on a one-day course to learn how to listen to children.

So for the next two years, I attended a local school at lunchtime twice a week, listening to kids aged six to eight struggling to read. Some of the younger children were willing participants in the programme, especially a dear little dyslexic girl called Lucy, who was cheerful, bright and intelligent, but at the age of seven couldn't tell the difference between the word 'Hi' and 'He'. I wondered what would become of her as she tried to make her way through mainstream education. On the other hand some of the eight-year-old boys were not so enthusiastic and declared themselves already able to read and not needing any extra help. They sat next to me, huffing and recalcitrant. After weeks of this behaviour, I felt like turning round to them and saying 'Listen, you little shit, you're a crap reader, so just be grateful people are trying to help you.' Hmmm - perhaps I wasn't cut out for parenthood after all!

During these two years, we embraced the idea of surrogacy as well. This was where a normal, fertile woman would be impregnated with Pen's sperm. She would carry the baby as normal, and give it up to us after its birth. I contacted Surrogacy UK and was told it was £600 for us to join as a couple. After a few forms were filled in, we could start going to meetings where the 'Intended Parents' (as would-be receiving parents were referred to) would be able to mingle with future surrogate mothers, rather like speed-dating or a cocktail party with a life-changing difference. If the surrogate mothers liked a particular couple, and vice versa, they could begin the process of meeting up and discussing arrangements for sperm donation. Pen would not impregnate the mother himself (he was sorry to learn). He would leave his sperm in a laboratory receptacle of some sort and she would insert it into her vagina at the correct time of her cycle.

The surrogacy UK staff warned us that would-be surrogate mothers might well be put off by our ages. After all, this was their child they were donating. Would I want a child of mine to be brought up by parents who would probably die in 30 years? Probably not. I wondered why we hadn't thought of using it before. I guess I had wanted to carry the baby myself. Now it seemed that surrogacy was such a simple solution.

I sent off the cheque for £600. They had said they would not cash it until we attended our first meeting. Then I suddenly had the urge to try one last IVF in Cyprus. I had the money and who knows

- it might just work. So in 2011 I returned to the same clinic in Nicosia, though I made sure it was at a different time of year - May - to avoid the gnats. Aisha talked me through the procedure again, I waited until my bladder was about to burst again, and then I went home to UK to wait out the usual fortnight. But nothing had taken. We had had eight IVF cycles, all, except the first, with multiple embryos. At least we wouldn't be able to look back and say we hadn't tried. Sometimes I wondered if the doctors had put placebos into my womb instead of embryos because none had survived defrosting or their quality was not high enough, and it was easier to pretend to insert a potential baby than to send me home empty-handed.

We had to admit defeat, and decided that it was definitely time to fall back on our two final alternatives. Surrogacy first. If that failed (and we hadn't decided how many times we would try it), it would be adoption. It was about this time that the government made a concession to women of 40 and below to allow them one IVF cycle on the NHS. It was too late for me, but I felt it was a step in the right direction.

Women who long for children and are denied them can live a life of silent sadness which might never leave them. They have to endure the births of nieces and nephews, of babies born to colleagues, and pretend to be pleased for them. They have to listen to other women talking about the amusing things their children did. They miss out on countless friendships formed between mothers.

They also have to endure comments from other people who think they have chosen not to have children and are career women. A colleague arrived at the office I shared with him, complaining of tiredness caused by his children keeping him awake during the night. As I am an insomniac I am often sleep-deprived, as I was on that day, so I thought I'd empathise with him. 'Yeah - so am I,' I said. He snapped. 'Do YOU have a child?' he almost shouted at me. I was utterly dumbfounded. He still tells me today how tired he is from time to time, and I now stay silent.

Another time a female colleague was telling me how she and her husband had decided to go ahead with her pregnancy even after a Down's syndrome test proved positive. As it turned out, the baby was completely normal. 'Gosh – how lovely' I said, and then her expression changed and she suddenly said 'Oh, but what would you know about wanting a baby?' I didn't answer, as I didn't want people's pity.

I met a woman at a social function and we discovered very quickly that neither of us had children and that we both longed for them. She summed it up for me in one sentence 'I feel it's a waste of a life.' I tried not to think like that, but sometimes it was hard not to. Just as transsexuals feel they have been born into the wrong body, it was easy to feel we had been living the wrong life.

★ ★ ★

In the meantime, Pen's career had changed from selling cars and motorbikes to property. He had joined a company selling overseas property and had found he had loved it and was very good at it. We had bought two condos in Florida and were renting them out via local agencies. They were paying for themselves, and we only had to pay the maintenance fee. Thanks to his increased salary and status, he had seemed happier. He felt he was contributing to the household and could hold his head up high.

We started getting on better. We hadn't had sex for about eight years by then, but remarkably the relationship had begun to blossom. We still held hands on walks. We watched films together under a duvet, with glasses of wine and the fire lit. From the outside we still looked like the perfect couple. No one need know that our sex life was zero. And no one could have guessed at the turmoil going on in my heart and soul at the lack of children. I played with my niece and nephew, and the children of friends, and then cried all the way home in the car.

I had continued to take part in several sports throughout my married life. I played volleyball, tennis, badminton and went to ceroc (a type of modern jive) lessons and dances. I was fit and healthy and looked about 10 years younger than my age, according to many people. I met a good-looking guy at badminton, and although 17 years my junior, we took a shine to each other. We had a brief affair that lasted four months, but I was not looking for anything long-term with someone so young so I rather faded him out. I think Pen suspected something, but never asked. He probably didn't want to know the answer.

I met another guy at dancing. We started arranging to meet at other classes and dances together, and I could see that if things developed, I could fall for him. I didn't know if I would be prepared to leave Pen for him. Deep down, I still loved Pen, I had been just frustrated with his behaviour. I also missed sex. As it turned out, within weeks the dancing guy had fallen for another, much younger dancer, who was extremely attractive and sexy and annoyingly nice as well.

Pen, on the other hand, took almost no exercise. Sometimes when I was dancing to an aerobics video in the sitting room, he would stand next to me, moving his forearm up and down in time to the music, as if drinking a beer, jokingly saying 'Lift that pint, lift that pint'. Mostly because he wasn't hand-eye coordinated, as I luckily was, he couldn't enjoy the cheaper, more readily accessible sports like tennis and badminton. His hobbies were all expensive. He wanted to carry on jumping but didn't have the money. He was an excellent sub aqua diver, but that also needed spare funds. He wasn't mountain climbing any longer. He loved motor racing, but that required mega-bucks.

He still smoked. I begged him to give up, saying he would leave me a widow, and citing the damage it was doing his body. 'Did you know that cigarette smoking is more addictive than heroine?' he replied. 'You non-smokers haven't a clue how hard it is to give up.' He gave up for about a year once, but slowly found it too hard and eventually went back to it.

He started putting on weight round his waist. Pen did most of the cooking, saying he didn't trust me not to poison him. It was true that I was probably a little more slap-dash than him. He produced good meals, but nearly always with a dessert added, which he ate and I didn't. He also loved pizzas and would have about three a week. He once saw an article that said pizzas were one of the worst offenders for causing fat to build up around the waist, and that was known to be a leading cause of heart attacks - but he couldn't help himself.

Then, as far as hobbies were concerned, his luck changed for the better. The building where his property company was housed was also being used by two very talented computer contractors, Keith and Richard. They had their own company, and more money than they knew what to do with. They would chat to Pen on the stairways sometimes and found out that he used to race Formula Ford cars. One day, on a whim, Keith decided he wanted to try his hand at racing FF cars too and decided to buy two - one for himself and Richard to race, and the other for Pen to use, if he would teach them how.

Pen was ecstatic. They started going down to the race track for whole weekends. I was very happy for him. In a way it hadn't seemed fair that I could go off and do my hobbies and he was stuck at home doing the cooking, even though he had brought most of it on himself. We had stopped jumping years before, partly because I had become fearful of the danger, partly because it stopped us doing anything else at weekends, whilst not achieving very much because of the frequent rain and wind, and partly because I refused to pay for his jumps any longer. I felt that my paying for all the food, household goods and bills was enough, and it was unhealthy for our relationship if I paid for anything else. Pen now had his own money, although he still didn't seem to have very much. I wondered where it all went sometimes.

Unfortunately, the UK had sunk into the worst recession in years by this time. The banks had given out too much credit, with too few checks on their debtors. Pen's property company went under, and he was made redundant. At the same time, the US was hit with the recession and within the space of two months our renters for our two condos in Florida dried up and stopped. I was left with three mortgages to pay, as well as all the household goods and bills.

After a few more months of struggling on, I decided to drop the two condos. There was no other way, if we wanted to keep our UK house. Pen was furious that I should give up so quickly. These condos were to be our pension. We had no other savings. That was rich, coming from someone who hadn't contributed to either the condos or the UK mortgage!

But I had made up my mind, and I held the purse strings. Within a few months, I had started foreclosure proceedings on both condos. I was free of them. Now I only had to pay one mortgage payment per month. What a relief, even though we had probably lost about

£100,000 in total.

Amazingly, after a few weeks, Pen suddenly declared that he could see my point of view about debt. He didn't want it any more. Halleluiah! He said he was going to try and consolidate all his debts by taking out one huge loan. He would then only have the one repayment, and then he would be clear. He tried to get a loan from several sources, but his credit rating was too low.

I sighed. 'OK' I said, 'I will take out a loan for you in my name, transfer the money to your bank account, and you can pay me the monthly repayments.' He agreed, and I did believe that finally he wanted to be rid of his debts. I got a Tesco loan of £20,000 within days, and transferred it to Pen's account. He seemed to be relieved that this had taken place so smoothly and quickly, and I wondered just how much he owed. I knew I wouldn't get a straight answer, so there was no point asking. And amazingly, I was so convinced that he wanted to start afresh with no debts that I don't remember ever checking that he was sending payments into my account.

CHAPTER TEN

Affairs of the heart

In early 2011, Pen started having chest pains. The doctor sent him to have an MRI scan, and the results were encouraging. 'I am very pleased to tell you that there is nothing wrong with your heart,' said the consultant's letter of March 2011 after the scan. Well that's OK then. Pen could continue with his life as before. But the pains continued. He would sit on the sofa, rubbing his chest. He saw a chiropractor, in case it was just a muscular spasm which just happened to be in the chest area. She confirmed that it was just a muscular strain. Phew.

Even though Pen's property company had been dissolved, he was quite upbeat about his situation. He had made a good business contact in Spain with an English guy living there called Bill. Pen found would-be UK investors in Spanish villas and sent them to Bill in Spain to complete the sale. When their property company went under, Bill and his wife Julie were about to take advantage of the world recession and their savings, to embark on a world tour... until Pen rang him one evening. Pen wanted to set up a property company between himself and Bill. Pen would find the buyers, and send them to Bill on the ground in Spain to complete the sale, just as they had done previously. They reckoned on only three or four sales a year to make a profit. Sooner or later, they reasoned, the recession would attract investors eager to take advantage of the rock-bottom house prices, knowing they would eventually start to rise.

Bill readily agreed. He would set up the company with Pen for a year or so, and then go round the world with Julie. They set to work on a brochure and the website. Many an hour I spent with him, proof-reading the wording for both. But I didn't mind at all. It was fantastic that Pen was so enthusiastic about a career for once. He never wanted to work for anyone anyway. His dream had been always to be a pilot. He had been an RAF cadet and sailed through all the exams – until the medical. The medical revealed that he was colour blind, and would never be able to fly with the RAF. He was utterly crushed, and never found anything else he wanted to do – until now. Now he had found something he was good at and was interested in, and it would be his to control.

He started telling friends and neighbours he already had his own property company – more lies to defend his pride. I didn't condone them, but I understood them. I was hopeful that Surrogacy UK would come to our rescue and produce our longed-for child. If not, there was adoption. With his own company, Pen wouldn't need to lie any more. He would be proud of himself. He would feel head of the household, as we both wanted. I had no interest in earning more money than him. As ever, I just wanted to be a stay-at-home Mum. We actually felt happy for the first time in years.

Pen's happiness seemed to be sealed when I said I was thinking we should renew our sex life. 'Oooooh yeah,' he said, with a grin, without any recriminations for the lack of sex for the previous nine years.

That July was our 14th wedding anniversary. We had been together for 19 years. I sent him a short text: 'Happy wedding anniversary. OMG. 19 years!' He replied: 'Happy wedding anniversary to you too. You are the best thing that ever happened to me... love you squillions.'

Pen's company was progressing well. The website was finished and the business plan had been presented to the bank for their approval of a loan. Three weeks went by and then a credit card with their new company name and logo was sent through the post. A couple of days later a chequebook arrived. Pen was convinced that this was a sure sign that the bank was going to approve the loan. He was a happy man, full of hope, which made me happy.

The weekend after the chequebook arrived, Pen was planning on going down to the race track. He had been going down quite regularly recently, and I wondered how he could afford it. 'They pay my petrol when I get down there. I sleep in the truck overnight, and I don't pay any race fees because I am racing for a team down there, so it's very cheap. Why don't you come down this weekend?' he said.

'I might another time,' I replied. 'I would just get in the way. I'm not really interested in cars or racing, as you know.'

'Well you might not get another opportunity, I'm trying to sell my car in the race magazines.'

'Why don't you sell it on ebay?' I asked, in passing.

'No, you just get time-wasters there.'

I thought no more about it. On the Thursday, Pen rang me, unusually, at work. 'Shall we have a take-away tonight and watch a film?'

'Oh sorry – I can't. I'm playing badminton.'

'How about tomorrow tonight then?'

'No. I'm seeing Sarah.'

'Oh.' He sounded hugely deflated. 'OK. I'll see you later then.'

I felt slightly guilty, but I needed to keep up my exercise for my health, and I hadn't seen Sarah for weeks and didn't want to let her down at short notice.

On the Friday night, I came back from Sarah's at about 11 pm. I found Pen sitting on the sofa with his hand on his chest, complaining of fairly severe pains. He was quite stoical as a rule, so I knew he wouldn't be complaining of any minor ailment. The previous week he had been to the doctor about it, and his blood pressure had been 180. 'You should have seen the doctor's face when she saw the reading.' he told me, with some concern. She had put him on statins straight away, but hadn't said not to exert himself in any way.

I sat next to him and rubbed his back for him. These pains had been coming and going for the last few months, so I hadn't been paying too much attention to them, especially as the letter in March had said his heart was fine.

'Would you mind ringing my work and telling them I'm sick tomorrow? I'll leave all the details on this note,' he asked.

'Sure.' I was used to having to ring his work to lie.

About 8.30 am the next day I awoke to hear Pen moving around the house, getting ready to leave for the day's racing. I got out of bed in order to see him off. He was in a normal state of panic, trying to remember everything. He didn't really want to have a chat with me at the same time, so I wished him good luck quickly to get out of his way and went upstairs. Then I remembered we hadn't decided what film we were going to watch that night, or what take-away, so I called down from the top of the stairs to ask him.

'What?' Pen called, though I could hear the rising panic in his voice. He walked halfway up the stairs to speak to me. 'You decide,' he said patiently. 'Yes, sure. Sorry. Have a nice time.' I said quickly, not wishing to hold him up further. Then I heard him gather up the last of his gear, and he was gone. We hadn't thought about having a quick goodbye kiss, which normally he remembered.

I waited until 10 am and then tried the number of Pen's office. An answering message said the office was closed on Saturdays. I wasn't sure what to do, so I left Pen a message on his phone to warn him that they would still be expecting him in. I went back to bed to try and get some more sleep, since I hadn't slept very well that night.

An hour or so later I was woken by a gentle knocking at the front door. I ignored it and hoped they would go away. The knocking stopped, and then after a few seconds, continued, so quietly.

'Surely they can see by now that I'm not interested,' I said to myself. It eventually stopped. 'Good' I thought, and tried to go back to sleep. But I was awake by then, so I decided to get up. I came down the stairs, and noticed a little card on the mat. It was from the police. A note was scribbled on the back: 'Please ring telephone number _____ and quote incident number _____.'

I began to feel rather uneasy, but tried to brush it aside, hoping that Pen might have been involved in a minor accident but his car was a write-off and he needed me to go and fetch him. I rang the number and a female police officer answered straight away. I gave the incident number.

'Ah yes,' she said gently, 'an officer will be with you shortly.'

'Can you tell me what it's about?' I asked.

'Er no, I'm afraid not. The officer will arrive shortly.'

Just then there was a knock on the door, so we abruptly ended our conversation. I began to feel sick. I opened the door, and an extremely tall young sergeant stood there. He must have been at least six foot five. He asked to come in. As he ducked his head to come into the hall, I noticed a long truncheon strapped to his side. He sat down on the armchair and began by establishing my identity.

'First of all, is your name Anna Skye?'

'Yes.'

'Are you Mr O'Neam's wife?'

'Yes.'

'OK. It's just that you have different names, so we had to establish your relationship.'

At this point, I began to clutch at very flimsy straws. He had been seen playing truant from work and his boss had sent the police after him, and now they were telling me he had been arrested and needed someone to bail him out of jail. That must be it, even though it seemed a bit extravagant to send a police car to his house. But they had sent a police car round to my house when I was arrested for drunk driving, so it all made sense.

'There was an accident at the race track and Mr O'Neam was involved,' the sergeant continued, very quietly and seriously. I was silent. But I had to find out before he told me, as I couldn't bear it. 'He's dead!' I blurted out.

He looked at me and just said 'Yes'.

I threw my hands up to my face in utter disbelief. Very bizarre thoughts raced through my mind: 'Is this a joke?' I actually looked outside the window at the police car in my drive, to see if I could see balloons tied to it. Pen had a wicked sense of humour sometimes, and liked playing practical jokes, especially on me. But there were no balloons. My second thought was: 'Why has he done this? Who am I going to watch the film with tonight?' Crazy! My third extraordinary thought was that everyone else had a husband, and now I had nothing. And it was just about at the end of all these outrageously selfish thoughts that it occurred to me to wonder if Pen had suffered at all.

And then I felt utterly, utterly alone. In the blink of an eye, I had lost someone to share 19 years of memories with, and at least as many years of life still to come. No one else knew what we had been through. No one else had our crazy, stupid, idiosyncratic, private jokes. We had come so far, Pen and I, and felt we were just on the brink of happiness. I was stunned by the cruelty of it.

'I must go to him, I must see him,' I eventually said.

'Unfortunately that's not a service the police do,' the officer replied. 'The body is in a different county.'

BODY? I had been talking to Pen about three hours before. How could this be? I wanted to be left alone with my thoughts and tears, which would surely come. Now there were none.

'What happened?' I finally asked.

'It appears Mr O'Neam had a heart attack while driving his racing car at the racing track. We don't have full details. The air ambulance was called, but then sent away since Mr O'Neam was pronounced dead at the scene. I cannot leave here until you've contacted someone,' he added regretfully.

I understood. I suppose people in my position do strange things – like commit suicide. I called my younger sister, who lived locally.

I got the answering machine, so I didn't leave a message. I didn't know who else to call, so I called my mother. She answered straight away.

'Hello Mum. Where are you?'

'I'm at home. Why?' I didn't know if she could hear the anguish in my voice.

'I've got some bad news. Pen has just died...' and then through the tears which came trickling out, '...and I can't get him back.'

'Oh my poor darling Anna,' I heard her say, completely shocked.

'So now I'm a widow like you' I went on, almost too overcome to speak.-

'Would you like me to come up?'

'Yes please,' I wailed.

★ ★ ★

I can't remember whom I told then. Things started becoming a blur. My sister knocked on the door – I don't know how she found out – and I remember the sergeant saying he could go now. He seemed a really kind guy and was genuinely sorry to be telling me such awful news. He made to hug me as he left, but then thought it wasn't appropriate, so he just shook my hand. Mum rang to say she was leaving and would be with me in a couple of hours. My sister Louise and I sat around talking about Pen and crying.

Then things took a turn for the worse, as if things were not already dire. The phone rang. It was a young man who introduced himself as Matthew. He asked if I was related to a Janice Skye. I said I was her daughter. He said he and a friend had been parked in a layby on the North Devon link road when Mrs Skye had knocked on their window and asked them to tell her where she was. They had decided that she looked very confused and needed help and had taken her to a nearby café, where staff were looking after her until someone arrived to take her home.

It turned out that the shock of what had happened to me had been too much for my 85-year-old mum to handle and made her forget where she was going, so she had automatically followed a route to North Devon, where we had just spent a family holiday. Once on the North Devon link road she started wondering what she was doing, and had stopped to look at a map and ask directions from a car that was also parked in the same layby. Luckily they were good people. They had asked if she had a mobile and dialled the first number that came up on redial, which happened to be mine.

I thanked him profusely for taking the time to help her, and said we would be down to collect her. Louise and I got ready to drive down to the café near the link road. In a way it helped take my mind off Pen's death. I wanted to have my car available so that I could drive on to see Pen's body the next day, so we drove separately.

I remember driving down the motorway in the dark and feeling so strange, without Pen in the world, but relieved to be by myself finally, and alone with my thoughts. I was glad Pen and I had ended on such a good note. He was supremely happy in his life on the day he died and full of hope for the future. He had loved me unconditionally. And I realised that I had loved him, but his debts and lying had side-tracked me from feeling that love. Now that those two issues were no longer a problem, I could appreciate that he had been fundamentally 'a nice guy'. He had just been consumed by his lack of a successful career compared to mine, and that had driven a wedge between us.

Something else I realised – no one now in the world knew me properly. There was no one now who really cared about me. Yes, my mother did, but she didn't know much about my life. Pen was the only one who knew me. Really knew me. Death can be so isolating for the people left behind.

We reached the café, where two members of the staff had stayed especially late to look after Mum. She was very pleased to see us, but bewildered about why she was there and why we had arrived. She went in Louise's car down to Emerton. Louise told me afterwards that Mum had shown classic signs of short-term memory loss, asking again and again why she had been in that layby. Towards the end of the journey she had suddenly said: 'Has Pen died?'

When we got home the family doctor was called out. He gave Mum and me sleeping pills and confirmed that she was suffering from shock. He couldn't rule out the possibility that she had had a minor stroke.

The next day I had breakfast and got ready to go and see the dead body of my husband. How weird to be even contemplating such an outrageously awful journey, but I couldn't wait to see him again.

I drove to the hospital to where his body had been taken and a doctor led me to the room where his body lay. Just before she opened the door, she turned to look at me. I had begun to cry again. 'Would you like me to come in with you?' she asked gently. 'No thanks,' I sobbed. She opened the door and I walked in.

Pen was lying under a sheet on a very narrow single bed. The room was cold and I wondered if it would be too cold for him. Then I remembered. He no longer needed to keep warm. I also kept thinking that he might fall off the bed, knowing he didn't like narrow beds. He was still wearing his race clothes but they were torn around the chest, I assumed from when they had tried to resuscitate him. One half of his face was suffused with a red flush. The doctor had warned me about that, saying it often happens with heart attack victims. Apart from that, he looked just as he always did. Still handsome.

I just sat there, numb with disbelief and grief. I tried to put my hand into his, but rigor mortis had made his hand brittle and I couldn't get my hand inside his fingers. I kept pulling back the sheet to see his chest and then quickly pulling it back up for fear that he might get cold, before remembering again that he couldn't feel the cold now.

I sat for about an hour by his side, wondering what was going to become of me. All my current plans had just gone skyward. Who would love me now? Who would want to have a baby with me?

I drove to the racetrack, where I had arranged to meet one of the organizers. He took me to where Pen had died and told me how it happened. One of the race stewards watched Pen's car taking the bend near him and then he suddenly noticed his head fall back, and saw his car leave the track and trundle to a halt by itself in the nearby field. No other driver was involved. The steward rushed over to him in seconds, saw no sign of life, and raised the alarm. Medics were there in moments and applied CPR. Defibrillators were applied, but there was no sign of life at all. They tried to resuscitate him for 49 minutes. The air ambulance was called, but was sent away empty. One of the medics knew Pen and broke down in tears, and had to be removed from the scene. Pen was officially pronounced dead at 11.02 am. He had been talking to me on the stairs of my house at about 8.45, our last, rushed conversation.

So Pen, it seemed, had not suffered at all. One moment he had been enjoying his favourite hobby, the next he was dead. What a way to go. I was really relieved that it had been so quick.

After telling me the story, the organizer suddenly asked me if I would like to stand in prayer with him for a while, in the very spot where Pen had died. *What?* Don't tell me how to grieve for Pen, and don't impose your religious rubbish on me. I would do it my way. 'Ah no. That's OK thanks,' I said. I hope he didn't notice my gritted teeth.

He took me to Pen's car so that I could collect some of his belongings. In the driver's side pocket I found two packets of cigarettes - one opened, one sealed. Another lie. Pen had kept assuring me he had given up a year earlier.

★ ★ ★

Mum came up to stay for about a fortnight. Unfortunately we didn't get on at all. I could work from home and actually found it therapeutic to continue to work. Not knowing how to help her newly-widowed daughter, Mum kept asking me if I really had to work, and couldn't that piece of work wait? Well it could, but that was what I chose to do. I didn't want to have to justify my movements to anyone. She also kept asking what she could do to help round the house. Oh god, stop asking me annoying questions! Poor Mum. What a nightmare I was. I feel so guilty about the two weeks Mum stayed. I just wanted her to leave me alone.

I also decided on another course of action to deal with my predicament. I wanted to set up an online dating profile, so that I wouldn't feel so lonely, but I couldn't until she had gone.

My sister came over a few times and the three of us sat around, making falsely cheerful conversation. I was too polite to tell them that I wanted to be alone for the next three months.

As the news spread, people started ringing up to express their condolences. After the 10th person had told me how sorry they were and asked what had happened, I couldn't bear the pity and the 'aaaaaahhhhh' coming from people, and I just wanted to get out of the house. It reminded me that my life seemed such a failure – no husband, no children, even if it wasn't my fault. They couldn't win.

What is it about people and death? People seemed to think that suddenly I wanted or needed their advice. I knew it was because they didn't know what else to say, and were desperate to help in any way, so advice seemed the right path, but often their words would not be well chosen. One neighbour knocked on the door and said 'Why don't you go to the local cinema? You won't be the only singleton.' *Singleton?* Two weeks ago I was a married woman. Another friend said (un)helpfully, 'Now don't go rushing into anything.' Someone else said 'Keep busy'. I felt like saying 'I'm bereaved. I'm not stupid,' but all I said was 'Yeah. Thanks.'

Most people couldn't bring themselves to use the word 'dead' or 'death'. They would say 'passed on', 'crossed over' or 'no longer with us'. I wanted to scream that he was DEAD, and that's it's a completely natural state, and we shouldn't be ashamed to talk about it, but luckily I kept it all inside. I recently talked to another widow and I was relieved to find she had a similar experience. She hated the pity she could see in people's eyes, their desperate need to avoid this taboo subject, when all she wanted to do was talk about her husband. My niece and nephew have never uttered Pen's name since the day he died. They are lovely kids and I know it's because they don't want to upset me, but it's sometimes as if he never existed except in my mind. I sometimes mention him in a conversation, not because I want to reminisce, but because it's relevant to the subject matter. Quite often, there's a little pause, no one knows what to say, and then someone changes the subject.

Grace kindly tried in her own way to help me through the first Christmas without Pen. 'You could send all your Christmas cards very early and sign them all with just your name. That will remind everyone to send you a card addressed only to you so that you don't have to keep reading Pen's name.' Unfortunately, that's exactly what I did want, in order to feel married again, and with a partner, if only for a fleeting moment.

My cousin very generously invited me to stay the weekend with him and his wife. I dreaded it, but couldn't find an excuse to refuse. Just as I had expected, it made me feel terribly lonely. They both had high-powered jobs and had just moved into a huge seven-bedroomed house. They sat opposite me at the dinner table, holding hands, while I sat alone, trying not to notice. Their two adult children already had successful jobs. I had nothing in comparison. As my cousin gave me a lift to the station, he said: 'I feel really sorry for you'. Gee thanks, that makes me feel SO much better! But then I thought back to things I had said to bereaved people, and I realise they had been just as inconsiderate. I had asked one lady who had just lost her second husband if she had any children. 'No,' she said, looking at me in exasperation. I had been going to say it was nice for her to have their support. I suppose there is just no easy thing to say.

An aunt, not normally known for tact, did, however, manage

to offer words of comfort: 'You're lucky dear. My husband took sixteen years to die.' Actually that was so true. Pen had not needed to be cared for in any way. I was now free to live my life as I chose.

After three days of answering the phone, I decided to let the answering machine take it and go and play tennis at my local club, where I didn't tell a soul what had happened. It was the best thing I could have done. No one pitied me, gave me advice or treated me with kid gloves. I watched as people bickered about line calls and the score, and felt I was back to normal life again. My strange, surreal, upside-down world back home was temporarily put on hold. And even stranger, no one realised at the club. When I eventually told some of them two years later, they were amazed that they hadn't had an inkling and that I could hide my feelings that well.

The funeral was weird. I kept wondering where Pen was and why he wasn't helping me arrange it, and then I'd remember within the next second. It took place on a wild, windy overcast day, up in the ancient little church on the hill near the village, the same church Pen had declared about a fortnight earlier that he was going to try and run to, every day, to help his blood pressure come down from 180. Pen would have approved of the funeral. I had the song *Angel* played, the chorus of which was '*In the arms of the angels, fly away*' by the sweetest of female voices. About 40 people from various aspects of Pen's life managed to squeeze into the rickety little pews. I turned round occasionally from my front pew and wondered who some of them were.

After the funeral was over, Pen's property company colleague, Bill, introduced himself and let me know that he had just heard from the bank that their fledgling company had been approved the loan! I couldn't believe the sad timing.

A group of racing drivers had driven all the way up from the racetrack location to pay their last respects to Pen. Unfortunately, although one of them kindly agreed to give the speech, he decided to use the occasion to advertise the fact that the racing track had a Trust and that they would welcome donations! During the lunch that followed at my house, he surreptitiously left leaflets of the Trust next to photos of Pen that I had placed on the table in my lounge! I was flabbergasted at the audacity of it, but at the time I didn't want to offend him and have a showdown, so I decided to leave the leaflets where they were.

★ ★ ★

I appointed myself executor to Pen's estate and started going through the papers in his room. Financially, things were not looking good. He was in much more debt that he had let on. He had at least five credit cards maxed out, with a total balance of about £20,000. I could find no trace of the £20,000 I had lent him and wondered what he had spent it on. Luckily the credit cards were all in his name and would die with him. Unluckily for me, the £20,000 I had lent him would live on until I paid it off. I had taken it out in my name, since his credit rating was so bad that he couldn't get a loan.

Then I remembered a conversation I had had with him about six months before he died. I had asked him if he was still paying the monthly premium of £20 for his life assurance, and he had answered very emphatically 'Oh yes!' as if he wouldn't dream of doing anything else. I had been paying for everything – household bills, council tax, mortgage, most of the food – but I had asked him to pay for his own life assurance. Fatal mistake. That was the only thing that I should have made sure I paid for, since it was only me that was going to benefit. As I looked through the papers I came across a letter that showed that he had cancelled the payments three years earlier. What a liar! I would have received £54,000.

Further lies bubbled to the surface. He had told me he had been given the racing car as a present from the two computer contractors, but that now he was trying to sell it in racing magazines. I rang one of the other drivers and asked if there had been any interest in Pen's car.

'Well, he wasn't trying to sell it,' he said.

'He told me he was advertising it in some of the racing magazines.'

'We know all the racing magazines and we would know if he had been selling it in them,' he said. This man would have no reason to lie to me.

The same guy kindly offered to advertise it for me. When I went down to the track a few weeks later to collect the £3300 that it eventually sold for, he commented: 'We were lucky to get this in this climate. That's just about what Pen paid for it.' I didn't let him see my surprise. He must have paid for it with his credit cards, while letting me pay for all our living costs.

I wondered what else I would find among the papers in his room. And I certainly made some finds. There were hand-written notes from Pen to unknown women. First of all, lists of women's names. Then small, hand-written notes as if he was rehearsing phone calls to them: 'Matt and I would like to meet up with you. We promise we will go to your level and at your pace. If at any time we go too far, you only have to say and we will stop.' Matt was a fellow car salesman. He had come to the funeral with his wife. Pen often used to meet up 'for a drink' with him. Now I knew better.

In the same folder as these notes were many photos of women in various stages of undress, posing with basques, many with their hands tied behind their backs, lying on beds, looking mock-scared. In among these photos, I was somewhat surprised and disgusted to find one of my 19-year-old niece with wet hair down her back. She had just been surfing in the sea, during one of our family holidays. I was present when he had taken those photos of her and remember wondering at the time why he was taking so many, but just assumed he wanted to make sure he would get at least one good shot. I could only shudder to think what he would do with such a photo.

I actually didn't mind these revelations and didn't feel betrayed. He and I had not had sex for nine years when he died. He had wanted a sexual relationship and hinted many times, but I had rejected his advances. What did I expect him to do? At least he had stayed with me. Many men would have left. I was quite sure he wouldn't have harmed these women. It would have been consensual, harmless, erotic fun to make him and Matt feel better.

CHAPTER ELEVEN

Back in the dating game

The funeral was over, Mum had gone back home and I had the rest of my life to think about. I was still stunned by Pen's death. Although I knew how much he had lied to me, I knew the fundamental reason was money. And I was glad for him that at least he had pursued his hobby until the end, especially now that his credit card balances would be voided. In effect he had enjoyed his pastime for free.

There was something else – a baby was effectively impossible now. How could I look after a child, while trying to keep down a full-time job, look after a house, keep fit and look for a mate all at the same time? Nevertheless, I wanted to try anything I could to salvage every tiny ounce of hope from my seemingly hopeless situation.

I wrote to Surrogacy UK to tell them that Pen had died and asked if there was any way they would still consider me as a future parent, if a donor father could be found. I received a very sweet reply from the girl I had been liaising with over the recent few weeks, saying how staggeringly sad that was, and saying she had voided my £600 cheque, and that, with huge regret, they couldn't start any surrogacy procedure with single people.

I knew adoption was an option for single people, but I couldn't face it. The child would have to be about 11 years old or older, given the rules on age difference between parent and adopted child. Imagine trying to take on a child by yourself that age, one who would probably have a good many issues. It wouldn't be fair on the child or myself.

The post mortem showed that Pen had died of furred arteries, leading to a massive heart attack. I put it down to smoking, eating too many pizzas and desserts and lack of exercise. I wondered if, had I been an excellent cook and prepared healthy meals for him every night, he would still have been alive at that moment. But I didn't dwell on this. It had been his choice to stuff himself with rubbish – and he had positively relished these meals, knowing the harm they can do.

★ ★ ★

So now I had to try once again to find a mate. How long should widows and widowers wait around grieving? What's an acceptable time in society's eyes? I was pretty sure it wasn't a fortnight. But Pen had gone. He wasn't going to mind me trying so soon to find someone. What on earth was the point of waiting another few months, or even a year, until society might deem it appropriate for me to start another relationship? I might be run over by a bus the following week. Pen and I had not had a conventional relationship, in that our sex life had died a death long ago. Even if we had restarted it, I wasn't sure I would have found the soulmate in him that I was looking for, especially given my recent discoveries. Or perhaps I was trying to convince myself of that, while I looked out into the void that now seemed to be my future. But I certainly didn't feel I owed him any more of my time.

One thing was certain - I wasn't going to sit around for weeks feeling sorry for myself. Society could think what it liked. I was very sad about Pen, but surprisingly, I refused to sink into depression. So a fortnight after Pen's death, on the same evening Mum left, I logged on to a dating site and created a profile. I was 56 and not bad looking for an old gal. I used one photo, which ironically Pen had taken in our kitchen about two weeks before he died. My profile stated that I was athletic and toned, and wasn't looking for a churchgoer, a walker or a smoker. I was 'fairly sociable but preferred the company of one'.

Within a few days I received three or four email replies, and a few winks. Rather vainly, I had thought there would be more. One photo was of a 59-year-old guy who lived just up the road. He was quite good-looking, so I thought I would give him a go. We exchanged a few emails over the next few weeks. He was divorced, with two children. I found I wasn't very keen to hear about his children, as it made me jealous. But I realised that I couldn't avoid coming across people with children. Unfortunately they were everywhere!

I arranged to meet him at a local pub. We had become quite friendly over the emails and I was quite nervous as I drove into the car park. I might be about to meet my future partner!

I parked and rang his number. 'Hi. I'm here.'

'OK. I'm in the back car park. I'll walk round.'

So this was it. The moment had come.

I got out of my car and waited. Round the corner walked this weedy little guy. This couldn't be him! But I recognized his face from the photo. I had forgotten to check his height. I like big guys, of about five foot ten and above. This guy was five foot six, only three inches taller than me. How heightist was I! He was also of slender build. I felt I could push him over with one finger.

My heart sank. All that emailing for nothing. Now I had to face at least an hour of false conversation, pretending I liked him. Luckily I had limited our first meeting to an hour, telling him we could always reschedule.

Actually he was very nice, but I just couldn't find him attractive enough. At one point he asked me when my husband had died and when I said 'five weeks ago' he was astonished. 'I feel I am taking another man's wife!' he said. Society's rules coming home to roost again.

After an hour and a half, during which he did most of the talking and not much listening, I said our time was up. 'Ah right. I've had my lot then,' he joked. I said we could always arrange another date via text, knowing full well I didn't want one. Phew – glad that's over. Next time I would take more notice of finer details like the height, and not waste so many hours emailing.

Later that evening, he texted to say he'd enjoyed the date and would I like another one sometime. I said with regret that there had been no chemistry. He replied that he 'would put his chemistry set away then'. It was all a bit sad and I didn't enjoy hurting his feelings, but I was secretly flattered that he had wanted to see me again.

The second guy I met was a completely different kettle of fish. He was five foot ten and muscular, and spoke with a Brummie accent. We arranged to meet at a dance lesson half way between our houses near the M42. We got on well, although I wondered about our different backgrounds, but when he asked for another date I was pleased. I just thought I didn't want to confine myself to middle-class people, as I might never meet anyone.

We arranged to see a film at the Showcase Cinema in Erdington. Unfortunately I was almost exactly an hour late. Satnavs are only ever any good if you have the number of the house as well as the postcode. I rang him from my car, which I'd parked in some back street. He tried to give me directions to get to the cinema, but he couldn't know my exact location. After giving me a few directions, he said, 'Have you started the car yet?'

'No. I was waiting for you to finish your directions first.'

'Christ – you would test the patience of a saint,' he said nastily. That should have been a warning for me, but I had liked him on the first date so I wanted to see if I could make it work between us.

I eventually got to the cinema and we just made the film. We held hands and chatted and it felt nice. Afterwards we tried to find a bar to have a drink, but everywhere was closed. He was about to say goodbye for the night, but as I'd driven for over two hours to get there, I didn't want the evening to end so soon, so I suggested having a drink at his house, only 20 minutes away. He asked if that was a good idea, as 'we know what will happen'. I answered that nothing need happen.

Once inside his house, we had a glass of red wine and began to chat. I commented that I didn't think it was a good idea for us to start anything sexual at that moment. Suddenly he leaned over onto me and kissed me. It was quite nice, so I kissed him back. Without even wanting to, I started getting turned on, and asked if there was a bed anywhere. Within minutes we were upstairs and naked on the bed.

That's where things started to go wrong. There was plenty of foreplay, and I felt ready for penetration, but I hadn't had sex for at least three years by then, and as soon as he started trying to penetrate, it hurt, due to the laser operation I'd had years earlier, and I cried out. He stopped and withdrew, then tried again more slowly. But the pain was still there and I ask him to withdraw again. When I said 'Ow!' for the third time, he suddenly raised his voice menacingly and said, 'Shut the fuck up!' Then he started ramming into me.

I froze and just lay there, while he continued to enter me. He was a big, muscular bloke and I had no chance against him. The pain actually eased after a while, and intercourse resumed as normal, if you call being taken by force normal. Just as in Italy with the Algerian, I acted calm. I chatted to him during sex and afterwards, as if nothing untoward had happened. We didn't arrange another date, but said we would text. That night the insides of my vagina were hurting and felt bruised.

The next day I googled the definition of rape: 'Sexual penetration using force or intimidation'. Well, he had used both of those. Had that constituted date rape? I didn't know, and I wasn't going to find out. I had gone to a stranger's home on the second date, and got into bed with him. If things had gone smoothly and it hadn't hurt me, there would have been no rape. He was just an impatient man, although that in no way excused his actions. Although I hadn't said the word 'No,' I had said 'Ow' loudly enough, and he had no right to ignore my protestations. But I thought my case would be very flimsy indeed.

I texted him. 'My insides are still hurting by the way,' I said. He replied 'Lol' and made a jokey comment. He obviously didn't view it as a rape. I decided I couldn't be bothered to do anything about it, partly because I didn't think it would ever stand up in court. But I wanted him to know that what he did was wrong.

'You shouldn't have done what you did,' I texted. 'You hurt my insides and used intimidation, saying 'Shut the fuck up'. But don't worry. I'm not going to do anything about it.'

Luckily he didn't know where I lived, but I still didn't want the heavies turning up on my doorstep. Within a day, an email was posted on the dating site, covering himself in case I took legal action, the gist of it being: 'You accused me of intimidation just because of an in-bed comment. You were trying to make out you didn't want sex, when it was you that wanted more.' I knew he had been scared by my accusations. I didn't want to cause any more trouble, either to him or to myself. But I felt that I had alarmed him enough to think twice before he acted so impatiently again with another woman. I guess this sort of leave-well-alone attitude of rape victims exasperates the police, but I just wanted an easy life and to be left alone to find a mate. On with the search…

★ ★ ★

Over the next few weeks, I met one man after another. Luckily for me they all seemed to like me more than I liked them. I say 'luckily', since it wouldn't have helped my confidence if they had all turned me down. But it was unlucky in that I couldn't find anyone who was anywhere near compatible. Most of them were just too working-class, or they talked too much and didn't listen. Was I so esoteric that there was no one out there for me?

I met one, tall, very good-looking guy called John at a café in the afternoon. When we met I noticed that he didn't look at me, but I put it down to nerves. It can be a very nerve-racking business, this dating online. We ordered tea and cakes. As he handed me my cake on a plate, I dropped the plate and the cake went everywhere. I burst out laughing, but he was not amused. He suggested very seriously that I take his plate, and we ask for another cake. No sense of humour. Exit John. Shame, as I had had high hopes for him.

I arranged to meet another guy, Sean, at the pub where I had met the short guy on the first date. I wondered if the staff had a good laugh, watching me turning up with a different guy every evening. He got out of his car and walked towards me in the car park. He was six foot with a big frame, and had a broad local accent. There was no way I would start dating him, I thought straight away. We sat in the pub and he talked incessantly, and I hardly said a word for the allocated hour. But somehow he seemed quite nice, and when at the end of the time he asked for another hour, I relented. I agreed to meet him again for a walk, and this time he was more relaxed and listened better.

I met him a few times, and began to like him, but I knew deep down that he was not right for me. I guess I was just lonely and it was nicer to have someone to go for meals with and watch films with than no one. I went out with him for four months. I credit him with allowing me to feel normal again, part of society again, after Pen's death had made me feel so isolated.

We decided to go for a weekend break to Auschwitz, the Nazi death camp in Poland. Unfortunately Sean had been badly let down by Jewish business associates in the past, and he couldn't bring himself to show much respect to the poor people who had died in the camp. I was disgusted with his attitude. He had also shown himself to be impatient at times, and unhygienic. As soon as we landed at Heathrow, and went our separate ways, I knew I wouldn't see him again. I needed to meet middle-class people, however snobbish that sounded. I decided I wouldn't meet anyone unless they were a professional. This would tend to ensure they had the same background and level of education, and way of behaving towards others. I hoped it would mean they had been taught to listen!

Soon after this ground-breaking decision, I started chatting to a nice-looking chap called Andy who lived about an hour away. He sounded really easy-going and fun-loving on the phone. Height: 5'10'. Occupation: actor. I reasoned that acting can be well paid.

After a few conversations, we arranged that I would go to his home in Bristol. On the appointed day, it was already dark when I punched the postcode into the satnav and set off. I reached Bristol within 35 minutes and kept following the instructions of the satnav, as it made its way to... St Paul's, an area of Bristol known for its poverty and vice. The faces got blacker and blacker with every street I turned down, the buildings poorer and more tumbledown.

'You have reached your destination' the satnav insisted, without remorse. I looked around to see a row of dilapidated Georgian buildings. I found Andy's basement flat and wondered if I should bother ringing, but then curiosity took over.

As soon as he appeared at the door I saw that he was about three stone heavier than his photo indicated, and I knew instantly he wasn't for me, but I was too polite to turn around and go home. His flat was tiny and dingy and had very old furniture. This guy was obviously not well-paid. However, he was as friendly and nice as he had been during our chats. He told me he couldn't find much acting work and money was scarce. He seemed honest and sincere

ANNA SKYE

– but not what I was looking for. I didn't want another guy with no money and no career prospects.

After a while he suggested going for a drink. I thought I might as well, since I'd driven all that way and it seemed churlish not to accept. We walked round the corner to a small, dark pub. Outside stood a huge black guy as if on guard, wearing a black coat and a cowboy hat. He had long dreadlocks and looked like a character from a gangster movie.

'Hi Ken,' called Andy as we approached. Ken stood aside and let us in. Inside there was one small room with a minute bar and a pool table that took up most of the room. Three black guys sat near the table, chatting in the darkness.

'Hi guys – want a game?' Andy asked cheerfully as we entered. These were his friends. And why not? But this wasn't for me. I would never fit into a black world. He bought me an orange juice and then started playing pool with one of the guys, while I watched from the bench, somewhat bemused and wondering if he thought I would be enjoying myself sitting alone while he played with his friends.

I plotted my escape without looking too rude. After about 20 minutes I made an excuse that it was late and I needed to get home. He looked a little disappointed, but saw me to the door and said he hoped to see me again soon. I just said 'OK' and walked away. The feeling of relief as I reached my car and drove out of the area, up the motorway and away from such a seemingly dismal life was palpable. But maybe he was happy like that. He certainly seemed it, so who was I to judge him?

I joined a dating agency, which did the searching for you. Membership cost £2400 for the year and they matched you with people of the same education, background, interests, goals in a partner and location. Within a week or so I was introduced to Anthony. We chatted on the phone for ages, and talked about flying mostly, as he had a pilot's licence. He spoke with a plum southern English accent, and I thought we might be getting somewhere.

We met as usual in a pub. He was better-looking than his photo and I liked him. Five minutes into the conversation I dropped a bombshell: 'I think all religion is bollocks', thinking he would agree with me. But I saw him visibly sink in his chair, looking very disappointed. It turned out he was quite religious, went to church fairly regularly and had many friends from the church. I also let slip that I didn't find Shakespeare very funny! Apparently an inexcusable statement. 'Well millions of people DO find him funny you know,' he said with disdain.

At the end of the hour, we made excuses that we had to get home. Outside in the car park, he suddenly asked if I wanted to see him again. I didn't think we were at all suited, but politeness made me suggest we go and see a play at the Royal Shakespeare Theatre in Stratford. He said he would get tickets and let me know. It turned out we were both too embarrassed to admit that the match wasn't right, although I would certainly have gone on the second date as I wanted to try out the famous theatre.

I heard nothing for three days, which I thought was an ominous sign. Then I received a text saying he didn't think there was enough chemistry to see me for a second date. My first rejection. However much you try and rationalise it, it's never nice to receive a rejection, even if you fundamentally agree with the decision. I wouldn't have wanted to fit into his church-going world and all his dinner parties at all, but I would still have been prepared to go on a second date with him. I had to find out why he had suggested a second date, so I asked him. He answered with obvious honesty that he couldn't bring himself to turn me down on the night face to face, but that I wasn't his type, and he was very sorry. I understood. I said he wasn't my type either, but it sounded like a lame excuse since he had got his rejection in first!

I did meet a lovely guy on one of the sites. He took a bit of persuasion, but we eventually met up to go to a play. He was 59, lived locally, height six foot two inches, spoke with a BBC accent and had a lovely sense of humour. I decided during the first half of the play that he was perfect. He even had lovely thick hair, rather than the many baldies I was coming across.

Then came the interval. As we queued for drinks, I asked him in passing what he did for a living, thinking he'd say he was manager of his own company or similar. 'I'm an artist.' he said rather apologetically, 'I sell paintings at my own exhibitions.' I tried not to look disappointed. Then he dropped another bombshell. 'It's a hard life. I often don't have any money at all. I lost my marriage and my house because of my passion. Galleries often only pay you about 30% of what they owe you, as they have a cashflow problem. They owe me many thousands of pounds which I will never see. I haven't been on holiday for years and years'.

Oh. Another Pen, although a very honest one. I couldn't bear the thought of being partner to a penniless man again. How long would it be before I would have to pay for him if I wanted to go on a quick weekend break? Exit the painter. I felt shallow but I felt justified in requiring a man at least to be able to go halves.

Online dating turned out to be a rollercoaster ride. I would be elated one moment on having just been contacted by a nice-looking guy and arranged a date with him. The next moment I would feel crushed when I'd met him and he hadn't looked anything like his photo.

In three years I've met 39 men. Thirty-three of them wanted to see me again. Five didn't feel any chemistry with me, or didn't like me enough to feel we would make a good couple. Quite a good track record, I told myself proudly. Of the five that turned me down, I was actually ambivalent towards them anyway but would still have gone on a second date to make sure: one was a smoker, one was the religious, Shakespeare-loving pilot, one was a manic depressive, one was rude and impatient, and the last of the five was a working class, streetwise ex-soldier.

It always took me a few days to get over one guy before I could move on to the next. But I found that the best remedy for a rejection or disappointment was to meet the next guy as quickly as possible. It's amazing how the human heart mends and forgets. I can't even remember now some of the names of the guys I cried over.

I probably spoke to double the number of men from the sites that I actually met. We would have liked each other's profiles, exchanged a few emails and then mobile numbers. In this supposedly non-male-chauvinistic society, it was nearly always the man who suggested ringing me, which was fine with me, even though it was nearly always me who first contacted him. (And it was *always* the man who bought the first drink on the first date, and very often he who insisted on paying for the first meal as well. I found it refreshing that even today some chivalry still existed and that our roles could still be defined, even in such a minor way.) But during the initial conversations on the phone I would often find something I couldn't accept in a partner, such as the fact that they didn't listen, or they didn't understand my sense of humour, and I became quite adept at cutting short the conversation with some excuse, saying that perhaps we could chat again another time. In the meantime I would send them a text saying that on reflection I didn't think we had enough in common.

One guy I never met (luckily) seemed by his profile to be a very good-looking 52-year-old American. He contacted me one evening while I was online. I should have known something was amiss from the fact that he had got in touch first. Why would a dishy 52-year-old from the US contact an older woman so far away? He could have his pick. Over the next few nights we continued to email but whenever I hinted at chatting on the phone, he didn't seem keen. He said he was working abroad at the time but was soon due to come back to the UK, where he lived. After a few days of emailing, he suddenly went quiet for about a week without warning. Then, just as suddenly, he came back online (a clever ploy to tug at the heart strings), saying there had been a terrible accident at work and one of the guys under his supervision had fallen from a bridge and was now in hospital. The machinery the guy had been using had crashed to the ground and was now out of action, and he couldn't now finish the work to complete his contract. He wouldn't be paid at all if he didn't complete the work, and would have to go hungry. He just needed £2000 to buy another machine, and could I please just lend him the money. A scam! I didn't let on I knew what it was, and said I needed to talk to him. He eventually agreed to a phone call – and within a second it was obvious why he hadn't wanted to chat in person. This guy was black. I saw from the phone number that he was ringing from Nigeria, where I knew this sort of thing was rife. I wrote him an email saying how disgusted I was with his behaviour, but he kept protesting his innocence during many subsequent emails (which I didn't answer), saying he was about to starve, and how could I abandon him?

Although I was annoyed at the waste of time, and the deceit, I did realise that his life in Nigeria probably wasn't easy. He probably thought all white people from developed countries could easily afford £2000, and that amount of money would be likely to sustain him for months. Perhaps he had a family to feed and extortion was the only way he knew how. Although I didn't give him the money, I felt sorry for him, and felt grateful to have been born in the UK.

I heard other stories of dating horrors. One girl apparently drove to an arranged meeting in a car park. She recognized the guy in a car nearby from his profile and wondered why he wasn't getting out of the car, so she got out and walked over. He wound down the window and said 'Could you help me get my wheelchair out of the back?' He hadn't told her he couldn't walk!

Another guy told me about a woman he'd met on a previous date. They'd arranged to meet at a pub. She was a bit late when she rushed into the pub, having been driven there by her ex-husband, which he found unusual, but he didn't see why he should mind that. 'Sorry to be late' she said breathlessly, 'I haven't got my teeth in at the moment. I'll just go and put them in.' And she dashed off to the ladies. She came back, still flustered, and they began to chat. Unfortunately in her haste she hadn't put her teeth in properly, and throughout the evening he watched fascinated while they kept falling down from her top gum. He couldn't bring himself to ask her for a second date.

Unfortunately for me, I relayed this anecdote during my first phone call to a good-looking chap who I had contacted on the dating site. I had just told him the story about the wheelchair and he had laughed. I pushed my luck and told him the one about the false teeth. There was a silence, and then he said 'I have false teeth'. Within a few minutes he had brought the conversation to an abrupt close.

That was the trouble with our age group. It had already started to deteriorate. Not only did that mean that our looks had often taken a dive, a seriously deep dive in some cases, but quite a few of the men I spoke to or met had ailments or diseases. When one guy got out of the car, I noticed his walking stick and saw that he was limping heavily. Our date was strolling around Stow-on-the-Wold for an afternoon. He was in a fair amount of pain and I felt sorry for him, but I did need someone who was fairly fit, since otherwise I would become a carer early on in the relationship. He kept emphasising that his knee did often suddenly get better, but coupled with bad breath, it put paid to any hopes of this relationship heading off into the sunset.

I had been chatting by email to another guy, a lovely 57-year-old, with a great sense of humour, before what I hoped was going to be a first date. Then one of his emails became suddenly serious. 'There's something I have to tell you. I've just been diagnosed with Parkinson's disease.' Poor guy. As if being diagnosed with such an illness wasn't bad enough, he had to face telling potential partners. He said 'I think you've been through enough, so I wanted to warn you first.' I thanked him sincerely for being so considerate, but said I couldn't face having to deal with that. He said he understood. I felt very disablist (if there is such a word), but I had to look out for myself at this point. I was fit and healthy as far as I knew, and wanted someone similar.

Another guy was just about to have a hip-replacement at the time I met him. How could I be contemplating going out with someone so decrepit? He was only 63. You forget that time has crept on and your age group IS the group that has hip operations, and other 'old' illnesses, despite the fact that you might still feel 32 inside.

I went out with one guy for four months. He had type 1 diabetes and always had to be aware of what he ate. While I ate a knickerbocker glory in front of him, he would have a glass of water. I chatted to another guy, who revealed that he had had cancer of the tongue. I didn't even know you could contract cancer of the tongue, but had to admit to myself that, very selfishly, I didn't fancy kissing anyone with that ailment, even though I knew that cancer was not infectious.

When it comes to finding a mate, we instinctively look for healthy specimens. I suppose it goes back to wanting to procreate with them. We are also attracted to people with good skin, as it is an obvious sign of good health, which is why the day I was diagnosed with facial eczema in 2012 I was not pleased. I've since managed to control it with emollient creams and steroid creams so that most people wouldn't know I suffered from it at all, but when I was told, I thought I could just do without it, thanks, at this time of mate searching.

One day a good-looking guy of about six foot two walked onto the dance floor in our local dance class. I thought he looked rather dishy, so I went and asked him to dance. He wasn't friendly and hardly smiled during the dance, but I still thought he was rather gorgeous.

Two weeks later he walked into the tennis club and put his name down for social tennis. I happened to be selected to play as his partner in the next doubles game. His name was Giles. I introduced myself and said I'd recently danced with him; he didn't remember. A few days later, I noticed him on the dating site. He was 63. Six years older than me. Perfect I thought, so I contacted him. I said I recognized him from tennis and dancing. He said he didn't remember me but would I like to chat. We chatted and he invited me round for supper that evening.

Just before I put the phone down, he said 'oh - how old are you by the way?'

'56.'

There was a pause and then 'Oh - so I'm not cradle-snatching then.'

Hang on a minute, mister. You're six years older than me. What a cheek! I know a lot of guys on the dating sites are very ageist, whereas women can be very heightist. But all I said was 'Yes I know. I'd like to be 40 but there you go.' I should have just put the phone down. Hindsight is a great thing. But I didn't want to fly off the handle and reject people at the slightest provocation.

He couldn't get out of supper, but I knew then he wasn't keen to see me. It was a challenge now to try and get him to like me. I certainly preferred guys who were not all over me, sycophantically hanging on my every word.

We had quite a nice supper and chatted about all sorts of things, but he was a bit surly, and abruptly disagreed with me a few times. At the end of the evening, he saw me to the door. 'So I will see you on Saturday for tennis,' I ventured. 'Yes,' he said, unconvincingly.

The next day I received a text from him. 'Hi Anna. Very sorry but some friends have decided to pay me a visit this weekend so I won't be able to make tennis on Saturday. We'll sort something out when you come back from your trip.' (I was about to go away for a fortnight for work.) 'Yeah right,' I thought. 'Pull the other one.' That was one of the worst excuses not to see someone I'd seen. For one thing, he could have told his friends (had they existed) that he was busy that weekend. For another, since they were going to very rudely turn up unannounced, if he was so desperate to see them, but still wanted to see me, he could have still had a quick game of tennis with me. I nearly texted back 'Bollocks. I wasn't born yesterday. If you don't want to see me, just say so.' But I wanted to appear easy-going and not paranoid, so just texted back 'OK'.

On my return two weeks later, Giles was mysteriously busy and couldn't quite make dancing or tennis for a few weeks. He was the first of my dates from my own area. He had similar interests, so annoyingly I would keep bumping into him. When I eventually did come across him at a dance lesson four months later, he put on a false smile and pretended to be pleased to see me. 'I haven't seen you for ages. Nice to see you. We'll have to have a dance together later,' he said. I smiled politely and said 'Yes'. Hell hath no fury... It was more the deceit and patronising excuses that annoyed me. Somehow he forgot to ask me later for that dance.

I was curious about the reason for the rejection, and decided to ask him. After all, it would only help me. But he avoided answering directly, and in the end I just said he was obviously not going to tell me. I think people should give people they meet and have rejected the reasons for the rejection. Ultimately we're all in this online dating lark together and are all just trying to find a mate. We meet up on dates with many more people than we'd ever agree to date in normal society. Most people you meet 'normally' are subtly rejected on looks, or attitude, or lack of sense of humour, or lack of wavelength with you, or social behaviour through different background, or that all-important, unexplainable ingredient – chemistry. But none of that is evident via the dating sites, or even on the phone during the initial chats. It normally makes itself known during the first date, which is why second dates are quite an achievement.

We should expect to reject and be rejected many more times from first online dates. We're all fairly set in our ways by the time we reach our fifties, and can't help to a degree what we've grown into. We should accept that we are not going to be compatible with many people. Nevertheless it doesn't seem to make it any easier to reject people, or be rejected. It's such a personal matter to be rejected as a lover. You can't exactly blame anyone else. It's also very easy to build up hopes and dreams, not only from people's profiles, but from emailing them and chatting to them over the phone once or twice so when you meet them and you don't like them as much as you thought you would, it can be a huge disappointment. You realise in a split second on meeting them that you will have to start all over again. It also means that you are single again, whereas you had come to think that you might have found a partner at last. It means you have a tiresome evening ahead of you, pretending to be interested in someone, when you know you will never see them again, with any luck.

I wanted to know the real reasons for my five rejections, but I couldn't get three of the five guys to tell me. I even wrote one an email as a joke giving him a multiple choice of reasons for my rejection: 1. Boring 2. Smelly 3. Too fat 4. Too thin. 5. Too posh. 6. Too working class. 7. Too old. (he was 52, I was 56) 8. Too young. 9. Lived too far away. 10. Not enough interests in common. 11. No sense of humour. 13. Too laid back. 14. Too serious. 15. Too intense. 16. Bad breath. 17. Too stupid. 18. Laughed too loud. 19. Spoke too loud. 20. Irritating character traits.

His reply was 'Not for me'. Very unhelpful, but from his point of view a nice, neutral, unhurtful comment. Trouble is, it makes you wonder even more. So I had to glean the answers from their behaviour. I *think* it was because I became suddenly shyer than normal with them because I was attracted to them, and they didn't think the conversation flowed, so they didn't think there was much chemistry. It couldn't have been coincidence that the five guys I liked enough to try out a second date were the ones that rejected me. I would want to know if I had bad breath or talked too much, or laughed too loudly, however much it would hurt to find out. But I think most people don't want to get involved in giving their rejectee a damning criticism of their performance, partly because they don't want to be the one to hurt their feelings, but also they can't be bothered with the aftermath of the ensuing texts pleading that they will change if only they could be given one more chance. In addition, I think most people feel it's not their responsibility or right to try and 'improve' people they've only met once.

Two guys I dated and slept with after the third or fourth date were too overweight for me to continue to find them attractive. I only saw how overweight they were when they took their clothes off. It was horrible to be in bed with someone I found revolting. They had worn cleverly disguising clothes, so I thought they were just stocky and muscular. When they got the rejecting text, they both asked me why there had been a sudden change of mind after going to bed. So I did tell them, because their weight is something they can do something about. Was I right to hurt their feelings like that? I don't know. One didn't take the rejection well.

'Good riddance. Well rid of you,' he spat through the text.

'As for me, I really enjoyed meeting you,' I answered, determined to remain polite, and admittedly feeling rather smug and superior in the face of his ignorant rudeness.

'You're just a slut. Did you come up here to fuck me?'

'Yes, partly. But because I really liked you and that's what we agreed. It wasn't my fault that I didn't fancy you because you are overweight.'

'I hope I haven't caught anything from you.' The spitting continued.

It wasn't pleasant to receive these texts, but I understood the reason for the bitterness - hurt pride and disappointment. But I was disappointed as well, in that I had really liked him and wondered if we could make a go of it.

He contacted me a few months later through the dating site, and told me he had lost a lot of weight and had found an attractive 50-year-old. I was pleased for him, and felt I had actually helped him, even though I could tell he was letting me know in revenge, to show me what I was missing. I had no regrets and as the tone of his emails became slightly nasty again, I blacklisted him on the site so that he couldn't contact me again.

Another guy was the date from hell, the religious kind. He had put on his profile that his religion was Christianity and that he was practising. I thought that if he only practised about twice a year, we might be still all right. We went for the normal drink and within minutes of sitting down I asked him about his religion, not wanting to repeat the mistake with the religious pilot, Anthony. He started telling me that religion and God were very important to him. Mmmmm. Oh dear. This was going to be another wasted evening,

I thought. Then he said, 'Do you know who Jesus Christ is?' His voice was slightly raised. What had I started? 'In what way?' I asked, innocently.

'So – you don't know. You should study your Bible.'

'I was brought up a Christian, so of course I know who he is. I think we ought to leave in fact' I said, and started to get up from my chair. I looked around for the nearest exit, while he carried on berating me for not reading the Bible. I walked out of the pub, and then ran as fast as I could towards my car, my heart thumping. It occurred to me that I probably wouldn't see him again.

CHAPTER TWELVE

Subs and doms

It was now about 15 months since Pen had died and I was no nearer finding a partner, and not making much headway into paying off the £20,000 debt he had unwittingly landed on my plate. In addition, I had had to fork out about £18,000 on fertility treatment, which had made quite a dent in my coffers and was still having a knock-on effect. I couldn't face the idea of having an evening job on top of my normal day job as a computer programmer. I also wouldn't contemplate going cap in hand to my parents. They had given me such a good start in life – a lovely home, secure surroundings, a good education, not to mention a sizeable lump sum towards my first home. How could I then turn round and say I was in debt and could they bail me out?

One evening I noticed my bottom in the mirror. It was a pretty good size and shape. I fetched a slipper from the bedroom and gave myself a few whacks with it. Pah - that was nothing. I could take a good spanking I reckoned. I wondered if I could find a way of being spanked for money. I imagined that men might put me over their knee, fully clothed, give me about 10 playful slaps and then I would go home. Very occasionally some of the more daring ones might raise my skirt and slap me over my knickers.

I googled 'spanking', and among the results was a site advertising for girls to be spanked. I entered the site, and felt my heart rate increase. This to me was a dark world, veering on prostitution. It was probably dangerous and sordid, and I didn't know if I was brave enough.

I found the home page and saw a note on it that said a website could be created for free for would-be spankees. There was also a contact email. I thought it could do no harm to ask, so I wrote there and then, before I could change my mind. I sent off the email – and my heart rate rose even further. I asked about rates, what spankers expect, and how dangerous it was for girls, while not believing that I could actually be doing this.

Within a day or so, I received a friendly reply from a man called Duncan. The spelling and grammar were immaculate, which surprised me. I thought I might hear from some backstreet pimp with no education. He confirmed that he could produce a web page for me for free if I gave him some text and some photos of myself in whatever pose I wanted. He said he could put me in touch with an existing, experienced spankee who could tell me the advantages and pitfalls. I asked if I could charge for being spanked, and he said he thought it was about £100 an hour. For doing something I quite liked anyway? Blimey! He gave me the email of a girl called Emeralda, which I took to be her spankee name.

I was encouraged by Duncan's friendly helpfulness and the seeming accessibility of the spanking world, so I decided to venture further and email my fellow spankee. She was also friendly and replied within a day that clients were mostly married men who just wanted 'a bottom to spank'. They were normally not interested in a relationship. She charged £100 an hour.

'Do they spank hard?' I asked, 'and do they take your knickers down? Do they ever follow you home, or try and have sex with you?'

'No they don't spank hard' she replied. 'Yes, they nearly always take your knickers down. They've never followed me home. Some of them ask if they can have sex, but they don't pursue it when I refuse.'

'Where do you do it?'

'Mostly their homes, or my home. I met my first client at a pub and then followed him to his house. I was absolutely terrified. But it was fine and now he's a regular.'

'Do they stop when you say stop?'

'Yes, although I've heard that just occasionally spankers don't stop when spankees ask them to stop.'

This answer worried me slightly. I found out a few months after this that Emeralda had been in a hotel room with a spanker who had started to cane her, with her permission. After her normal quota of strokes, she had asked him to stop, but he decided he hadn't had his money's worth, and continued to thrash her as she writhed on the floor, trying to escape him. Somehow she managed to get hold of her mobile and rang a spanking male friend, who spoke to the guy mid-caning and calmed him down. She hadn't mentioned this to me during our initial email conversation. Presumably she didn't want to put me off.

'Do you get any cranks?'

'No I haven't so far. Some will email you and after a while it's obvious they are not interested or brave enough to meet you. So I just say to them 'If you'd like to arrange a session, just email me'.'

'Gosh. You sound so normal!' I remarked to her.

'Lol. Of course I'm normal!'

I went back to Duncan and said I would like him to go ahead and create me a website. I would send him some photos. One thing bothered me: 'I'm 57. Are clients going to want to spank me when there must be so many other younger spankees available?'

'Oh don't you worry,' he replied. 'Many spankers are in their sixties. They quite like older spankees since they can relate to them more easily. I'm nearly seventy, so you are all young to me! One thing I would recommend is to put a sort of disclaimer on the bottom of your web page, saying that you will not perform sexual favours.'

I couldn't wait to start taking photos of myself in various rude poses. I looked at some of the other girls' photos on their websites. They were all quite different. Some showed faceless men's hands about to slap their bare bottoms. Some spankees were alone and completely naked, bent over a chair or table. Some were just bent over themselves, fully dressed, with their skirt raised, knickers round their knees, while an anonymous male hand could be seen holding a strap and about to strike an already reddened bottom.

I put my Instamatic on 10 seconds delay, took down my jeans to below my knees, pulled my lacy knickers half way down my buttocks and bent over my armchair. The first 20 photos or so were awful. I was off-centre or the cellulite on my thighs stood out like veins, or my bottom looked too flabby. So I dimmed the light, took up position again and started producing sexier photos. I pulled my knickers all the way down past my bottom and took a few more.

Then I put on a lacy white summer dress, pulled it up to reveal half a bare bottom and took the final photos. I was ready for my life as a rooky spankee.

★ ★ ★

The website was ready within a few days. It showed my new name (Lily-Rose) and email address on the bottom. I also noticed that my name was tagged as a new entry in the list of spankees. This was it. I was about to display my bottom to the world.

I waited two days - nothing. Then on the third day I received about three or four replies, polite, well-written emails from men in their 50s and 60s. Some wrote quite long emails about what they would like to do to me for a session. Some just wanted to know what I would charge, where I operated, and if I switched. Switched? What did that mean, I wondered? I guessed that it meant switching positions from say, over a table, to over a bed. Yes, I thought I could manage that. It turned out to be where the spankee spanked the spanker. Yuck. That didn't interest me at all. The idea of having to deal with a man bent over the bed, with his hairy arse and balls on display, was an instant turn-off to me. I never felt the need or desire to dominate someone else, either verbally or physically.

It was scary and at the same time exciting to receive these replies. I didn't know if I would have the nerve to actually meet any of these guys. It felt so like prostitution. But at the same time, there should be no sex involved. I really did like the idea of being spanked by a strange man, and especially for money. I wouldn't do it without the money, I decided. I would feel too cheap and desperate, strangely enough, almost as if I needed the excuse of the money to justify why I would take part in, and enjoy, such activity.

★ ★ ★

One 65-year-old man contacted me, then once I replied, asked to meet up, so I gave him my mobile. He rang immediately and we started chatting. But after a few minutes I noticed that his voice was becoming slightly breathless. I had an inkling of what was going on. He suddenly said: 'I want you to treat me like a naughty schoolboy. You are my school headmistress and you are about to cane me.'

No thanks. This was not what I wanted. If this was the only type of caller, I wouldn't be pursuing this new career at all.

'Go on,' he pleaded, 'just say a few words.'

I suddenly felt sorry for him and said, very unconvincingly: 'you're a very naughty boy. Bend over my desk.' I heard this quiet, exhalation of breath and he just said, 'That's it. I've come. Thank you.'

'You're welcome,' I said, and quickly put down the phone. I felt disgusted. I wouldn't give out my mobile so readily next time.

A guy named 'Joseph Joseph' aged 50 plus, contacted me: 'Dear Lily-Rose, I would be pleased to here [sic] more about your spanking services. I am a professional white gentleman in my early 50s who is an experienced spanker. My interests are purely pleasure related and I have no interest in, or any desire to hurt my spankees. I particularly enjoy playing with an older lady and one who has other interests around which we could perhaps create some interesting role play scenarios. If you are interested in playing you will find me to be reliable, discrete [sic] and good fun. I am based near Dringham and can travel to suit you. I look forward to hearing from you. Joseph.'

I replied in the same polite vein: 'Hi Joseph, Thanks very much for your reply. You sound like just the sort of spanker I would enjoy being spanked by. I would do any role play you would like. I may not have the clothes to begin with, but could probably build on that. I am also reliable and discreet. This is, as you say, just a fun session for both of us. We would have to talk on the phone first (5-10 mins), if it's OK with you. My rates are £100 for the first hour, and £50 per hour after that (pro rata). I am about an hour south of Dringham so we could meet half way, or I could come to your house. I would prefer to go for a quick coffee/drink (10 mins) before following you back to the house/hotel. If this sounds all OK so far, I can give you my mobile number. Regards, Lily-Rose.'

We had a brief conversation on the phone, and I detected an unkind, bullying tone, but I assumed this was normal for a spanker talking to his spankee. Afterwards I realised we hadn't discussed what I should wear. 'I would be happy for you to wear similar knickers [as the web site] but they won't be staying on for long!' he replied. 'For this to work for me I have to find you attractive and you need to excite me. The pictures I have seen certainly do that and I like what I learned about you over the telephone. Are you brave enough to send me more pictures to whet my appetite? I want to see one of your face and of you dressed.'

I sent him the three photos I had used on the dating sites.

'That's good. You have a good figure and I am looking forward to playing with you. You will be going naked with me and spanked very hard which will wipe that smile off your face. Do you understand?'

Mmmm. I wasn't sure about the naked part at all. 'I didn't agree to going naked so I might not do that,' I replied. He backtracked hurriedly. 'Naked in terms of knickers down and shamefully around your ankles, legs apart and bent over a chair or the hotel bed ready to take a firm hand spanking and slippering. That is what I meant by you being naked.' Good god!

We arranged to meet at a pub so that I could feel safe with him first before going to a nearby Travelodge. A huge man of about six foot three met me in the car park. He seemed normal, didn't have two heads, and spoke with a very educated accent, so I decided I would at least have a drink with him. It felt weird to be having a drink with a guy who was soon going to be taking my knickers down and spanking my bare bottom, having only just met me. He told me that he'd been with his previous spankee for years, and that unfortunately she had had to move away. As he talked, I realised he was in love with her. That was a revelation in itself. I thought men would consider spankees as inferior prostitutes, not equals with whom they could fall in love.

We walked over to the Travelodge, chatting slightly awkwardly. As soon as we were inside the room, his personality changed. 'Stand over there,' he ordered, pointing to a spot near the bed. I did as I was told, feeling very nervous and excited all at once. Then he took off his jacket and handed it to me. 'Hang this up!' I took it from him, but instead of hanging it up I decided to give him an excuse to spank me, so I threw it onto the bed behind him, where it lay in a crumpled heap. He stared at me with surprise. Instead of grabbing me and putting me over his knee, as I envisaged, he just turned round and picked his jacket up and hung it himself on a hanger, looking slightly embarrassed. (I later learnt that most dominants just want submissives to do as they're told and not put up any fight.)

Then he came and stood right next to me at right angles to my body, and grabbed my arm. 'Stand up straight!' he barked. I did so. And without hesitation, he bent over me and started to spank me hard over my jeans for a few minutes. It stung, but it was easily bearable at this point.

Then he pulled my jeans down to my knees. How weird. I was still standing up. And how vulnerable I felt, in the grip of this huge man. He slapped me hard on the buttocks with his enormous hand 10 or 12 times. This time it stung a lot. Then he pushed my shoulders very slightly forward so that my bottom was sticking out. He roughly pulled my knickers down to my knees and continued the spanking. Another 10 or so slaps reigned down.

'Can I see your breasts?' he asked.

'No,' I answered.

'Then take off your knickers and jeans!'

I took them off where I stood, and as I bent right over to finally jerk the jeans from my feet, I was almost bent double in front of him. 'Stay in that position' he said. Then he spanked me hard again for about five minutes. 'Right, stand up, and bend over the bed with your feet apart.'

Blimey. He wanted to look at my private parts. I started coming out of myself and watching myself going through the motions. I was way out of my comfort zone and couldn't believe that I was going through with this. I bent over the bed with my hands spread in front of me and placed my feet about a foot apart. He took a chair, placed it directly behind me and sat down. I could feel his eyes on my body.

'Feet wider apart,' he ordered.

'No,' I said defiantly.

'OK,' he said. 'Turn around and put yourself over my knee.'

I could do that, I thought, although my bottom was beginning to feel quite beleaguered. I placed myself over his knee, and to my surprise he started caressing my bottom gently and chatting to me again, as if we were just friends. After about 10 minutes of this, he asked what I felt like doing.

'Well, I've got a slipper if you want to try that,' I said. He agreed and I naively took out of my bag a man's heavy ribbed slipper which I had bought that day. He grabbed it eagerly, commanded me to stand up again, and walloped me hard another 10 times with it. That hurt – but I just stood there and took it, thinking this was normal.

Suddenly he stood upright, took a look at my buttocks and said 'I can't use this bottom. It bruises far too easily. I think you've had enough.' He gave me back my slipper. I felt quite disappointed that I seemed to have failed as a fledgling spankee.

'How much do I owe you?' he asked rather gruffly.

'£100 is fine.'

'Here's £120 – for the petrol.' He handed me a wadge of £20 notes.

'I won't count them,' I said to him, slightly embarrassed at being paid for our interaction, and trying to show that I trusted him.

'Well I counted them out in front of you,' he snapped. Oh. I mumbled that I hadn't been watching him count it out, but the atmosphere had changed, and he was clearly slightly annoyed. Then, bizarrely, he suddenly took me in his arms and started caressing my head. I came up to his nipple line. I realised that he could very easily break my neck with one little twist of his huge hands, but instincts told me that a guy who refused to carry on slippering me for humane reasons would probably not then want to kill me.

'You OK, small person?' he suddenly asked gently. I assured him I was. Then he thanked me, told me not to ring his mobile because of his wife, and left quickly.

Phew. I'd survived. I'd had my first spanking session. My bottom hurt. I hadn't really enjoyed it and I hadn't liked the guy very much. He was a bully, but perhaps that was normal.

I walked over to the mirror and turned my back to it. My bottom was very red, and was flecked with tiny blue bruises all over. The next day when I surveyed the damage, it was a bruised mess. Not only was it covered in small black and blue bruises, but two slipper-shaped marks were magnificently obvious.

I was unashamedly proud of having taken such punishment with no complaints. I took several photos of my rear with the slipper held next to it to compare bruise mark sizes and shapes. I was about to send the best one to him when I saw that he'd sent an email: 'Hi – how are you and that gorgeous bottom of yours?'

I was surprised he cared or bothered to get in touch again. 'Strange to get an email from someone who's just thrashed the shit out of me, asking about my welfare,' I joked in reply. 'Here's a photo of your handiwork.'

He didn't seem amused. 'I didn't thrash the shit out of you. I like to spank hard, that's all. Thanks for the photo. I've seen worse. It reminds me of what a nice little body you have.'

'Thanks for the extra £20. Sorry I was so wilful – that was just play-acting, so you could have something to spank me for, but that obviously wasn't what you wanted. And I hope I didn't crease your jacket. So if we do meet again, I will just be subservient.'

'Not a problem. It's always a challenge to deal with my subs' different behaviours. Thank you for your note. I hope your bottom is still stinging but that the marks and reddening are reducing. You have a delicate bottom that you will need to be careful with. Anyway it was a pleasure to meet you and if you enjoyed yourself I hope that we may be able to do it again sometime.'

I assumed that by 'subs' he meant submissives. I quite liked the idea of being a submissive within a spanking context, although I wasn't sure the verbal bullying when the spanking had finished was ideal, but perhaps that was all part of the scene. I never heard from him again, so it was probably a combination of the fact that my bottom couldn't take his strength of spanking, that I refused to undress and that we hadn't got along that well as people, however polite his emails seemed.

Interesting though. That first encounter had demonstrated two things to me: that it was much more of a social interaction than a financial arrangement, and that spankers can care about their 'subs'. I later learnt that the spanking world doesn't like terms such as 'beat' and 'hit' as that sounds like abuse. 'Spank,' 'strap,' 'thrash' and 'smack' should be used, as these words denote punishment, the premise behind every interaction. Also frowned on are terms such as 'arse,' 'bum,' 'butt' and 'backside'. They are seen as crass, with no decorum. 'Bottom' is easily preferred to anything else, although occasionally I've heard people saying 'behind', 'seat' and 'derrière'. Hence Joseph's dislike of my 'accusing' him of having 'thrashed the shit' out of me, even if I had been joking.

The second email I received turned out to be typical of many I would get over the course of the first year. Here it is verbatim:

My name is Tyson. I'm a 50-yr-old male and live on the Staffs/Derbys border in the Midlands. I am totally genuine and would be keen to hear from you with a view to a session together. I've been an occasional [sic] player in CP for a few years but struggle to find the time, like role play, secretary or school scenarios. I enjoy putting a naughty lady over my knee and giving her the spanking she deserves. I am much into the fun and mutual pleasure of it all rather than pain. So come on let me put some colour into your cheeks! - Tyson.

I discovered that CP meant 'corporate punishment' and is a widely-used term. People refer to the CP scene, or someone's CP preferences. Unfortunately he was too far away for us to meet up.

The third email was from a surprisingly young but experienced spanker who had been a spankee himself. 'Hi. Lovely pictures, you have a gorgeous bottom. Mid 20's, fit athletic chap here, especially like spanking the more mature lady, just wondering on your rates?' As a student he couldn't afford the £100 an hour, so we negotiated a reduced rate of £40 for half an hour. I needed all the money and experience I could acquire. It's entirely up to the spanker and spankee involved to make a financial arrangement and stick to it. It's almost a case of 'my word is my bond'. I've not so far come across any spanker who has either tried not to pay or changed the rate once agreed. This young guy said he had once allowed himself to be spanked by someone and then the guy had not paid up, so he warned me against it.

We met for a quick drink at a Travelodge, and then went straight up into the room. He wasted no time and quickly put me over his knee fully dressed, where he proceeded to give me a gentle spanking to warm me up. Being warmed up makes a big difference to how much you can take later. Soon my dress came up and my knickers went down and a harder spanking continued, for a solid five minutes.

'Take your knickers off and put yourself in the wheelbarrow position,' he suddenly said.

'What's that?'

'OK. Lie on your front on my thighs with each leg either side of my body. Your hands on the floor. Your bottom facing me and the ceiling.' OMG, how personal is that going to be! I lay in that position while he spanked my buttocks.

'Nice view' he remarked, with a laugh. He never touched me anywhere other than my bottom. It might have felt strange to have someone young enough to be my son feeling my body with his fingers – but I decided I would have let him, had he asked. The agreed half hour extended to an hour, but that was fine. I could have left at any time if I had wanted. I accepted the £40.

* * *

Soon after my website went live, I received another very polite email from a 62-year-old man called Jeremy:

Hello Lily-Rose, This is Jeremy from Chasenell. I am an experienced player and have been active in both the party and 121 scene for about 10 years. I've just seen your profile on the web site. As a newcomer, I expect that you are inundated with enquiries, but in due course I would be very interested in meeting you for a 121. So, if you'd like to, do please get back to me when you have the chance. All the best for now, Jeremy x

I liked the sound of him and the fact that he was experienced, so I emailed back straight away. I wasn't quite sure of some of the terms he'd used but from the tone of his email felt that he wouldn't mind explaining them to me, since I was a novice.

Hi Jeremy, Thanks very much for your email. I've had several enquiries but I'm certainly not inundated. I imagine the age does not help. What is a 121? I assume it's one woman with two men? I would only try that after I had met you once or maybe twice. My rates are £100 for the first hour, and £50 per hour after that. Would you prefer to meet in a hotel/lodge or your house? Regards, Lily-Rose.

As predicted, I received a kind explanatory email by return:

Dear Lily-Rose, Thanks for getting back to me. It's true I suppose that most of the girls in the 'scene' (as we often refer to it), are somewhat younger. But nevertheless there are still a number of very attractive spankees of various levels of experience who are in their 40s or 50s. Although age might be a factor in the level of response you are getting, on the other hand, your profile on the whole is highly attractive. The term 121 is a very confusing 'text-style' abbreviation of the phrase 'one-to-one', meaning 'one on one' or one man/one woman. (Other numerical combinations like 221 or 122 are of course also possible, but quite rare.) A 'party' has multiple players of both genders, normally in a ratio of between 2 and 3 men to each woman. But don't worry, I'm just enquiring about a straightforward 'one on one' meeting. I would prefer to meet at my home, where I live alone. Before arranging a meeting however, I would appreciate the opportunity of having a brief telephone conversation with you. Best regards, Jeremy.

We arranged for me to spend an afternoon and probably an evening with him in his house, since it was one and a half hours away. He assured me he would pay me for the petrol. He said he had a play room, which I was very eager to see – but not necessarily try out. I had read *Fifty Shades of Grey* and imagined it would be decked out with chains and whips and whipping benches.

I arrived at the appointed time and knocked on the door of a big, detached Victorian house in a very well-to-do residential area. A slim, clean-shaven man with short, dark hair and dressed smart-casual, opened the door, smiling, and greeted me with a hug. 'Come in and have a cup of tea,' he said, taking my coat, and leading me into the conservatory, which looked out onto his lovely garden, with a bowling green behind. 'Would you like some biscuits?'

We sat and had afternoon tea, while members of the public played bowls yards from the garden. How quintessentially English, I thought. Little did they know what was about to happen, and what, it transpired, frequently happened in large numbers, behind closed doors here. We discovered that we were on the same dating site, which gave us two good subjects for discussion. He agreed how hard it was to find a partner who liked the spanking scene as well. (Non-spankers, both men and women, are described as 'vanilla'.) He said he had once dated a girl for a few dates and then decided to tell her about his spanking interest. She was horrified and he never saw her again.

I finished my tea and looked expectantly at him. Sometimes it was a little awkward finishing the social chit-chat at the beginning of a session and starting the spanking itself.

'Right. Shall we get going?' he said. 'I think a little role play would break the ice, don't you?'

'Yes that's fine,' I said, trying to sound confident, but inside I was dreading having to do my first role play. I was a rotten actress. I had never volunteered in schools for parts in plays. I was just too self-conscious.

'What would you like to play?' I asked. We had discussed by email different scenarios, and he had asked me to invent one. I was surprised that many spankers like to do role plays of the spankees' choice rather than theirs. They told me it means they know the spankee is more engaged in the interaction. I was also surprised how many of them want the spankee to enjoy herself during the session.

'I want you to stand outside the play room, and knock on the door,' he said. 'I will be inside behind the desk. Come and report yourself like we agreed.'

I waited for him to go into the room, and then knocked on the door, with my heart thumping. 'Come,' he shouted. As soon as I opened the door, a completely different character sat behind the desk, staring at me gravely. The room had no whips, chains or whipping benches. It was just an ordinary carpeted room, with a desk, two chairs and a sideboard.

'Come and stand in front of me,' he said sternly. 'Why have you been reported to me?' I tried to tell my agreed story - that I had been caught red-handed stealing apples in his orchard by his gardener and been ordered to report to him (the rich landowner) to be dealt with accordingly, or he would go to the police - but whenever my eyes met his, I was just aware that this was the guy I had just been having tea with, five minutes before, and I started to smile. So I kept looking away, trying to concentrate on the scenario, so that I could look contrite. Nerves were playing a part.

He kept up the solemn pretence of the role play well, even in the face of my fading prowess as the leading lady.

'You have to choose between a severe spanking from me, or the police.'

'But what's wrong with taking those apples? They were on the ground. No one would want them anyway.' I tried desperately to get into the part.

'You know very well that stealing my apples and trespassing on my land is a crime. Choose what your punishment is to be.'

Then my eyes met his, and I committed the mortal sin of laughing. I really didn't want to, but it just escaped out of my mouth. I wondered if he would be annoyed that I didn't seem to be taking this role play seriously. I was annoyed with myself, since he seemed a nice guy, and deserved to be treated with respect, and moreover to get his money's worth from this spanking session, which would only be enhanced by a good initial role play. I managed to say that I didn't want him to go to the police.

'Right. I will wipe that smile off your face. Come and stand over here.' He got up and sat down on the chair in the middle of the room and pulled me roughly over his knee. He had even put a small stool for my elbows to rest on. I was sorry that I had almost ruined the moment, but he seemed to have forgiven me. It was a great session, which I thoroughly enjoyed. I was spanked over several different pieces of furniture – over the knee, (often referred to as OTK), over the desk, over the table, over the end of the chaise longue. He had quite an array of implements which I'd never seen or tried, or even heard of. He tried them on me one by one, very gently to begin with, and only if I wanted him to, and always stopped immediately if I asked him to. There were several types of strap (a thick short leather belt), a paddle (a round malleable leather implement, shaped like a huge lollipop, which made a lovely, loud thwack on my bottom, with not too much pain), a riding crop, and a flogger (a small cluster of light leathery thongs attached to a handle, which made a loud thud but was surprisingly unpainful). There were also several canes of different lengths and thicknesses, but I said I didn't think I was ready to try them out yet.

He tried the flogger on my bare back very lightly. I liked it. Throughout this first session with him, he never touched my genitals. My knickers did come off completely at one point and my legs were pushed apart over the desk. I looked round and he was squatting down between my legs, having a good gawp at the view. Fine by me. After the first spanker had asked to see my breasts and crotch, I had decided that I might quite like men to look at me, and I did in fact find the whole thing extremely erotic, as Jeremy could tell from the amount of lubrication oozing from me. It was actually dripping onto the floor, so much so that he kept having to hand me tissues, and on one occasion helped to dry me off himself.

'I'm glad you're enjoying yourself so much' he chuckled. 'It's much nicer for me that I see you are so turned on by it. And by the way – it's disgraceful.'

I explained that I was on HRT, which helped the body lubricate. We agreed that perhaps I was on too high a dose!

The session ended and we had another cup of tea. He wondered about taking me outside for another spanking session in his garden, but people were still playing bowls on the nearby green and might hear the slapping noises, so we decided instead to have another spanking session in his bedroom, with me bent over the end of his bed. He placed several mirrors around the room, so that I could watch myself being spanked. Very sexy! The juices flowed! Then we had a game of table tennis (which I won!) in one of his rooms. Slightly bizarre in the circumstances, but hey, life is bizarre.

That evening we decided to have a meal at a nearby restaurant. Jeremy remarked that the day was turning out rather like a date. I agreed, but started to wonder what he was thinking. We did get on very well. He said it was lovely to have someone his age to talk to about spanking, as none of his family knew, and sometimes he longed to chat about it freely. I drove home rather elated after my day's exploits.

The next day I received an email from Jeremy saying how much he'd enjoyed our session and wondered if I'd like to go out on a real date. I liked him and we had much in common, but he was just too far away. I'd tried long-distance relationships before and they were hard work. I hoped though that we could still be friends and spank. I was relieved to find that he continued to email me and invite me up to his house for regular spankings even after I gave him my answer.

* * *

I still wasn't sure if I wanted spankers to come to my house - a great topic of gossip for the neighbours, but rather detrimental to my street cred. Or perhaps it would enhance it? I thought if I met them first, I might let some of them come, as long as they disguised their implements. It would obviously cut down my travelling costs and time taken for a session.

By the time I had been a spankee for a year I had allowed three of them to visit my home. One came specifically to introduce me to the cane. He asked me to wear white stockings and suspenders for the session. He always turned up with a bunch of flowers, which touched me, especially at the beginning when I thought I was entering a near-prostitution scene. It seemed to show that despite my baring my bottom to strangers, he respected me.

After the initial polite chit-chat and cup of tea while I placed his flowers in water, he declared that not only was he going to cane me, he wanted to shave me if I would allow him to! I thought about it. It could do no harm. I might quite like it!

He placed a towel on the arm chair and asked me to lie on my back on it with one leg on each arm of the chair. He had already removed my knickers, so everything was on display. He took out a razor, dunked it in shaving cream and proceeded to shave my public region all over. It was rather relaxing and erotic, once I'd got over the embarrassment of the revealing position in front of a strange man.

Most spankers seem to want their spankees to be hairless down below. 'No hair below the eye-lashes' one said to me. The reason, he said, was because it makes the spankee look more feminine, more vulnerable, younger, more innocent, more in need of discipline. Then he asked to spank me over his knee on the sofa. After a good, quite lengthy spanking to warm me up, he requested the wheelbarrow position. This time I didn't mind so much as with the young guy. This guy had just shaved me after all, and he was only a few years younger than me.

Then he got up, took hold of the cane and started swishing it through the air. He led me through to the kitchen and told me to bend over my kitchen table with legs apart, my hands grasping the sides of the table, and wait for him there. He had laid a cushion on the table. I had to go on tiptoe to bend over it. It pushed my bottom up higher to present it for the caning.

I could hear him behind me fetching the cane from the other room, and then I was aware of him walking slowly back through into the kitchen, cane in hand. He took up a position to the left of me. He told me afterwards that my bare bottom was framed beautifully by the white stockings and suspenders. He said he would use the cane gently to begin with.

'Ready?' he asked quietly. I said I thought I was, very unconvincingly – but I knew I wanted to get used to the cane, as it's something most spankers seem to love, and I thought I might be able to ask for more money if I could take it well.

I felt the cane being placed gently on my buttocks in readiness for the first stroke. My palms had begun to sweat and I remember looking at my kitchen table, two inches from my face and completely out of focus. I felt the cane being removed, and then after a second, heard the swish of it flying through the air, and then a very sharp sting as it came down on both buttocks at once. Ouch! That was painful. But I wanted to try and take some more.

'Well done,' he said. 'Shall I go again? It's entirely up to you.'

'OK.'

I felt the cane placed on my bottom again. Seconds later came not one but two sharp strokes, one after the other, much harder than the first. I gasped. Oh my god, the cane hurt! Both strokes were so painful that I cried out, got up off the table, mumbled out loud 'I can't take this' and marched through to the sitting room, where I sat in a fairly huffy, annoyed state. (That was probably breaking some tacit spankee rule, but I didn't care – it hurt like hell.)

He came through after me, rather concerned, and sat down beside me to calm me down. 'I know – it does hurt. Well done – you've just taken three strokes of the cane'.

I was embarrassed by my petulance and sudden display of temper. I could have just said 'Ow!' and said I didn't want any more, in a calm way. He was very understanding, but the atmosphere had changed slightly. I would have to watch my anger, as I would be losing clients. All the spankers I've met just want a fun consenting session between spanker and spankee. If I continued to flare up like that when the pain got too much, it would become awkward and they would not return to me.

He remained polite, congratulated me on taking the cane, reiterated that I had done well, and left. I wondered if I would see him again. (To my relief he wasn't put off, and became a regular.) I inspected the damage in the mirror. Several bruises were beginning to appear, deep purple ones. It hurt to sit down. Did I really want to get used to such pain? I didn't know that I did. Perhaps I could be a no-caning spankee. How could other girls take it?

I was disappointed by my own behaviour, by the intense pain of the strokes and by my intolerance. At the same time I knew that I wanted to be able to tell people I could take whatever they wanted to throw at me - belts, straps, riding crops and most importantly, the cane. It seemed to be the pinnacle of most spankers' excitement.

CHAPTER THIRTEEN

Out of the Blue

One day I had an email from a well-educated, white male in his mid-forties who said he was looking for 'someone to spank regularly'. I will call him Blue. He was not interested in switching, as he was quite dominant, and mostly enjoyed bare-bottom over-the-knee spanking. He sent a photo, which surprised me. I could have done anything with it - put it on Facebook, for one. Not that I would dream of giving anyone's identity away, but Blue didn't know that. As it turned out, and as I got to know him over the coming six months, he wouldn't have minded. Most people knew his antics anyway, and he was proud of them. But there seems to be a tacit agreement among the CP community that you do not kiss and tell.

Blue said he had never been married, did not have any children and didn't intend either to happen in the future. I wondered what made someone decide on a life that solitary. It also made me wonder if he was a weird, axe-wielding recluse who just liked to spank vulnerable women in his home and then bury them in the walls.

However, we arranged a date and time. I asked him what I should wear to meet him and if jeans were OK. He answered that he wanted me to wear whatever made me feel at ease. He then said he wanted me to get to know him as much as possible so that I would feel relaxed in his company. I thought that was nice, but at this stage I was still naive enough (or cautious enough) to think that all spankers could be rapists and murderers, so was this approach a trick to lure me in?

My satnav had broken, so I decided to look at a map beforehand and memorise the route. I was to arrive at his house at 7 pm, without ever having met him or even spoken to him beforehand. Crazy? I had so far not been wrong about my instincts about people, going by their emails. Their spelling and grammar often give their level of education away. Words like 'too' and 'their' spelt wrong are often indications. Sometimes there are no full stops in a paragraph, no capital letters at the beginning of a sentence, and apostrophes randomly scattered at the ends of words.

I'm not saying that being poorly educated is a prerequisite for being a rapist or that being educated means you are not going to rape someone, but a well-constructed, grammatically-correct email means to me that the emailer is likely to have a similar background to me, and that we will be more likely to reach an understanding and have more fun together. Having said that, I've had sessions with brickies and A & E surgeons and had just as much fun with both. It's sometimes the tone they use, or the abruptness with which they request details of my rates and CP preferences. The ones that say they don't want to hurt me but just have some fun with me are more likely to receive a positive response from me.

At 7.05 pm I was still driving along some dual carriageway a few miles from his house, trying to find somewhere to stop to explain that I hadn't in fact arrived, in case he hadn't noticed. I turned into a forecourt and, with some trepidation, phoned him. A very well-spoken, young-sounding male voice with a BBC accent answered.

'Hello – where are you?' he asked. I described where I had turned left down a Wellington Road, and thought now that I should have turned right.

'Right,' he said patiently, without any hint of irritation, 'turn round and just carry straight on until the High Street'.

'Don't I have to turn right?' I said.

'No – just go straight on'. Oh yes. 'Damn. You're right.' He was too nice to make any comment. He gave me a few more directions and I felt sure I had it straight in my mind.

I set off and about 40 minutes later I was no nearer. A text came through: 'how are you doing?' I rang him, feeling an idiot. I described my location, and he gave me further directions, saying at the end 'Do you think you are going to be all right now?'

'Who knows?' I said. He laughed, and said I should be with him in a few minutes. I wondered if he thought I was just some dumb blond.

At about 8.20 pm, still lost, I spotted a pub and rang him. 'Could you come and meet me? I've come into the car park of the White Swan'.

'Sure' he said, 'be there in five minutes.' Sure enough, within about five minutes, I saw a little white car with a missing hub-cap drive into the pub car park. A tall, slim guy looking no more than 30 got out and strode confidently towards me. Should I get out and kiss him? No, too forward. So I wound down my window and offered him my hand. He seemed nice, and friendly, even though I was by now one and a half hours late.

I started blurting out that I thought it was easier for him to come and meet me. He waited patiently for me to finish my sentence and then just said 'Sure. You follow me.' I followed his car in the dark to a small residential back street in the centre of the city. He indicated where to park and I wondered if I was going to be able to get my car into the space offered. Cars lined both sides of the road, with few gaps, so I thought I had better try to park where he said. I managed it, and got out.

Up the road, I saw a tall, slim, silhouetted frame waiting for me. This is it, I thought. I could run for it, but knew I wasn't going to. I walked towards him and then followed him into his house. The house seemed to have bare floorboards and little furniture. I felt slightly uneasy, but he'd been very kind on the phone, and was now offering me a cup of tea, which I accepted. I said I needed to go to the loo, and he said 'I thought you might. I made one earlier for you'. I chuckled at this reference to the Blue Peter demonstrations on TV from the 60s, and felt further at ease.

When I came downstairs he handed me a cup of tea and sat on the sofa next to me but a little way away. He asked me why I had started being a spankee and I saw for the first time how handsome he was. His photo didn't do him justice. We chatted about the spanking scene, and then he suddenly said 'I like you. I'd like to see you often. We can develop a good interaction, and do more than just spank. I will spank you regularly and pay you every now and then. We can have so much more fun than just a spanker-spankee relationship. What do you think?'

I was flattered but didn't know quite what he meant. Did he

mean a relationship? He was 12 years younger than me, and I hadn't contemplated dating any of the spankers, as I had been told by a fellow spankee that the vast majority of spankers are married and just want some harmless fun, which suited me fine. But I didn't want to offend him, so just said 'I like you too. Er – that sounds interesting'.

Then his attitude changed slightly. He got up, sat down next to me and put his hand on my thigh. 'I will need you to be naked now,' he said, in a way that wasn't really a request. The room was brightly lit. No gentle, soft light to make my body look anything other than 57. Did he want me to undress like a stripper while he watched?

I felt suddenly embarrassed and inexperienced, and said 'I think you will have to help me'.

'OK – stand up' he commanded. He stood behind me and bent over me. He was six feet tall. He reached round from behind, unzipped my jeans and pulled them down without hesitation. Then he bent over me from behind again, and said 'By the way, I'm OK. You don't know me, but I am OK'. It was a relief to hear this, although I had already decided that he probably was OK.

He roughly pulled down my knickers to where the jeans were round my knees, and then took off my jumper, T-shirt and bra. He sat down on the sofa again, and roughly pulled me over his knee, where he proceeded to give my bottom about 10 quite firm slaps with his hand. He then pulled off my boots, jeans, socks and knickers and I lay there across this stranger's knee, naked and utterly vulnerable, with only the instincts that I had developed over years of meeting people to guide me.

But I have to say that it felt surprisingly right – and very exciting. He was quite a hard spanker and I started to complain about the pain. He immediately stopped for a while, and rubbed my buttocks. When I got to know him later, he said he'd never known a spankee whinge so much. He had a way of giving an extra-long massage just before the spanking started again, so I grew to recognize the signs of the impending smacks even during that first encounter.

We changed positions a few times, from the sofa to over his knee on a chair in the middle of the room, where my feet and hands hung down in mid-air either side of him. Throughout the spankings he would chat to me amicably, as if we were discussing the weather. But when anything to do with spanking came up, there would emerge a dominant character that I found hard to argue with, although feeling confident that I could at any time get dressed and walk out of the house. It was a world of make-believe, where he became a dominant, and I got to be dominated in a sexual way. And I was being paid!

'Want to try the riding crop and cane?' he asked at one point. I agreed rather hesitantly, more out of curiosity, so he told me to kneel on the sofa and bend over, with my hands on the back of the sofa. I felt suddenly vulnerable, bent over naked in front of a man with a cane – but wasn't that part of the attraction? I also felt confident that I was 'safe' with him, and that if I said 'stop,' he would. We had never discussed a 'safe' word that I was to use if the pain were too much. He just said that I was to tell him if I wanted him to stop and he would do so immediately. I believed him.

He took a lethal-looking black riding crop out of a holder in the room and started sliding it down my back and over my bare, red bottom. Then I felt a light but sharp whipping pain on both buttocks. He gave me two strokes of the crop, but having been spanked quite hard for about an hour by then, my tolerance level was subsiding and I said I didn't want any more.

'OK. We'll try the cane.' He went back to the holder in the room, while I waited, naked, on the sofa. Out came a beige-coloured cane, seemingly made with a light, smooth bamboo or wicker, with a large curved handle. He laid it gently across my buttocks and said 'Ready?' It was just one light stroke, but the pain was intense. I had had enough and decided I didn't want to be spanked or caned or have any further implements used on my very red bottom that evening. I turned round and looked at him, and hoped to god he was going to oblige.

'I think I've had enough now you know.'

'OK. Well done. You did very well.'

The cane and riding crop were returned to the holder. To do otherwise would have been tantamount to abuse in the eyes of the law.

I assumed the evening was over, but he suddenly grabbed me and hauled me bodily over his knee again over the sofa, saying what a sexy girl I was. He asked if he could put his hand between my legs. I was taken aback by his boldness, since none of the other spankers had suggested sex, but it didn't alarm me. I was incredibly turned on by the whole experience. 'Yes, OK' I said. He pushed my legs wide apart. His fingers were experienced and I just lay there, revelling in this astonishingly sexy, exciting turn of events. He asked if I would go upstairs with him and have sex.

'Do you normally have sex with your spankees?' I asked him, looking back at him over my shoulder from my prostrate position.

'Only with two of them' he stated matter-of-factly, looking at me intently. It made me aware how closely sex and spanking can be interlinked. Inside I was thinking 'oh my god – this guy is paying me, and asking me for sex. How close am I from entering the dark world of prostitution.' But I didn't feel threatened by him.

I was also flattered. He was a good-looking, strong, fit guy, 12 years my junior. He'd seen my 57-year-old body in a brightly lit room – and still wanted sex. I didn't want to end the evening on a refusal and in fact didn't know at the time whether I wouldn't have sex with him at a later session, if I got to know him and we started a relationship. So I just said 'Well maybe – another time'.

Then he told me to get dressed, and said he would take me back to the motorway (three miles away) 'to ensure I reached home by morning'. He handed me an envelope with £90 in it. Although we had agreed a price of £70, he said he had added £20 for the petrol I had wasted trying to find him. I thought of counting it and then decided that would be very churlish. I hesitated slightly though. I thought we had agreed £70 for the first hour, and then £50 per hour after that pro rata. Blue had thought it was £70 for the whole session, however long that was. Spankees can charge whatever they are able to. There's no overall spanking association dictating charges.

He noticed my hesitation. 'We agreed £70. You should make sure you are clear about your charges before you meet clients' he said sternly.

'Oh – no, that's fine' I said quickly, bowing to his experience, and not wishing to ruin the evening.

Before I left, he stood in front of me and put his arms round me. I was fully dressed by then and I was surprised by this sudden show of affection. It was as if we were about to have a slow dance.

'My real name is _____,' he said, smiling. For some reason it hadn't occurred to me that spankers too would use false names. I had used a false name on the web site, as I didn't want to be recognized. I told him my real name too. The dominant, commanding spanker had disappeared, and was replaced by the nice, polite guy who had met me in the pub car park. Just a lovely, ordinary, considerate, funny guy who made me laugh so easily.

I asked him at one point towards the end of the evening if he wasn't worried that a completely strange woman now knew his address and could stalk him. 'No' was his immediate reply, 'because this particular woman would have to ring up for directions'.

* * *

So began a spanker-spankee interaction which lasted six months, led me into an intimate dom-sub world and allowed me to meet one of the nicest, most patient, most intelligent and humorous men I've ever met.

I didn't hear from Blue for two weeks and supposed that I hadn't been a very good spankee, with all my complaints. But then he texted to say he'd like to see me again. I knew I liked him more than as just a client spanker, but because of the age difference I didn't want to admit it even to myself. We arranged for him to come to my house. I live in a cul-de-sac in a quiet country village where neighbours can easily see other people's visitors and the last thing I wanted was a string of men queueing outside my house holding canes. Blue said he would disguise the implements under his coat, and anyway wasn't he the only spanking visitor? Yes, so far he was. I hadn't decided how many men I would allow to visit.

He turned up with no implements, I was relieved to see. When I greeted him in the hallway I found myself wanting to kiss him.

'I nearly kissed you,' I told him.

'Well why don't you,' he said immediately, and bent down to give me a slow kiss on the mouth. 'Now you can come over to the sofa' he said, 'and we'll see if you can take any more than last time.'

'I was going to make you a cup of tea' I tried to say, but in a trice he had me over his knee, jeans and knickers down to my knees, and was spanking my bottom which such a sting that I cried out. He caressed my buttocks and then continued the spanking.

After about five minutes he said, 'let's try you over the back of the armchair'. He turned the armchair round, led me into position at the back and continued to undress me until I was completely naked again in front of him, while he remained dressed beside me, looking down at me. I found out later that this scenario (called MDFN - male dressed, female naked) is all part of the dom-sub scene. The sub is vulnerable, naked, slightly humiliated and at the mercy of the dom, who is supposedly in control, dressed, not humiliated and deciding the fate of his sub.

'Bend over', Blue ordered quietly. I bent over the armchair, and felt his hand press down on my head so that my feet came off the floor and I had to use my hands to steady myself on the two arms of the chair. I had never felt so vulnerable, or so sexy, come to that. The juices started to seep out between my legs. 'You are such a sexy girl. Such a wet girl,' he murmured.

He started to spank me hard on my buttocks, one, then the other. I complained and he stopped each time, caressed me and then continued. 'Spread your legs' he commanded. I did so. 'Wider.' I spread them wider, and felt his fingers caress my lips again. 'I've brought a

Durex in case you change your mind, you know.' I thought about it. Would it do any harm? It was so deliciously rude being bent over the armchair, being felt up and spanked hard like this.

'Go on then' I said quietly.

'Yeah?' and quickly he got a condom out of his pocket and slipped it on. He started penetrating me, but I hadn't had sex in a while so it was hurting. I had to say stop a few times, which he immediately did, but in the end he came all the way into me.

'Do you always carry condoms with you?' I asked afterwards.

'Mostly yes. And I always practise safe sex, even if I know the girl well. And I don't come in the vagina normally. I only come in the rectum. We'll have to try that with you soon.'

I wasn't so sure about that. I had tried it twice as a teenager and got nowhere fast because of the discomfort. He was so matter-of-fact about this, as if discussing the type of tea we were about to drink. I was to notice this often with other spankers. They talk about spanking, sex, genitals, orgasms, even excrement, with utter seriousness, with no hint of embarrassment, giggles, smiles or laughter. Mention the word 'spanking' to the normal man in the street and a smile will almost always start to appear on his face.

Blue came to my house frequently after that. He would take my face in his hands when he arrived and kiss me fervently. I noticed him swallowing a few times and knew he really liked me. I was becoming fonder and fonder of him, but didn't like to admit it even to myself. He was 12 years younger, for goodness sake.

When he arrived, we would chat for a while and then I would often be hauled over his knee on the sofa, skirt lifted up and knickers taken down, and given a firm spanking. He had suggested we do this mostly for fun, but that every now and then he would pay me for my services so that he could ask me to act like a proper spankee, at his command. I declined to be paid by a man who was becoming a friend, which I think pleased him. Not because of the money, but because it meant I was liking being with him, and being spanked by him on a regular basis, and seeing him as more than just a client.

It emerged that he had envisaged having a dom–sub relationship with me after seeing me on the Internet. He wanted to train me to be his sub. I noticed that his attitude when spanking me was changing subtly to be more commanding. He started telling me to go and stand in the corner or face one of the walls after a spanking so that he could see my red bottom on display. I have a bad back, and standing still for more than about five minutes would make my back ache. While I was standing there, completely naked, facing the wall, he would make himself a cup of tea and deliberately not make me one – all part of the make-believe dom–sub world. He would come in from the kitchen with his cup of tea and accuse me of having moved from the position he had placed me in. He would make me use the word 'sir' to him. I quite liked this notion, but I felt a bit silly using it.

He slipped seamlessly into his role as a dom, having been in amateur dramatics and being quite a theatrical character anyway. As I have said, I was not a natural actress. I felt self-conscious playing this role with someone who I had started to view as a boyfriend, and who I knew in 20 minutes would turn into a nice, kind, non-dominating guy, who I could snuggle with on the sofa and watch a film.

'Did I put you in that position?' he would bark.

'No sir.'

'Come here.' And I would be told to place myself across his knee and be spanked again, often with 30 or more hard slaps. So sexy, even though at times quite painful.

The dom–sub interaction progressed slowly with each visit to my house. He would find issues with my recent behaviour, such as cancelling a visit, even though there was an unavoidable reason for it, and proclaim that I needed to be punished with a sound spanking. One particular time I texted him to say I would have to cancel due to work. He texted back: 'OK, that's fine.' Then five minutes later: 'Don't think I'm going to forget this.' A shiver of excitement went through me when I read this. Just before he arrived at my house on the following visit, he texted: 'When you open the door to me, I want you to be naked'.

When he arrived at my house, he wasn't smiling. I duly answered the door, completely naked. He came in, closed the door, marched through to the kitchen, grabbed one of the hard chairs and took it back into the sitting room. He came over to me where I stood naked watching him, and walked me over to the chair, where he sat down and then pushed me down over his knee. 'Now' he said sternly, 'I was disappointed with your behaviour this week, do you hear?'

'Yes,' I said, slightly flustered and nervous.

'Yes what?'

'Yes sir.'

'I don't like being let down like that.'

Silence from me. Then I decided to say something: 'I couldn't help it. It was work.'

'You can cancel on me whenever you like but I won't like it and you can expect to be punished.' And with that, he proceeded to slap my bottom hard for one or two minutes continuously so that it started to sting.

It was a bit unnerving having this changing character in my house. Even though I knew it was all play-acting for the thrill of the spanking scenario, and I knew I could put an end to it at any moment, I did sometimes wonder if I was doing the right thing. He would stop for minutes at a time, while instructing me how to behave like a proper sub. Then the spanking would continue. And all of a sudden he would decide that the punishment was over. He'd ask me to get up from being bent over his knee, and to stand next to him and I'd expect to be spanked again. Then he would gently sit me down on his knee and there he was, back again, the guy I was dating. He would start to smile and laugh, and say I had done well, and taken quite a good spanking.

I was becoming a good sub, and he made me feel proud of my progression. One part of me actually was proud, while the other half couldn't believe what I was doing. This was absurd, wasn't it? To stand in the corner, and be treated like a naughty schoolgirl? Yes, absurd, but somehow, deliciously sexy and rude.

I was starting to see other spankers who had contacted me from the web page. It was becoming less frightening and less strange with each contact to meet complete strangers, go to a lodge or hotel (which they always paid for without question) and be spanked, belted or thrashed quite hard with paddles or straps while they chatted to me quite amicably and sometimes fingered my labia. Blue would be very interested in these encounters. He wanted to know every detail I was willing to tell him. I think a small part of him was jealous, but he never told me that in words. I could just see it in his expression. He wanted to know if they had played with my crotch, and what positions they had placed me in, how hard they had smacked me, and with what implements. After all, he had no way of knowing how other spankers behaved unless he asked spankees, since he didn't go to spanking parties.

He suggested on more than one occasion that once I had paid off my £20,000 debt I might stop going to other spankers, which made me realise that he indeed did like me – or perhaps it was just the ownership issue rearing its ugly head. You can hardly be a dominant and simultaneously want your sub to be shared with other men.

While I was seeing Blue, the guy who wanted to introduce me to the cane and shave me came to my house. I emerged from that visit with several purple and blue bruises on my backside. That evening, Blue came to visit. He took one look at the bruises, and instead of abstaining from touching me as I thought he would, he started spanking me as normal. I was surprised it didn't hurt more than usual, but I guess a spanking stings the surface, whereas the cane had bruised me below the surface on the muscle.

After a few minutes of continuous spanking, I realised that it was going on longer than normal, and he wasn't being his usual chatty self. I began to complain about the severity.

'Taking the cane from someone else is a punishable crime' he said. 'You are my sub, and I am going to leave my mark on you.'

'No Blue, you're hurting me now!'

He stopped, and started to rub my bottom for me. He let me up and we started making a tea. But he was still ominously quiet. Then he tried to grab me again, to put me over his knee again, but I had had enough. I managed to escape his grip and dashed upstairs, locking myself in the bathroom. He followed me upstairs and banged on the door.

'Open the door!' he ordered.

'No!'

'Open the door now!' he commanded again.

'No! I can't take any more tonight.'

This wasn't what I had signed up for. It was slightly scary, even though I knew he was still in dom mode.

After a few seconds he said 'I'm going now, but I won't forget this'. I heard his footsteps going downstairs, and then heard the front door being opened and closed gently. I stayed in the bathroom for about 10 minutes, thinking that he could in fact have pretended to leave but still be in wait for me downstairs. 'This is utterly ridiculous,' I thought to myself. 'This is taking it too far.' But half of me was quite excited at the prospect of the next encounter with him, and I was also flattered that he minded that someone had got to cane me properly before him.

I gingerly opened the bathroom door and crept very slowly downstairs. I seriously didn't want to be spanked for a few days. Blue had gone. I was thankfully left alone to lick my wounds.

On one occasion he used a riding crop to whip me (gently mostly) while berating me for leaving him outside on the doorstep too long. I had been upstairs in the shower and hadn't heard his knock on the door. He made me lie on my back naked and lift my legs in the air wide apart. He stood over me with the riding crop and whipped my buttocks, then caressed my lips with the crop, then whipped my upturned feet so that I cried out. Then he hit my buttocks again.

'OW!' I cried out again, slightly annoyed. The spell was broken, and he instantly turned into the nice guy. 'Do you want a cup of tea?' he asked, a little too quietly.

'Why did you stop?' I asked, disappointed.

'Because you are not entering into the spirit of it. You are not embracing the notion of being a submissive. Submissives don't get annoyed. They take what their doms give them.'

'But it hurt' I said, actually rather deflated by my lack of success as a sub.

'There are ways to let me know, you know, without getting annoyed. I will never harm you intentionally. The punishment will sting, because that's the whole point of a spanking. But I wouldn't hurt you for the world. You have to trust me. I am your dom. You are in my care. You have to entrust your welfare to me completely. I am training you as a sub. I chose you from the beginning because I believe we can have a wonderful interaction as dom and sub. Don't throw this opportunity away. For example, stop watching what I am doing with the riding crop as if you don't trust me.'

'Well I don't,' I said truthfully.

'Then you are not embracing this interaction and it might not work between us.' Ridiculous to say, I felt ashamed that I had let him down. 'I cannot do this if you don't fully understand what we are doing,' he went on. 'If you undermine me by coming out of sub mode, like you did just now by getting annoyed, the whole scene with me as dominant is eroded and we are left as two silly adults playing around. You have to submit to me fully, and you will see the benefits. We can have such fun, and such exciting sex, if you embrace this properly.'

We carried on drinking our tea, making awkward conversation. Then he got up and I could see he was in dom mode once more. I was inordinately pleased that he was giving me another chance. This time I was determined to play the part. I allowed the riding crop whippings, and answered 'yes sir' and 'no sir' in appropriate places, while he continued with the tirade against my behaviour as a wayward sub.

That night I thought about what he had said. I would have to decide either to enter this dom-sub world properly, or leave it. He was keeping his side of the bargain. It was he who had to come up with the 'issues' between us that would make a punishment imperative. It was he who had to think up different positions to place me in and articulate the reasons for his 'disappointment', emphasising the expected behaviour of a sub. If I was going to be too embarrassed to join in properly, and keep to being 'me' whenever I chose to come out of sub mode, he was right – it was pointless and a waste of time, and made him look like an idiot.

He kidded me that I was the worst sub in the world and although I knew he was trying to say it in a jokey way, it was starting to gall between us. I didn't want to lose him. I had started to feel I could love him. So I decided to go all out, and try and be a good sub. I texted him this decision.

'What's brought this on?' he texted back.

'I thought I would just try and be a good sub for once.'

'Good girl!'

I never decided if I really liked the patronising-sounding 'good girl' or term 'young lady' he often called me (slightly bizarre since I was 12 years his senior) but for the time being I would take all that being a sub entailed. I was always conscious of the neighbours being able to hear the spanking noises. I had been told by someone who organises spanking parties that if he ventured outside into his garden while spanking was taking place, he could easily hear the slaps. After that I worried about my immediate neighbours in my semi-detached house hearing everything. I became slightly obsessed by this, which ruined many of the impromptu spanking positions I would find myself in as soon as Blue came through the door on his visits.

In our excitement at seeing each other and the thought of imminent spanking over the armchair, we would greet each other at the door, come straight into the sitting room where Blue would take me immediately over his knee without much conversation, take down my trousers and knickers in a trice and start spanking me, for me only to remember that we hadn't closed the doors that led to either the kitchen or the hall, which meant that the neighbours were only one wall away from the slapping noise. I would suddenly say in mid-spank 'The door!' and poor Blue would have to stop and let me get up, waddle in Guantanamo Bay style with trousers round my ankles to the doors, shut them, and waddle back to put myself back over his knee, to allow him to carry on spanking. All of this killed the mood, and once or twice he just stopped and said the moment had passed. This left me feeling hugely disappointed, as well as guilty for having failed as a sub once more to allow him the tantalising immediacy of an unplanned and sexy spanking as soon as he walked through the door.

He said once that whereas with other girls he had had relationships with, and had been able to spank as part of the relationship, he had been able to walk through the door, take their knickers down and have sex with them on the stairs, as well as spank them as part of the sexual act, I was too clinical and too preoccupied with the neighbours, or objects on the sofa, or on the armchair, for him to feel he could just have impromptu, raw spanking and sex. I was hurt by this but recognized that he was probably right. And for all my worries that the neighbours would hear, they probably heard anyway. And they probably didn't care. They probably chuckled to themselves and thought 'There's Anna having another spanking session'. It's not against the law, as long as there are only consenting adults taking part.

Blue and I did other things apart from spank. We played singles badminton and discovered that we had a similar standard. Some of our rallies went on for minutes and we ended up utterly breathless with laughter. We also went for meals out, and to the cinema. We would watch films on TV and snuggle on the sofa. It was to all intents and purposes a relationship, as far as I was concerned.

We had another thing in common – bereavement, and its effect on your life. Blue had lost both his parents in his mid-thirties, as well as four friends to various diseases within the space of six years. Like me, it had left him with a dread of wasting time before his final breath. He took it one stage further and refused to take part in group activities, saying that it's too stressful to make conversation with more than one person. People try to outdo each other with knowledge and witty repartee. For this reason he only ever saw his friends one by one. He hated being forced to go to places in which he had no interest, as this was also using up valuable time. I, too, had begun to avoid group situations much more after Pen's death, and it was a relief to discover that someone else felt the same.

★ ★ ★

After one game of badminton, we were just about to get into our respective cars when I noticed some thick bushes and small patches of woodland surrounding the car park near the sports hall. Feeling sweaty and lusty, I suggested we try and have sex in one of them, to which Blue readily agreed.

We found a little clearing inside a particularly thick slice of wood, with a birch tree in just the right position for me to lean up against. Blue wasted no time, as usual. He had my shorts and knickers down to my ankles and pushed me over, so that I could lean against the tree. He penetrated me, and after quite a bit of pushing and shoving, we decided it wasn't really going to work, mainly due to our relative heights and the upright position. Then Blue suggested we try anal sex again (we had tried it rather unsuccessfully once before over the armchair). I wasn't too enamoured with this idea, but was willing to try it again.

He used lubrication and gently put two fingers inside my anus. It felt uncomfortable, as if I needed the bathroom. He did this for a few minutes and then tried with his condom-covered penis. It felt as if he was trying to shove a large cucumber up my bottom, and I began to think 'there's no way it's going up there'. He was being very careful and gentle, but it was beginning to hurt. Slowly, slowly he was inching into my rectum, but I was very tight, probably through nerves, and it just wouldn't go in.

He came out. And then started again, with some lubrication on two fingers. It was again uncomfortable. The fingers came out, and I felt this rod-like object trying to enter my anus, a very alien sensation. Again, there was no give from my body and Blue was beginning to lose his erection. He came out, and we were talking about giving up.

'OK' he said, rather resigned, 'let's just try for the last time – then we'll give up'.

I reluctantly agreed. I knew that this was the ultimate in sexual stimulation for him. He found it hard to orgasm in the vagina, as he thought of it as 'too normal, not special enough'.

'Don't take this the wrong way, but loads of men have been up your vagina,' he would say. Thanks, Blue, why don't you just say I'm a slut, I thought with a smile? Although it has to be said that I *had* slept with quite a few men over the course of my life.

'It's about ownership,' he explained. 'I want something of you that no one else has ever had'.

I understood this notion, and despite not liking the concept of ownership, I thought it was within the context of our dom–sub relationship. I liked the fact that he wanted something unique with me. In went the lubricated fingers, trying to widen the rectum. Then the seemingly huge penis that felt like it would split me apart. Suddenly I felt my anus widen, and he edged in a bit more. Then it widened again, and he was fully in! Now, apart from feeling the pressure against the side of the rectum, I couldn't feel him inside at all. It was as if he was moving around in a void. How peculiar! And how comical to have lost my anal virginity in a sports car park, with traffic going to and fro, yards from our tree. There was no pain, just a rather uncomfortable full feeling.

And then I noticed the strangest noises coming from behind. Blue was uttering low, breathless grunts and roaring noises like I'd never heard before. Within a minute or so, they reached a crescendo – and then it was all over in about 20 seconds. I felt him withdraw slowly. I was slightly concerned that this action would take the rectal lining with it, but it seemed to remain intact. After all, gays seem to survive it, so I suppose I would.

I looked round at him. He had a happy, breathless, spent look on his handsome face. I felt very proud that I was the reason.

I had opened the floodgates. Blue wanted anal sex all the time after that. I did like him a lot, and wanted him to enjoy sex with me, so I wanted to like it too, and hoped that it would get easier with time. Well it certainly got easier with time – but I didn't grow to like it. After a month or so, he barely had to use his fingers to lubricate me, and my rectum started to allow him to enter almost straight away. The bull-like noises were sometimes so loud that I had to ask him to keep it down, because of the neighbours.

But I had started to dread it. I realised that I wasn't looking forward to him coming to my house as much as I had been. I knew I would be spanked, quite hard, and that I would then be asked to bend over the armchair naked so that he could sodomise me. We often didn't have vaginal sex at all, although he would have if I had asked for it. But I found it hard to enjoy vaginal sex, knowing I was about to be sodomised, so I chose to go straight to the anal sex to get it out the way as soon as possible. Then I would be able to snuggle on the sofa with him, and tell myself we were having a normal relationship.

We discussed spanking outside, as we had both enjoyed the odd sexual encounter al fresco, so we waited for a very dark, warm night and then drove into a field near my home. I was wearing green wellies and a yellow dress. We got out and Blue pulled off my dress and pushed me over the car bonnet. Bra and knickers were removed in a trice, but I insisted on keeping my wellies on. He took off his belt and thrashed my bottom with it as I lay over the bonnet, completely naked but for my green wellies, bottom raised and breasts resting against the warm car. While I clung to the top of the bonnet he took me from behind, and lay on top of me for a while, panting and elated. It was a very sexy moment.

I had started noticing that the skin on my backside was becoming much thicker and rougher, which enabled me to take harder and harder spankings and to enjoy them more. The Heathrow guy, who had become a regular, gave up after one spanking and said it was obviously hurting his hand far more than it was hurting me. Blue was able to spank me, then cane me, then give me a belting of a hundred strokes (he sometimes counted). 'You've become a phenomenal spankee,' he remarked once. My chest swelled with pride!

One day we were sitting watching TV together when I said I had to go to the bathroom. He asked if I was going to have a poo and I said I was. 'Can I come and watch, and wipe your bottom afterwards? Or perhaps I could manually evacuate your bowels ?'

'What? Christ, No. No you certainly can't!' I was disgusted.

'OK. No worries. It's not a huge fetish of mine. It's just about ownership. I would know that I had done something that no other man has done with you.' And then he added as a passing comment: 'I did it with my previous girlfriend.'

Whooaaa! You did WHAT? I had to hear about this one! Apparently he had asked her the same thing and she had agreed, after a little persuasion. So he had sat on the edge of the bath while she had a poo in the loo. When she finished, without looking at her poo, she just put herself over his knee where he sat on the bath, and let him wipe her bottom clean. That happened twice. On another occasion she let him manually evacuate her bowels with two fingers. I asked if she had then needed to have a poo. 'No,' he answered proudly, 'I evacuated her real good'. Yes, well that's as maybe, but being a poo extractee was not on my web site - or my long-term radar.

After two or three months I noticed changes in Blue's behaviour. When he came through the door on one of his visits, he stopped looking nervous, stopped swallowing when he tried to speak, and worst of all, he stopped trying to kiss me hello. He started saying we were having an interaction, not a relationship. I hated the idea of what I had with Blue as not being a relationship. I mentioned the lack of kissing and he said he wasn't really a kissing type of person.

'Well, you were at the beginning' I commented.

'People often do things out of character at the beginning of relationships, and then after a few weeks settle down to their normal selves,' he retorted. I wasn't entirely convinced or happy with this explanation, but I had to accept it for the time being. He also said at about this time that he wasn't at all romantic, wasn't sure what love was, didn't know if he had ever been in love and wasn't looking for it. That to me seemed just an excuse as to why he was going off me, and why he didn't love me. He said snuggling on the sofa was 'OK', but he could take it or leave it.

One day I asked him if he would like to go to London for the day to see the London Eye. His texted reply had been 'OK'. I commented that he didn't sound very enthusiastic. He said he loved his everyday life so much that he didn't want to disrupt it for a day by sitting on a train for hours, waiting in queues, only to have to do the same journey at the end of the day. He also said he wouldn't want to go on day trips to any city, and especially not three-day European city breaks, which I had hinted I loved. The hassle of waiting at airports, packing, preparing his work and life before the holiday and then catching up on return rendered it too stressful to be worth it, according to Blue.

At about this time, we had what we came to call the 'sofa conversation'. We had the normal spanking session, had had a meal and were just settling down to watch TV. He suddenly became quite serious and turned to me on the sofa and said that he knew I was looking for a long-term boyfriend and that he would never be it. He would never be the 'real deal'. He would never want to meet my friends, or my family, or want to go for afternoon trips to see a National Trust house. He was utterly happy to see me for what we did, and didn't want anything else. This consisted of the following: spanking, sodomy, meals out and in, cinema and singles badminton. And that was it. Nothing else, apart from maybe a lesson in golf from him, was ever going to change or develop about my life with Blue. He didn't want me to be anything other than completely warned about what he wanted from, and for, me.

'What we have is pure' he said, straightforwardly. 'I will never have to resent you because I have to go and drink tea with your mother, or spend time doing something I don't want to do, because you want to do it. I'm with you now because I really like you and want to be with you.'

It was clear he would never love me, although I think in his own way he was very fond of me. He admitted that he 'very much liked my company' and would miss me if I wasn't around. He did make time for me in his week, I realised, but how much of that was because he had a very high libido and needed sex?

I was finding it easier and easier to let him in to my anus, although I still didn't enjoy it. It didn't turn me on, and there was no sexual feeling to it for me, like for some girls. I did it to keep him around, because I had begun to have feelings for him, although I could never really let myself fall completely for him, because I knew it wouldn't be reciprocated. I sometimes felt like a convenience for him.

He explained once that he had many friends, and he did many different things with all of them. With one, he could play badminton, with another he could watch DVDs, with another he would watch the football. But he couldn't have sex with any of them, so that's what he liked about me. I said relationships were about more than sex. They were about companionship, sharing experiences, closeness. He said he had enough people already who loved him and cared for him. He didn't need closeness with a woman. He had companionship, shared experiences, and closeness with his friends. A most extraordinary outlook on life. I didn't know whether to envy him or pity him. But it wasn't my job to do either. He wasn't asking for my approval for this approach. He was just explaining it to me, so that I would understand where I fitted in to his life. He said he was glad I was in his life and happy he had found me. On the night we had the sofa conversation, I cried when he left. To me he was letting me down gently, telling me to go out and find a long-term boyfriend, that he was just interim. But after a few days of thinking about what he said, I realised that, true to form, he was just being kind and honest with me, wanting me to see what I had with him for what it was – a pure, utterly sexy interaction that could be enjoyed for the now, for the moment. He was actually being fairly selfless, since he would know that I would probably start looking elsewhere.

And I did want more. I didn't want to re-marry, and I certainly didn't want to live with another man, after my husband's financial disasters. I didn't even want to be included in Blue's friends' lives or meet them. But I wanted him to love me, and he clearly didn't.

He had had a girlfriend two years before, whom he had loved. It was a difficult family situation into which he had integrated himself, and coped with, because he loved her. After six months, she had decided against any more sex but he stayed with her another year, because of his love for her. That relationship, he said, had convinced him that conventional relationships were not for him. He had felt trapped and resentful that she had denied him sex for so long.

Here was I allowing him to sodomise me and spank me harder than I wanted, just so that I could be with him. And he couldn't love me. It wasn't his fault. That was life. You can't make someone love you. And the more you try, the more likely they are to be pushed away and irritated.

And I wasn't convinced that he couldn't fall in love. He had loved once, so he could love again, and it wouldn't be me. I asked once, nonchalantly, what would happen if he met a 40-year-old woman who didn't want kids, didn't want marriage, didn't want to live with him, but did want to be spanked. Would he go after her? He didn't hesitate: 'Yes, I would.' Where would that leave me? Getting old, alone.

Blue's point would be that that can happen anyway. He knew many couples who are miserable together, but stay living together out of guilt, or financial reasons, or fear of being alone. Which is worse, he would ask me, in one of our 'relationship bollocks' (as he called it) conversations - being happy alone, able to see friends/lovers when you and they want, or being trapped in a relationship, and a house, that make you miserable?

Yes, Blue, I see your point. But I wanted you to LOVE me. And I can imagine him saying even now 'but how long would that last, even if I loved you now?' Yes, I did see Blue's point of view, and he might well have been right. Many couples split up. Many couples remain together without love. But – sometimes relationships DO work. In fact relationships often work. And I was going to try and find one.

A seemingly minor issue, but one that was actually quite important to me, was the issue of holidays. Blue would never want to go on holiday with me, not for three days, or a week or longer. I was not going to spend the rest of my life either not going on holiday or going on holiday with other women.

That night I knew I had to move on. It made me feel sad and empty, to think that after six months I would lose a lovely, funny guy with whom I had sometimes laughed so much that I had literally felt faint. But I needed to move on to someone who needed me.

I turned once again to the dating sites.

CHAPTER FOURTEEN

Back to online dating

I continued to see Blue, without telling him that I was looking for men on the Internet. I didn't think there was much point, since nothing might come of it. Also, he had said we were having an interaction, not a relationship. What's more, he had almost encouraged me to go out looking for 'the real deal'. Actually now, I think I should have told him. It would have made the relationship more honest.

We continued to play the roles of dom and sub, but I was finding it increasingly difficult to take it seriously. I found saying 'sir' to someone I had been laughing with as an equal only moments before harder and harder, and one day I told Blue this. He looked at me seriously and said 'In that case we should stop this dom–sub role play from now on. It will just undermine my role as your dom if you can't call me sir.'

I started regretting telling him, and felt I was letting him down again. 'Why can't we just carry on as dom and sub, but I don't have to call you sir?' I asked. 'After all, it's just a word'.

He fixed me with a grim stare. 'If it's just a word, why can't you use it?'

'I feel a bit silly saying it to you,' I admitted.

'Well that's fine. We won't do it any more,' he stated matter-of-factly.

'I suppose I could try again,' I said, without much conviction.

'No. Now that I know you don't like calling me sir, I know that you've not properly entered into the spirit of being a submissive. I'd rather not continue with you as my sub.'

There was a long pause, and although I felt disappointed that I had failed as a sub again, I knew it was the right thing for me. I *had* tried hard to be a good sub, but I suppose like anything, it's horses for courses. A part of me was wondering whether being so submissive that I was willing to lie on my back, legs apart, lips and anus on full display while someone whipped my buttocks and caressed my anus and lips with a riding crop would eat into my confidence, and start affecting me as a person in society. I had been bullied by three people as I was growing up. Although this current situation was consenting play-acting, being willingly controlled and 'bullied' by my dom, I had traits of personality that made me try to please too much, that wanted always to be accepted, and I think I was probably too likely to let this dominance seep into my 'normal' life, fun and sexy as I did find it. I really just wanted Blue as a normal boyfriend, with a bit of spanking, and normal sex thrown in. To keep him, I had been willing to go out of my comfort zone, but I knew inside it didn't feel right, and he was right not to want to continue.

I also knew that he wasn't going to change, not for me, not for anyone. Blue was Blue, a free spirit.

'Are you disappointed?' I asked him. His answer surprised me. 'No, not disappointed. It's not a big thing with me. We can just carry on spanking and having sex, without the role play.' Oh, well that was OK then. I wasn't going to lose him completely at all.

And then he smiled wickedly at me. 'I can still dominate you, you know.' We laugh about that now. He claims I resigned as his sub. I claim he fired me. I suppose it's a bit of both.

He told me about a woman who had been his sub for about eight years, before he knew me. She had been a real sub, not a pretend one like me. He had spanked her so regularly that her bottom was nearly always sore. Apparently as he started spanking her, the bruises would start appearing very quickly. I asked if she ever complained about the pain of the spankings. He said she often wriggled when she was over his knee, and complained he was spanking too hard, but he continued anyway, knowing she could take more, and ensuring his dominance over her. She was a top corporate executive, at the head of a big company, and often had to chair large board meetings. She told him she loved sitting there, with a very sore bottom after he had thrashed her, knowing no one would suspect it of her. So it was clearly not an issue for her, being a dominated, sometimes humiliated, sub one moment, and then switching the same day to a position of authority and decision-making. I wondered which was the real her. Did she long for someone to dominate her all the time, if she hadn't needed the job? Or was she really just a dominant, natural business woman, who liked to play submissive for the sexual excitement?

I decided I needed a break from Blue to wipe the slate clean, so that I could concentrate on two guys I had met on the dating sites. I wrote him an email explaining my reasons and truthfully telling him that I would miss him. He later told me that he had been quite upset to receive the email. His reply made me laugh, as usual. Part of it read:

And what I will always tell you is that, although I will never be the 'real deal,' I spend time with you because I very much like you and enjoy your company, and I do the things that I do with you because I very much enjoy doing them with you. Is that really such a shitty deal for somebody, Anna? Does there have to be some well-constructed endgame to make something have a value and a worth? The endgame is that we're all going to die, so if you find somebody in your life whose company you enjoy, why keep pawing over the interaction that you have with them? Why not just enjoy it?

Now, I'm not suggesting you should prioritise such an interaction over the business of finding somebody to be miserable with for the rest of your life. You shouldn't, and you're right to be pursuing these online options. All I'm saying is that if you do, at some point, come back to what we have, please, please, please will you embrace it for everything that it offers, and stop fretting about what it doesn't offer, or thinking that it should somehow offer something more? Let it be what it is - you might enjoy it more! And it's not as though you can't then investigate other options, is it, as this current scenario ably illustrates.

So, yes, cheerio, at least for now - I will miss you too! And the very best of luck in your search for the 'real deal'.

PS: Although I'll always be willing to 'take you back,' you should know that any-or-every time you return to me after a caper like this, your arse is going to be in for one helluva session, as punishment for the inconvenience you will have caused me by your absence!

PPS: Remember during these dating shenanigans that your anus remains my exclusive property, and is for the pleasure of my cock only!

★ ★ ★

Blue and I still see each other as friends to this day and have the occasional spanking, caning and belting session, just for fun. I still whinge a lot, but in fact I need the spankings to help maintain a thicker skin on my buttocks. We go out for meals, go to films, don't have sex but still make each laugh until we are helpless. And even better is the fact that we will never have to end the relationship with each other, because there isn't one.

★ ★ ★

I had often wondered about spanking parties, without really wanting to take part. I wanted to be a fly on the wall. Jeremy sometimes organized parties to which about nine or 10 men came, and three or four girls were invited. It was nearly always a similar ratio of men to women. Apparently it starts off like a normal party. People mill around, chatting and drinking and then the organizer starts the spanking. All the men sit in a big circle on chairs and all the girls go over their knees, moving round the circle one by one. Their skirts are lifted up and knickers taken down to their knees with each encounter, then raised back up at the end of each spanking so that they can get up and walk on to the next man. The girls are never nude above the waist. He is very strict with the code of behaviour at these parties, and if people transcend these rules they are not invited back.

Throughout the party, 121 spanking sessions are arranged between individuals and they disappear upstairs and then reappear an hour or so later. Food is also served at some point during the proceedings. The caning round seems to be the pinnacle of the party, and is taken quite seriously. Each girl takes it in turn to stand up from the circle of chairs, lift up her skirt and take down her knickers in front of everyone and bend over the caning bench. Then each man will give her six strokes of the cane in turn. This is not with excessive force, but enough to sting and leave a few red marks – 'party level' as it's called. Everyone watches each stroke in silence and smart-alec remarks are not allowed during these caning sessions.

I heard of a girl who boasted to one of the men during the social part of a party that she could take any number of strokes of the cane, executed with any amount of force. The man took her up on her challenge and the whole party watched as she bent over the caning bench. He took up position and started caning her, using more and more force until her bottom was purple with cane marks. She refused to give up, and in the end he couldn't bring himself to continue, and conceded.

Apparently if you cane someone enough to make them bleed it can cause a weakness in the skin, which has a tendency to bleed easily thereafter. Some spankees have had to give up the scene entirely due to severe canings. I heard about a spankee new to the scene who was trying a spanking party for the first time. The organizer (not Jeremy) had also invited a spanker who was known to give generously and who was keen to cane the new girl. He started caning her over the back of the sofa while everyone watched. The girl's bottom was becoming very striped and then began to bleed, but she was too shy to complain. One of the other spankees started to protest, but the organizer insisted that the spanker got his money's worth. In the end the protesting spankee made so much fuss that the proceedings were brought to a halt, but she was never invited back to that organizer's parties. The new spankee left the CP scene soon afterwards.

I went to see a spanker recently who told me he had had a previous session with a spankee who asked him to cane her. He started caning her with the usual amount of restraint, but she wanted him to do it harder and harder. He noticed she was getting extremely aroused. He continued until her bottom was so covered with angry purple welts that he was afraid he was going to make her bleed, so he refused to carry on, to her great disappointment.

How someone could take that amount of pain and actually enjoy it I will never know. You also wonder why the men should always pay when we women do seem to so enjoy it sometimes (or often).

Jeremy told me of spanking parties where the men sit round in the usual circle. A girl will strip naked and go on all fours on the floor in the middle of the circle. One by one the men spank her and then use their fingers to try and make her have an orgasm (I wondered how many girls faked their orgasms). Jeremy said he would never have such parties. He did on occasion invite me to take part in a spanking party, either as a spankee or as a hostess where I would only be helping to serve food, organise the drinks etc, while being allowed to watch the proceedings to gauge if I wanted to join in either then or at a later party, but I felt that at 58 my body wouldn't match those of the 30-year-olds. I also wasn't sure that my current tolerance had reached party level.

He sent me a very kind email: 'As for a party, rest assured I wouldn't invite you if I did not think it was suitable for you, or if I didn't think you would fit in, or if I thought it was beyond your limits. On the whole, levels of play at my parties are less exacting than 121s. It's true that the OTK round(s) are quite intense, but I carefully moderate the use of implements and cane... You should have no worries about being outclassed in looks, and remember you are only ever naked below the waist. Looks-wise, the main focus of the guys' attention will be your bottom, and believe me, you can take 'pride' in that part of your anatomy.'

But I still felt dubious about being spanked or caned in front of several people. I didn't mind men seeing my genitals, but I wasn't sure I wanted other girls to see them. What if their bits were neater than mine? What if people noticed how much I was lubricating?

I did, however, accept an invitation to Jeremy's house to have a different type of session from just a 121 with him. He was sensitive to my dislike of group activity so he had invited one other guy and one other girl. I didn't mind about one other guy being there, but I wasn't sure about having another girl there. What if she was about 20, and unfriendly?

I arrived first and helped Jeremy prepare lunch. Stan arrived, and I immediately felt at ease with him. He was one of the friendliest guys you could hope to meet. Over lunch he told us about a caning session he had requested himself from a mistress (as women are called who do the caning) as a punishment he felt he deserved for some misdemeanour. He said he'd taken 72 hard strokes of the cane on his back and bottom and felt cleansed afterwards. I couldn't imagine the bruises his body must have sustained, and I wondered what he'd done to think he deserved such punishment, but I didn't ask, and he didn't offer an explanation.

I had a 121 with Stan as soon as lunch was over, in one of the upstairs bedrooms, while Jeremy did the washing up downstairs. I wondered if he could hear the slaps. Stan soon had me naked and spanked me quite hard over his knee. He chatted amicably throughout the spankings and never went into domineering spanker mode. He kept asking if I was OK, and if the severity wasn't too much for me to bear.

We tried several different implements, and he then caned me about 10 to 15 times as I lay over the bed. It hurt, but the thicker layer of skin on my bottom by then allowed me to take it without too many yelps.

Then I heard the doorbell ring. I was really nervous about meeting a fellow spankee, but I needn't have worried. Laura was a lovely, friendly, down-to-earth girl, aged about 40. She told me there was a strong sisterly sentiment among the spankees and never any bitchiness.

Jeremy called us all into the lounge. He asked me and Laura to bend over two chairs with our elbows resting on the chairs, with our backs arched, our legs straight and feet apart. Apparently spankees often round their backs rather than arch them, which doesn't present their bottoms for spanking as nicely. He told us both to raise our skirts, then he walked over to Laura and pulled her knickers down. Stan stood behind me and I felt my knickers being taken down to my knees. I looked across at Laura bent over the other chair, in the same position as me. She was grinning. I was enjoying myself too.

Stan spanked me with his hand for a few minutes, and then he and Jeremy swapped over and I was spanked by hand by Jeremy while Stan spanked Laura. Then we had an OTK session with both pairs swapping over.

At one point I looked across the room at Stan spanking Laura over his knee. They were chatting away to each other and clearly having a good time, but I felt something was missing. I guessed it was because there was no mention of punishment or discipline between the two. They seemed to be talking about a non-spanking subject most of the time. I suppose in a group situation, it was harder to role play and take a scenario of punishment seriously, as the atmosphere was so jovial.

Then Jeremy said he wanted to show me an example of a party caning, but didn't expect me to take part. He asked Laura to raise her skirt, pull down her own knickers and bend over the caning bench in the middle of the lounge while we watched. The bench was about three feet high, shaped like the struts of a collapsible table, with a padded top to it.

Stan took up position with the cane and I watched from the safety of one of the armchairs. Jeremy reminded everyone that this was the part that was to be taken seriously. Jokey comments, as in a normal spanking party, at this point would be silenced. Stan showed Laura the cane he was going to use, but she decided she wanted another one. Jeremy remarked to me that this was called 'topping from the bottom' – where the spankee is in fact in control of proceedings by strength of character.

Stan gave her six light strokes of the cane as a demonstration for me, making her count each one. 'One, thank you, sir. Two, thank you, sir'…

'And what do we say about the last one, young lady?'

'It's the hardest,' giggled Laura. Even though an atmosphere of punishment was still missing, since they had kindly set it up just for my benefit, it was still fascinating to see someone else being caned. Not something you see in your lounge every day. I asked Laura if it had hurt her, and she said simply no. She had been in the spanking business for years, so the skin on her bottom must have been nicely thickened by then.

Then Laura and Stan disappeared into a bedroom for a 121 while Jeremy and I adjourned to the playing room. He had placed a piece of A4 paper with a letter typed on it, in the middle of the desk. He told me to bend over the desk so that my face was about a foot from the letter.

'Now Miss Skye. Read the letter out loud – slowly,' he ordered. I began reading. 'More slowly'. I slowed down. I reached a word that was spelt wrong and wondered if Jeremy realised. I didn't have to wonder for long. A sharp spank as I read it out told me he was fully aware of the spelling.

'That word is spelt wrong. You will have to retype it. Carry on reading.'

I read out the next sentence, where there were no mistakes. I felt Jeremy behind me, ready to pounce. I could see a misspelled word in the next sentence. As I reached the misspelled word, I braced myself for the next punishment.

Wallop! 'Another mistake. Retype that one as well!' He raised my skirt and the tirade continued over my knickers, and then on my bare bottom.

In the middle of this session, Laura knocked on the door to say her goodbyes. I was bent over the desk with my bottom on full display facing the door as she walked in, but she didn't bat an eyelid. She walked up to me, gave me a big hug and said she hoped I would enjoy the rest of the day.

With the door open, Jeremy called Stan into the room. Then followed one of the sexiest moments of my life. I was stripped naked. Jeremy placed a chair in the middle of the room, and pulled me over his lap. He started spanking my already red bottom on the buttock nearest his body, and encouraged Stan to start spanking my other buttock at the same time. So there I was, completely naked, in front of two men, being spanked by both of them at the same time. The spanking lasted only three or four minutes, but I will remember it for the rest of my life.

When the session was over, Jeremy called me into the lounge, where he gave me tea and biscuits. He had set up the film *The Secretary* at a certain scene which he thought I might now find familiar. I watched as the girl in the movie went through the same spanking scene with the letter that I had just endured. I told him I had found the session *very* sexy.

I had another 121 session with Stan. While bent naked over the side of the bed at one point, I asked him if I looked as if I was turned on. He immediately felt my wet lips with his fingers and told me he thought I definitely was. Then suddenly I felt his lips between my legs. He had decided to go down on me without asking my permission or warning me. I wasn't sure I wanted this at all, but didn't want to ruin the atmosphere.

By the end of the session Stan reckoned I had had enough of being spanked and caned, since my bottom was very purple. But I had promised another session with Jeremy in return for all the food and drink he had provided, and didn't want to renege on an agreement. So I had yet another session with Jeremy that day. Both had used the cane in their two respective sessions with me and my bottom was feeling very sore. I took about 100 strokes of the cane through the day. I was paid £150 by Stan and £30 petrol expenses by Jeremy, who had the spanking sessions with me free of charge, by prior agreement, since he had provided food and drink, and the accommodation, and done all the arranging. Apart from the occasional over-enthusiastic stroke of the cane, I had enjoyed every minute.

The following week bruises of all the colours of the rainbow appeared on my bottom – I likened it to the Northern Lights – but I just felt proud of myself. I reckoned I had turned from rooky spankee to party-level spankee.

'No need to worry about your level of tolerance now,' Jeremy commented as I left.

* * *

Even though none of the men I had met for spanking had turned out to be dangerous, I felt I had to vet them quite carefully. I had heard of a spanker who had used a cane that seemed to be made partly of metal on a spankee. It was only after the ferocity of the first stroke that she realised it was no ordinary cane. She managed to escape, but was extremely bruised.

I mainly used the emails they sent to accept or reject them. If it was a one-liner, I tended to answer that I wasn't available. Two examples: (verbatim):

'Can we use my car so u can so i can spank u'.

'Hey, wanna talk U reply if u read this mail;'.

If their spelling and grammar were good, and it was basically a civilised letter, treating me as if I was a human being, I replied positively. One such email read:

I am going to be in Taunton in a couple of weeks' time and wondered whether you might be around that sort of area. You could come along to my hotel where I am staying and we could then if you wanted have dinner together either before or after playing. Hope to hear back from you.

('Playing' is the term used for having a CP session. I wasn't in that area, so we never met up.)

One young man started off in an acceptable manner:

Hi saw your ad on the site, you look perfect, I am 23 years old 6ft tall and live in market Drayton shropshire, I love giving a good spanking and you seem like you like receiving a good spanking. How hard can I spank U? How good is your pain barrier? I like to give a good hard spanking but need to no you would be able to take it? What may I get to spank?

So I replied that he could only spank my bare bottom with belt, strap, slipper, flip flop and paddle, and that my pain barrier was not bad I'd been told. His next reply led me to reject him, although I think he was probably fine. He WAS only asking about sex but I had to be careful, especially as I thought it unlikely a 23-year-old would have the sort of money he quoted:

Wow that sounds good to me ;) so is what has been talked about the only kind of service provided by you? If not id like to hear more, and do u travel? Getting to you isnt an issue just work ect be easier if you came to me? Your sounding perfect so far and I have £5000 to spend so what would that get me from you?

I received this very polite email from a spanker in Ireland:

I hope you are well. I saw ur ad on the _____ website. Im visiting UK next week exact date not settled yet its flexible depending on when ur free and so on. There is a very specific fantasy I want to act out and I'm seeing if you'd like to do it. Can I say at the outset apologies if u don't like the idea or I'm being too graphic.

Ok here goes…The fantasy is as follows:

Girl wears a school uniform pleated skirt, shirt tie and jumper white socks and pink knickers.

Here's where it gets a little eccentric. I then want u to wet ur knickers and stand in front of me in the wet for about five minutes. Then say Daddy I've wet myself. I will ten give out to u for doing such and spank u with hand, belt and paddle then make u go in the corner.

Ok so that's it is it something you would / could do. Anyway that's what I'm looking for thanks for reading and again I hope it was ok to be so direct.

Yours…

I surprised myself by accepting his invitation, but said I would only be able to produce a few drops of urine and would definitely not be able to urinate fully in front of him. On that basis, he politely declined to meet me.

I came across some other strange fetishes over the course of my first year as a spankee. A second guy wanted to shave me, so I was paid to lie on the bathroom floor while he pasted turquoise shaving foam all round my labia and then proceeded to gently shave me. Actually it was very soothing. He then made me wear a skimpy dominatrix suit and crawl on all fours round the room while he beat me with a spatula and a wooden spoon. It really hurt, and I didn't enjoy it. When I reached the door, I started turning round to begin the return crawl back across the room, but he ordered me to carry on in the same direction. 'Er – there's a door in my way', I commented, but he insisted, 'Just keep going. Did I tell you to turn round?' So I had to pretend to crawl through the solid door. Whatever floats your boat.

Another guy, who chain-smoked throughout the session, gave

me three strokes of the cane bent over a chair in the middle of his sitting room. Then he asked me to undo his belt, and I immediately said I wasn't going to perform sexual acts. He calmed me down and said he just wanted me to undo his trousers and his shirt, so that I could suck his nipple while he masturbated. Oh god, how utterly revolting! But I needed the money, so I clamped my mouth round his nipple, while he felt me from behind to speed up the process. I didn't go back to see him, even though he invited me to go to New York with him, all expenses paid, for a long weekend.

Two other guys masturbated with one hand and spanked me with the other, and then proceeded to deposit their load on my back. For some reason I was surprised each time how warm it was. They were then at great pains to wipe my back up afterwards. I wasn't sure how proud of me my mother would have been at this point.

Another man tied my hands behind my back with metal handcuffs and blindfolded me, while I stood in his lounge completely naked and he played with my body. I found this very sexy. He had spanked me over his knee but then said he wanted to cane me with a big heavy cane. I said I didn't think I could take it, so he said he would do it quite gently. I took about 12 strokes of medium force without complaining too much.

'Can I just try one hard one?' he pleaded. I wanted to know what that would be like, so I agreed. After all, it would be over in a second. I didn't realise that the harder the stroke, the more likely it is that the cane will miss the right spot and fall too high or too low, both of which can be very painful and give deep bruising.

The cane was long, thick, unbendable and just under half an inch thick (he kindly measured it for me later). He placed it on my buttocks and asked if I was ready. I said I was, and then I heard the swish of it through the air before it landed with a sickening thwack on the top half of my buttocks, missing the accepted target area of the more fleshy part. I shuddered with the agonising pain as it shot through my body. I let out a loud howl and my hands curled up to my face in agony. He saw that it was way more than I could take, and put his arms round me, saying 'oh sorry, sorry. I won't do that again.' The bruise that was produced was a large, round, purple, black and blue one, about two inches in diameter. It stayed for three or four weeks, and at one point I was actually worried it wasn't going to fade completely. I had to cancel three other spanking appointments, partly because spankers normally like a blank canvas to work on, but also I couldn't bear the thought of anyone going near the bruise. But it wasn't the guy's fault. He had asked me and I had said yes! More fool me.

One guy had asked me to wear a very short skirt to the session. When I walked into the hotel room I noticed a number of Opal Fruits scattered on the floor. He asked me to bend down with straight legs apart and pick them up slowly while he watched from behind. He also caned me with what he called a 'pipe' in the diaper position, where I was on my back and he was holding me by the ankles with one hand, and caning my bottom with the other. A pipe is a bendy, fairly malleable round stick of rubber or leather about two feet long.

This same guy suddenly put on rubber gloves while I lay on the bed waiting for another spanking. I whirled round and asked what he was doing. 'Oh don't worry. I have a cut on my finger. I didn't want the blood to touch you while I feel your pussy.'

Another guy just wanted to use the riding crop on me. When

I first arrived he took off my dress almost immediately, sat me down on the sofa and gave me an orgasm with his hand. Throughout the session he would suddenly bend me over furniture and thrash me with the crop. He kept holding me in the slow dance position and staring into my face, which I found very disconcerting. He then ordered me into bed, where he tried for about 30 minutes, unsuccessfully, to give me another orgasm with his hand. Then he would take the sheets back, order me onto all fours and give me another four or five strokes of the crop. At the end of the session he said he'd never thrashed anyone as hard as he had done with me. I was so proud!

Some spankers go to great lengths to create a realistic and sexy scenario for a spanking session. One 60-year-old spanker asked me to make out a 'sin list' – a list of things I had done in the previous few weeks that I considered punishable. As soon as I started this list I realised there were quite a few. They included uncharitable thoughts about people, such as hoping a friend of the family wouldn't ring to arrange a visit, being pleased someone at work I didn't like had put on even more weight, and being too lazy to vacuum my house for a friend's visit.

He met me at Nottingham station, put my arm in his and walked me to a hotel. Once inside the room, he sat me down on a chair opposite him and proceeded to berate me for each crime in turn from the list, describing the number of strokes I was going to receive, the severity of each stroke, and with which implement. I was to be spanked, strapped, belted and caned. For some of the punishment I would be naked, and tied with rope to a chair. Over the course of three hours, during which he produced a delicious lunch and chatted to me amicably, I took 128 strokes of the cane and 126 strokes of the belt. He insisted with each one that I count them and say 'Thank you, Master'. If I ever addressed him I had to use the term 'Master' at the end of every sentence, otherwise he would add two more strokes of the cane to the next punishment. He let me off the first omission of 'Master' but on the second and third omission I received four more strokes of the cane.

At one point I was completely naked and tied with rope by my ankles to the legs of a chair. Another rope went from my ankles up round my elbows, down round my crotch, round my back and round the leather handcuffs on my wrists. I felt very vulnerable and decided not to agree to this degree of restraint again with any other spanker, but I had agreed beforehand to be tied up, and didn't want to renege. Part of me wanted to see just how far he would go. After giving me 12 strokes while I was tied to, and slightly bent over, the chair, he undid the rope round my ankles and ordered me onto the bed, still trussed up like a mummy. I could hardly walk. I was worried I would hurt my breasts when getting onto the bed as my elbows were still tied back, so he had to help me by lowering me gently onto my front. My bottom stuck up at a conveniently spankable ankle from the bed. I received another caning and belting, while he continued to berate me for the worst sins on the list. He seemed to be a very experienced spanker and had carried out the strokes in such a way that I was hardly bruised the next day. He had given me frequent hand rubs and caresses between sets of strokes, and then rubbed moisturising cream over my sore bottom every now and then.

The next day I received an email saying how well I'd taken the punishment, inviting me to spend a week with him on his boat on a Greek island and hinting that he'd like me to be his girlfriend.

Unfortunately I had to decline this delightful invitation as he held no attraction for me. If only!

Another spanker contacted me with a polite, introductory email so I replied and we agreed to chat on the phone. He sounded fun and emphasised that he only wanted to use his hand and a slipper. Not the cane, I was pleased to hear. We arranged to have our first session and then I received this unexpected email:

Dear Lily-Rose,

Your husband will have made you aware that you would be contacted by me.

Your current behaviour is quite unacceptable and your husband has made you aware of his displeasure, but lacks the fortitude to take remedial action to curb your behaviour.

You will attend my offices on September the 25th at no later than 19.00.

You will bring with you, your husband's slipper and a plimsoll.

You will be dressed and act in an appropriate lady-like manner, I can assure you now that you will be receiving a prolonged hand spanking and a severe slippering for your slovenliness and inappropriate behaviour

I would be grateful if you could confirm your acceptance of this punishment and I will report your cooperation to your husband

Kind regards.

I found the idea of being sent by one man to be spanked by another somehow erotic. We met up and the session was very sexy, cordial and fun. We then went for a plate of chips and a drink in a nearby pub.

One man kept emailing me from Lancashire for months before

daring to come and meet me. He said he had wanted to spank for years and years, but never had the courage. We arranged to meet in a field near me, where I could bend over a log or fence. We met up, and we found a fence. He gave me two or three slaps on my bare bottom with his hand, but then said he felt silly and didn't want to carry on.

I suggested going back to the hotel, in case it felt more appropriate there. We went back, but the same thing happened. After wanting to spank someone for years, and sending me many long emails about his fetish, when confronted with the reality of it, he suddenly couldn't go through with it. He then admitted that it was partly just an excuse to get me naked and feel my body, as he didn't have that much success with women. I didn't mind and was glad to help in fact.

Time and again spankers have appreciated the fact that I am very turned on by a session. Most of them don't enjoy it if they can see that the spankee has just turned up, bent over, taken the spanking, then the money, and left, with hardly any social or sexy interaction. Some spankees have three sessions a day, so I can understand that after a while it becomes more like a job to them.

A spanker recently told me about a session he had which he didn't really enjoy as the spankee was very unexcited by the whole affair. She was an attractive, slim 27-year-old girl who lived with her 67-year-old master, who was also her boyfriend. After the initial social chit-chat, the spanker finally got to spank her, but was watched the entire time by the master, who sat opposite them. After a while the master suggested the client feel between her legs. She was as dry as a bone, which made the spanker begin to feel rather emasculated. In order to try and get a sexual reaction out of her, the master ordered her to strip naked in front of them, stand facing them, hands on head and spread her legs, whereupon he started to spank her crotch from the front. Not a drip appeared between her legs. The spanker was then allowed to adjourn upstairs with her alone to have oral and vaginal sex. He likened the whole event to 'fucking a robot' since they had to use lubricant to achieve penetration. He had found it hard to keep an erection. He was relieved when it was all over and he could leave a session that hadn't given him anything but some dented male pride. Perhaps I should lend her some of my HRT !

Another young and inexperienced spanker wanted me to sit on a space hopper in his lounge naked from the waist down and face the corner. He ordered me to move backwards and forwards over the space hopper using my bum only, so that my buttocks and rectum stuck out backwards towards him over the side of the hopper. He squatted down and watched. Each to his own!

Later in the evening, after he had given me a belting over his bed, he suddenly disappeared from the bedroom and returned with cream on his middle finger.

'What are you going to do with that?' I asked, slightly concerned.

'I thought you liked this,' he indicated my bottom.

'Ah no. Sorry, I don't.'

'Oh. So sorry. I won't do it then.'

He never asked to see me again but later he had the cheek to ask me to give him a good reference in case he wanted to see younger spankees!

I also heard stories of girls being spanked for 'real' discipline. A man who liked spanking for fun one day discovered that his ex-girlfriend had become so jealous of his current girlfriend that she had threatened her with a knife. He thought of going to the police, but decided that a caning would actually be kinder. She would learn her lesson and not be tarnished with a criminal record.

He went round to her house and stood on her doorstep, holding a cane very visibly. Partly because she wanted him back and partly because she didn't want the neighbours to see, she allowed him into the house. He wasted no time in spanking her over his knee very hard for about 10 minutes, berating her behaviour, while she howled and screamed. He then hauled her over the back of the sofa and, holding her down with his hand in the small of her back, caned her 12 times – six over the knickers, and six with knickers down. They didn't have any trouble from her again.

Another man had been punished by a female friend of the family when he was a teenager. He had done no more than try and get her teenage daughter into bed. The mother found out and had put him across her knee, using a hairbrush on his bare bottom. He never forgot the humiliation of it, fearing his testicles and anus were on display. Years later, as a strapping guy of over six foot, he got his own back by spanking her over his knee with a hairbrush on two separate occasions. She thrashed around and yelled, but the punishment carried on until he had had his revenge.

The line between abuse or discipline and erotic fun must be fairly thin in many instances. I had heard of 'maintenance spankings', where a husband regularly spanks his wife to keep her on her toes. He might also give her an extra hard spanking before they go out for the night, saying that if she stepped out of line during the evening she could expect another spanking of equal severity on her return. But I also heard of a cruel case where a man tied his wife up over a bench in their garden shed for four hours, while he went out. When he came back, he thrashed her with a cane until she bled and then had sex with her while she was still tied up over the bench.

* * *

I had originally entered the CP world to get rid of the £20,000 debt my late husband had left me, but spanking had now become so much more to me. It had become part of my life, and I wasn't sure I wanted to be without it. It's just a convenient symbiosis. Spankers enjoy spanking, and spankees enjoy being spanked. Some spankees enjoy it so much they can orgasm from a spanking.

Only twice have spankers asked if they could penetrate me there and then. I refused (politely) and they didn't press the matter. It's not that I wouldn't contemplate it with one or two of them, and especially as I am hugely turned on by the whole event. But I didn't want to get the reputation of having sex for money, as surely that would make me a prostitute. I said this to one spanker, and he said 'No, you're being spanked for money. We could just have sex as two consenting adults.' I've since heard this argument several times. Spankers without a doubt don't view spankees as prostitutes at all, even if playful fingering is part of the spanking session. We are all just contributing to a fun, erotic scenario. The sex would be just a natural extension of the interaction – or so their argument goes.

Many spankers are in their 60s, so they come from the era when corporal punishment was allowed in schools and probably at home as well. I've spoken to them about why they want to spank, and no one really has an answer. They asked me the same question and I didn't have a comprehensive answer either. We came to the conclusion that it's obviously sexy to have or see a bottom on display, to have the hand–bottom contact, and to have the domination–submissive punishment issue going on. I assumed at 57 that I would be too old for the spanking scene, but quite a few of the guys told me they like spanking someone more their age, since spanking women of 20-30 sometimes makes them feel like dirty old men.

Some are looking to date their spankees and view it as just a way of meeting them, so if a spankee is nearer in age to their own, it's more likely to end up as a dating arrangement. And you would instantly have an activity in common. And what an easy way to find out if someone is sexy (and clean) and if there's any chemistry.

It's a difficult issue to overcome, this business of having a relationship with someone who doesn't spank (vanilla). Do you tell them or not? There was Jeremy, who had lost his girlfriend because he had told her the truth. This is a real problem, which can lead spankers to either try and find a girlfriend from the CP scene itself, keep their spanking fetishes a secret from a vanilla partner or give up spanking altogether, which can lead to frustration.

Most of the married clients I've met over the last year just have the odd 'business meeting' as far as their wives are concerned, which entails arriving home slightly later than normal. I actually feel I'm helping their marriage by providing an outlet for their fetish.

I asked a spanker if he would mind if he knew his spankee girlfriend was being spanked by other men, bottom and lips on full view. He considered this question carefully for some time before giving me his answer: 'Of course it would depend on the person, but I don't think I would have the right to mind. But it might be different if it actually came to that situation.' We came to the conclusion that if you do meet a potential partner who is vanilla, you could ask them nonchalantly or playfully if they've ever spanked anyone for fun. If they look coy and admit they have, you might be in with a chance at eventually admitting your lifestyle. If they look disgusted or disinterested, you probably don't have a hope in hell of keeping this person as a partner, once you admit your secret fetish.

But that leads to the sometimes very real issue of leaving your fetish aside and having a conventional sex life. Now that the fun of being spanked has been re-awakened in me, I feel sex without it may be rather mundane. I've heard that the CP scene fluctuates greatly because of this issue. Spankees find boyfriends and leave the scene. I've met some spankers who were genuinely sad that their regular spankees had felt obliged to leave the scene since their new men were not part of it.

CHAPTER FIFTEEN

Love match

My husband had died 18 months earlier and I had been meeting men from the dating sites for the same length of time (minus a fortnight) without much success. I didn't think it was likely that I would have an opportunity to meet anyone from the real, unvirtual world. People from my age group were mostly married, and anyway, without a convenient notice hanging round their necks declaring themselves available for dating, complete with a synopsis of their interests, it was difficult to know who was free.

I had begun to make a mental note of characteristics I couldn't put up with, and those that I definitely needed in a partner:

Must-haves:
1. Good listener.
2. Honest.
3. Sense of humour.
4. Kind.
5. Solvent.
6. Driving licence.

7. Caucasian.

8. Hygienic.

9. Healthy.

10. Intelligent.

11. Educated.

12. Sense of fun.

No-gos:

1. Smoking.

2. BO.

3. Under 5' 7'.

4. Bad breath.

5. Talking too much.

6. Main hobby walking.

7. Religious.

8. Bad-tempered.

9. Bullying.

10. Impatient.

11. Huge debts.

12. Loud.

13. Over 70.

14. Fat.

15. Lazy.

16. Over-sensitive.

17. Long nasal hair.

Nice-to-haves:

1. Likes spanking.

2. Funny.

3. Wants to travel.

4. Lives under 30 minutes away.

5. Sporty.

6. Kind to children, old people and animals.

7. Affectionate.

8. Sensible, mature and level-headed.

9. Calm when stressed.

10. Own teeth.

11. Over 5' 10'.

I wondered if I would ever find such a man. Was I being too fussy? Someone at work said I was looking for the perfect man. But you can't force yourself to be attracted to someone; chemistry is an inexplicable, elusive ingredient. And I certainly gave people second chances - people who I was 90% sure wouldn't make a suitable partner. Perhaps such a man didn't exist, or if he did, he would be married.

I started thinking that it was surprising that so many couples ever got together in the first place and stayed together for so long, given the large number of faults I was coming across with every man I met (while I of course was perfect). But then the more I thought about the sort of man I wanted, the more I realised there were other traits that I didn't think I could stand long-term: moody, selfish, self-obsessed, patronising, know-all, needy, unreliable, disloyal, unadventurous, arrogant, unsupportive, sarcastic, publicly flirtatious (with other women), obsessive - oh god! This was looking like an impossible task. It was surprising just how many bad traits people could have, and yet the world population was still increasing at an alarming rate, so presumably people were turning a blind eye to their partners' faults - well at least long enough to procreate!

In the normal world you would get to know someone and discover all their traits first. Most aspects of their personality would be fine and acceptable, and you might just detect a glimpse of one of the no-gos. With online dating, you have no history of their good or bad traits. You have just a few hours to make up your mind about the nervous individual before you. It's my experience that nerves don't bring out the best in people at all, which is why I would always accept a second date if there's even the minutest chance of chemistry developing.

★ ★ ★

While all these online dates were continuing, I spent many Saturdays and Sundays at the tennis club playing social tennis. I could turn up when I wanted, put my name tag up on the board to show that I was ready for the next game of doubles, and then stay there all day if I wanted, playing, chatting, sunbathing, drinking and eating with the other club members. It was a lovely way to spend two days with like-minded people, and it was especially nice for single people.

I kept a lookout for eligible bachelors, but none seemed to be around. Then one day I noticed a new name on the board – Steve Pall. We were trying to pick the next four names for a doubles game and no one knew who he was. We were in the middle of discussing the pronunciation of the surname when a voice from the back of the small group assembled uttered the name with great authority. I turned round to see a handsome, craggy face on a slim man of about five foot ten. He was my partner in the next set of doubles, and we trooped off to the grass court allocated for our game.

I was aware of Steve the whole time. He had a lovely sense of humour and we immediately had a rapport. He had the right attitude of trying to win while treating the whole thing as a huge joke, as I do, and playing only for the exercise and social interaction. Too many people (mainly members of the alien male species) at tennis clubs lose sight of why they should be playing – ie, to have fun! Nice, polite human beings off court, they turn into petulant children on court, huffing and puffing, and blaming their partner. If I'm their partner, I start losing concentration and confidence and play much worse. But with Steve as my partner I felt calm and confident.

Afterwards he seemed keen to chat to me. We had another game, and then he left. I didn't see him for about a month after that, but when our paths did cross again, he made a beeline for me in the clubhouse and I knew he liked me as much as I liked him. He clearly had a life outside the club though, so I had to be careful not to assume he was free.

We again played a few games, flirting and chatting and laughing, and then he left. I didn't see him for about two months. I was still trying my luck at dating online all this time, and getting nowhere, but I would much rather have met someone whom I'd met in the flesh already, and who I knew had an interest and sense of humour in common with me, and was local. But of course here's the problem with meeting people in the real world as opposed to online dating. Often you meet them as part of your regular activities – either at work, through friends or through your hobbies. If you start going out and it doesn't work out, you will be forced to keep seeing them. With online dating, you can put them back where they came from, and hopefully you will never see them again. It can also take so long to keep 'bumping' into them. At least in online dating, you know they are on the market and actively declaring themselves single and searching for a mate. It's been my experience that most people on online dating sites are genuine.

I had no idea if Steve was single or searching for his soulmate. I just knew he was doing rather too much flirting for a person who was already in a relationship. I intended to start engineering the situation, and devised a plan. I would pretend I'd found a wallet with the name of 'Steve P' written in it. It couldn't have his full name in it, as there weren't two Steve Palls in the club and it would be too obvious if a wallet was found with his full name in it.

I rang reception from my home and said I had found a wallet and could I ring the person concerned, if they could give me his number. There was £5 in it, and no cards, by coincidence. How brazen!

'Ah no. That's fine,' said the cheerful receptionist, 'We'll ring him. Thanks for telling us about it.'

Curses! I thought that might happen. And now I had to go out and buy a damn wallet and put £5 in it! The cheapest man's wallet I could find cost me £18. I handed the wallet into reception, and decided that on reflection, this had been one of my worse plans.

About two weeks later, I decided to go and ask nonchalantly at reception if anyone had claimed the wallet. It was a different lady behind the desk this time.

'Well here's the wallet, but there's no note pinned to it, so I don't think anything's been done about it. I'll give you his email, since he's allowed it to be given out to other members.'

So I sat down that evening to email the poor unsuspecting chap. 'Hi Steve, You may remember me from the summer when we were chatting about our tennis elbows. I found a wallet in the clubhouse with Steve P in it so I wondered if it was yours. I handed it into reception and although they said they would ring you, it doesn't appear that they have, so I thought I would email you.'

Within a few minutes, a reply arrived. 'Hi Anna. Thanks very much for your kind effort. Reception did in fact ring me about the wallet and I can assure you it's not mine. With no cards in it, it sounds as if it's a student's. How's your elbow coming on by the way?'

'Quite well. I've been playing quite a bit,' I replied. And then I had a brainwave.

'By the way, we are looking for people to play in doubles friendlies every now and then,' I wrote. 'Would you be interested? You will only be called on every now and then.'

'Yes – put my name down,' he responded. 'Very keen. I can only play every other weekend though. I have my kids every other weekend.'

Hah! I had engineered a cast-iron excuse to call on him, and I had discovered that he had kids and was probably separated or divorced.

For the next few months, over the autumn and winter, he played in my doubles games. We chatted every now and then between games, and afterwards in the clubhouse over tea. He would then leave and I wouldn't see him again for a fortnight. It was obvious he liked me but didn't seem to know what to do about it. I understood the dilemma though – if it didn't work out we would be forced to confront each other at the club, and probably everyone would know about it.

He was indeed separated from his wife, and looked after their three children every other week. The kids were really quite young – six, nine and eleven. He was 57, and owned five companies that he'd started himself. It all fitted together. I would go out with him, and I would have a ready-made family of young children.

For a week or two, I liked this rather flighty idea, but then reality started to kick in – did I really want to move in with another man and have my space invaded and valuable time taken up by other people's children? I had begun to cherish my independence more than I realised.

One day in early December 2013 I strained my shoulder, and was advised not to play for a few weeks to rest it. The few weeks turned into four months, and Steve and I had no contact in that time. I was finally on the mend and couldn't wait to start arranging doubles games again.

On the day of the first organised game, Steve walked onto court and I felt my stomach do a flip. I didn't notice that he had lost about a stone and a half in weight over the winter. During one of the changeovers, one of the other players noticed that he was eating a lot of bananas. 'That's very healthy,' she remarked as a jovial comment.

'Yes,' he said, 'I'm not well. I've been diagnosed with prostate cancer. I'm not going to have chemo so I'm fighting it with a diet.'

I couldn't believe it. As I walked back onto court I looked skyward. Was nothing ever going to go my way?

After the match I managed to get him on his own. Although it was obvious to both of us that we liked each other and had been flirting, nothing had ever been said, so I had to keep up the pretence that I was just a friend, rather than saying what was on my mind, which was 'How the fuck are we going to be an item if you've got cancer?'

What I actually said was, 'Did I hear that you're not well?'

'Yes. Cancer. I was filling in a life assurance form and I had to admit that I used to smoke sixty fags a day. They insisted on my having a medical and it turns out I have prostate cancer, and now they won't insure me.'

'Why aren't you going to have chemo?' I asked tentatively, not sure how far I could push this very personal subject.

'Because your life is crap afterwards. Don't worry. I'll beat this thing. I found out you can beat it with a diet of no meat, just fruit and veg, no alcohol, no tea or coffee, and no sugary stuff like sweets and cake.'

'How long do you have to keep that up?'

'All my life. Well, until I'm in remission.'

What a life that sounded. I was rather devastated by this news. I asked friends about prostate cancer, as well as researching it myself online. Apparently many men outlive it, and one friend told me he'd heard that about 90% of men have the disease by the time they die without even knowing. It's one of the least aggressive cancers. I felt a bit better.

Then about a week later, I was trying to sign into the online booking system at the club. I didn't have my glasses with me and called to Steve to see if he could read the screen for me. As he bent down near me to peer at the screen, I was aware of the distinctive smell of smoke on his breath. He was still a smoker! And this was about 10 am. I had told myself that I would never go out with a smoker again after Pen and what happened to him. People are not allowed to smoke in the grounds of the tennis club, so I hadn't been aware that Steve smoked.

I felt a deep disappointment again. Having decided I could live with the prostate cancer, I really didn't think it would be wise to pursue a man who still smoked, despite having cancer. I had in fact noticed the previous year that he had had a deep cough, but I had assumed it was the end of a cold. He still had that cough this year, so it was possibly the early symptoms of lung cancer.

I felt incredibly sad and actually quite depressed that morning as I played my doubles game with Steve. All credit to him, he was being very positive about the whole issue. I suppose he had no choice. I was impressed with his attitude to his situation in one way, but baffled that he should continue smoking. But there speaks a non-smoker.

Pen had brought it home to me that smoking cigarettes can be as addictive as taking heroin. It takes enormous will-power to give up, and smug non-smokers cannot possibly know what it entails. Unfortunately for Steve and me and any future romance on or off the tennis courts, I decided that I would have to turn back to the dating sites.

★ ★ ★

I had now virtually paid off my £20,000 debt, with the help of the spanking revenue, my own monthly payments and an £8000 gift from my mother, who conveniently was in the throes of trying to beat Inheritance Tax. But I still enjoyed the thrill of being spanked, and the money was useful, so I decided to continue with this double life. I was also becoming bored and frustrated with the idea of working. After Pen's death, my own mortality seemed so much more real and even imminent. There was so much I wanted to see and do in the world, and working was just taking up my valuable time. Spanking would never pay off the mortgage, but it could help towards it.

I wondered if my spanking world would ever cross paths with my online dating world. It would be so nice to meet someone who liked spanking already or who came to like it with a little encouragement from me. It could only enhance our sex life, after all.

In fact spanking and dating met in my 38th online date, but not quite the way I had intended. I joined a new dating site and spotted a guy within the first day or so. He was dark-haired and had a handsome face with strong, masculine features. He was sporty and lived in the area of Chadworth where I worked.

One of the difficulties of online dating is trying to form relationships with people living far away. With the thrill of meeting someone new you think it won't be a problem, but it nearly always is. Even meeting halfway between the homes takes time and petrol. If you do get as far as going to the other person's home, spending one or two hours there and then turning round and heading all the way home again seems a waste of time, so you stay for a day or even the night. That can be wearing if you don't know the person very well. For most people a couple of hours on the first few dates is long enough.

I emailed chap number 38 through the dating site, and said our profiles and attitudes seemed similar, and especially convenient was our location. Within a minute I got a reply: 'Hi Anna. You sound great. Unfortunately the chemistry is just not right. Best wishes – Tim.'

I was disappointed and, in a rather vain way, surprised. Then I rallied. Not everyone can find you attractive. You had let your thoughts run away with you. So I moved on. But it wasn't the end of number 38.

I had met up with number 37 a few weeks after my online exchange with Tim. Number 37 and I had two dates, during which he became very clingy and declared he'd fallen in love with me and would love me forever. His last girlfriend sounded horrendous, so I wasn't surprised that he was a bit of an emotional mess. She had been so jealous of him that if they were out shopping together and standing in a pay queue, she would stand in front of him so that he couldn't see any of the girls on the check-out desks. She also used to get furious if he didn't manage to give her an orgasm orally before they got up every day! I didn't want someone needy, so I had to let him go. During our last few sad texts he was kind enough to say that I was stunning, and that my online photos did me no justice at all. Even though I knew this was said by someone who was so-called in love with me, with blinkered eyes, I thought I would try something. With hindsight, I should have listened to that saying 'Don't waste your time on people who don't want to waste time with you.'

I never quite forgot Tim, number 38, partly because he was so close. If I really was so much more ravishing than my photo, perhaps I could persuade him to meet me, even for 15 minutes. And that's exactly what I suggested to him – 15 minutes. I didn't expect for a moment that I would hear from him. If I had been in his position, I'm not sure I would have replied after telling someone the chemistry wasn't right.

I didn't hear from him, so almost as a joke, convinced there would be no response again, I sent another email 'OK – 2 minutes?' And this time I received a curt reply: 'Where do you live? I live in Chadworth.'

It was either his style to be very succinct, or he was just going to give me the two minutes I'd asked for to get me off his back, and maybe see if I was indeed better than my photo. He had nothing to lose, as I saw it, apart from two minutes of his life.

We agreed to meet up for a coffee. He chose a brightly-lit cafe, which is never conducive to free conversation for me as I feel at 58 that I look better in a dimly-lit room. We managed to eke out the date for 45 minutes, but throughout I felt that he was only going through the motions of talking to me, while I was there looking for a soulmate.

I quite liked him but felt wavelength and humour weren't quite meshing – but I would have been willing to meet him again if asked, just to check. There was also the telltale hint of a Cockney accent. As a rule I don't get on with Cockneys – they are often streetwise and I tend to feel naive and out of touch with worldly affairs when talking to them.

When we left the café we parted awkwardly, mumbling things like 'It was good of you to finally meet me' and 'You do look better than your photo,' but no further date was mentioned. The next day I decided to find out if he had liked me, although I was pretty sure of the outcome. I texted, 'Would you like to go out for a meal some time? Pub or restaurant – I don't mind.' I only had to wait five minutes before I heard the phone alert me to a message: 'Dear Anna. It was nice to meet you but I didn't think there was a spark between us, so to go for a meal would just be leading you on'.

I was quite surprised that I was so hurt by this. I guess it's just never nice to be rejected. Tears welled up and rolled down my cheeks. I started to think back to the date and wondered when he had decided that I wasn't for him. But that was that. I had no choice but to accept his second rejection of me. However, I thought I would give him a parting chuckle and tell him I was a spankee, and that during the date I was wondering how I would have told him, had we started to go out together. Within about 30 minutes of my email I received the following reply: 'Hi Anna, Well well. I would never have guessed it... it must hurt. Not sure I could have coped with that in a relationship, but who knows. Please send the website details... I am fascinated. Tim.'

I sent the website details, and thought that would be the end of it. That evening I was busy trawling the dating sites again, when the phone rang. It was Tim, calling from his car, driving towards Basingstoke. He sounded completely different – excited, interested!

'It's Tim, Anna. I looked at your website. I think it's brilliant! Who would have thought it. You can come round to my house as a spankee any time!' Hmmm. I was very pleased to hear from him, but this wasn't the intended reaction. However, he hadn't finished.

'What are you wearing?'

'Er – a short black skirt... why?'

'I want you to find a table and bend over it. Lift your skirt, and take down your knickers, then put your hand...'

Phone sex! I'd never done this, and to me it seemed a completely pointless exercise. 'No, sorry,' I interrupted him, 'I'm not doing that. I'm not like that. Spanking is just something I do on the side.'

I'd forgotten that the general public would have a different attitude to spanking and very probably liken the entire scene to extreme sado-masochism and prostitution, just as I had done only a year earlier. He sounded a bit nonplussed by this piece of information, but still continued to ask questions about my spanking activities. After a while he suddenly asked if I wanted to go to the cinema the next day, and then put the nail in the coffin as far as I was concerned: 'And wear a dress and high-heeled shoes.' Going to the cinema in a dress and high-heeled shoes? Being told what to wear? Not my style at all. Then he added in passing: 'And grow your hair. Oh, and what you were wearing on the first date – I've got news for you – not sexy at all'.

Even said as a half-joke, that comment was enough to tell me it would never work between us. I had been wearing tight blue jeans and a tight white top. Thirty-three other guys had found it sexy. It showed what sort of guy he could be – chauvanistic and quite rude. He obviously felt he could treat me as he liked and wanted me to look like some dolly bird.

Then I remembered that unlike every other date, I hadn't spoken to him on the phone before our first date. That was the stage when, increasingly, most of the potential dates were falling by the wayside as I rejected them one by one. The next day I sent him a message: 'I think our backgrounds are too different, so I will say cheerio and best wishes. Anna'. Tears trickled down my cheeks again at the realisation that I would have to start my search all over again.

* * *

Another online date crossed uneasily into my spanking world and convinced me that dating and spanking don't necessarily mix, unless one is ready for the other. I spotted a good-looking, fair-haired guy from Oxford among the profiles. After a few emails he rang me for the all-important first chat. I'd had so many of these now that I no longer felt nervous. He was very well spoken and said I sounded nice, so we arranged to meet up. But just before the end of the conversation he said: 'There's something I should tell you – I'm a naturist'.

Oh for fuck's sake! Why couldn't I find *anyone* normal? (To my mind spanking had now become normal!)

'So where do you do that?' I asked, trying not to sound resigned and exasperated.

'Oh in my home, and sometimes in woods near my home.'

'Isn't that against the law?' I asked, amazed.

'I make sure no one sees me,' he said nonchalantly.

The next day he started an Instant Messenger conversation with me, so I decided I would return the compliment and reveal my CP inclinations. Maybe we could bond over our respective fetishes.

'Wow,' he replied, 'How interesting.'

I was pleased with his enthusiasm, but the more the conversation continued the more his attitude seemed to be changing.

'I'd love to try that,' he said. 'We could hire a room and I'll spank you. If I do it wrong you can guide me.'

I thought it might be different to the normal date – naturist meets spankee – so I agreed. We met in the beautiful little town of Burford. I felt it didn't deserve such depravity. We went straight up into the room and it was obvious this was not a date to him. He didn't want to chat at all. He was very polite and in fact quite charming, but he wasn't shy at coming forward. He pushed me face down on the bed, pulled up my dress and started spanking me. Then he lay on the bed and pulled me on top of him so that I was facing him, and carried on spanking me. He said he wanted to see my face move and grimace with each spank.

After a while he asked if he could take off all his clothes. I felt safe with him by this time and didn't see the harm. With his clothes gone I noticed that his testicles were completely shaved, and by way of explanation he said he was very fastidious when it came to hygiene. At one point he suddenly turned round so that he was facing my feet as I lay on my back on the bed, his knees either side of me with his bottom upturned, buttocks spread apart, and six inches from my face. I was treated to a view that I would rather never see again – a man's rectum, albeit very clean, looking at me from a very short distance away. I wondered what made a man want to show his anus to someone, but assumed that the naturist in him must have contributed to this strange display. It was all a bit bizarre and not that enjoyable. I'd spent a lot of time preparing for this date, had had to pay for the petrol for the 40-minute journey, only to find I was fulfilling someone else's fascination with a new fetish experiment. Moreover I had said I would pay for half the room, since I thought it was going to be a date.

After about an hour he said he didn't think spanking was for him, but he was glad he'd tried it. We parted amicably and neither of us contacted the other for some time. A few months passed and he suddenly contacted me. Did I want to have another spanking session with him? No, but I would have a date with him, I suggested. He declined. I decided not to mention spanking to any further dates, unless they broached the subject first themselves. The general public was just not ready.

CHAPTER SIXTEEN

Playing hard to get

About this time, the tall guy I had met at Heathrow Airport suggested we had an afternoon in London with a long spanking session included. He offered to pay me £500, as well as all expenses paid! We would have a meal and maybe go to a show. Did this make me an escort? No, because escorts are expected to have sex as well. I had heard of 'escorts' being just that though – companions for lonely rich men. In fact I didn't really care what it was called. It made me whatever I chose to be called. But it was a step in a different direction from being just a spankee, since he was paying me for my company as well.

Anyway, the £500 sounded like easy money to me, so I thought I would go ahead and try it. I met him at Waterloo Station (I was five minutes late), and we went straight to the hotel. I was wearing quite a thick knee-length skirt, which I assume he would remove, but he told me to bend over the chair and wait for him there, fully clothed. He fetched a cane and, without the usual gentle warm-up, started caning me fairly hard through the skirt, saying I had been late again. I was yelping at the strokes, but was determined to take it as long as I could.

After about 20 strokes, he ordered me to remove my skirt in front of him and bend over his knee, where he spanked me quite hard over my knickers for about five minutes. After the caning had already made me tender, the spanking hurt as well, but I didn't complain. I wanted to try and take it, since the money was so good, and I hoped there might be a repeat.

Suddenly he stopped, roughly took down my knickers to my knees and fingered me as usual, but this time he had one finger on my anus. He asked if I minded, and as I knew him well by then I said I didn't.

The session ended and we went for a meal. Over the meal he said he'd like anal sex with me, as he had always been fascinated by it but never ventured into it. What did I think about that? I said I would consider it. After the meal, we didn't have time for a show so we had another spanking session, with no anal contact, and then I got my train home.

In my mind I had taken a further step towards prostitution and I didn't know if I liked it. But again, what did it matter what it was called, as long as I got paid? Who would know? Why was it different from having sex with a boyfriend, as long as a condom was used? We hadn't discussed payment for anal sex. It wasn't to my taste, but I would have been prepared to consider it with him if he paid. He was a very nice guy, intelligent, clean and considerate.

He had said during the meal that he had previously had normal vaginal sex with another spankee and it had changed their relationship afterwards, so he didn't want to go down that route again. Fine with me. More and more spankers had begun to get to know me well enough to feel comfortable suggesting penetrative sex as well. Most hadn't wanted to pay extra for this service, and to them it was certainly nothing to do with prostitution. They just found the whole scenario so erotic that sex seemed a logical and fulfilling finale. I understood – but I only wanted to do it if I *was* paid extra for it. Most of the spankers weren't my type, although they were all nice people, and I certainly didn't want to have sex face to face, with kissing thrown in. In addition, I would only do it with condoms.

For a few days I considered this option carefully. I understood why women went down this road now, so much so that I found myself defending prostitutes in general to a guy at the tennis club – to his surprise, and even to mine. It was almost as if I felt I was one of them. He was talking about a holiday he'd just had in Spain and described how he wouldn't go down a certain road because there were prostitutes standing by the road junctions. I suddenly found myself saying 'Why wouldn't you walk down that road? They wouldn't have harmed you'. The guy just looked at me but decided not to say anything, which I was relieved about, since I would have had a hard time explaining my slight outburst.

I decided against any sex with spankers. I didn't mind them touching me if they wanted, but there would be no vaginal or anal sex, with or without condoms, and I would not be touching them in any sexual way. That was to be kept within the boundaries of a relationship. For one thing, there were STDs and AIDS to consider, and it might just change a spanker's attitude for the worse. He might become overly zealous, get violent if I decided against it on occasions, or even be jealous of other spankers. I didn't need the money that much.

The Heathrow spanker had in fact independently decided against pursuing this activity with me.

'It wasn't fair of me to ask' he said kindly. 'You made it clear on your website that you wouldn't perform sexual favours, so I shouldn't have even brought it up.'

I had heard from spankers that there were studios which spankees or spankers could hire for £20 an hour. Blue told me he had spanked a girl in one but had been annoyed by other spankees interrupting his session by entering the room to fetch spanking implements they had left there. He said it ruined the atmosphere of punishment he had created, and made him feel he was on a conveyor belt of customers. So when a spanker suggested meeting at a studio I was a bit dubious, but I decided to try it, for the experience.

We met in a petrol station and I followed his car down some narrow Birmingham back streets until we turned into a small courtyard surrounded by tumbledown ruins. Two men were waiting outside the door of one of the ruins, one of them smoking. If this had been a gangland movie it would have been a cliché. I felt I had stooped quite low, even for me, to have to use such a desolate place.

My spanker paid the smoking guy £20 and was handed a key. We went in through a dilapidated door and up some rickety stairs which looked as if we would fall through them at any moment. We reached the studio and I was pleasantly surprised. A large room was divided loosely into three smaller open-plan rooms. Each was expertly furnished to look like a headmaster's office or a manager's office. Each had a whipping bench, I noticed straight away, with some trepidation. There were chaises longues, armchairs, sofas, chairs, desks and tables to bend over. On one of the tables was an impressive array of canes, whips, straps, belts, paddles and riding crops for anyone to use.

We had the rooms to ourselves, so we knew we could role-play without interruption. I was becoming better at acting out my role as naughty schoolgirl, errant secretary or recalcitrant apple-stealer without ruining it now by laughing, through nerves or self-consciousness. This time I had been caught pilfering the petty cash and a good spanking was in order, followed by a caning over each of the three whipping benches in turn. The spanker said he sometimes tied girls to the whipping benches, but as it was my first time he didn't want to scare me.

He asked me to choose which cane I would like him to use, but then proceeded to use all of them anyway. And he didn't hold back when using the straps and paddles, as my bottom bore witness over the next few days. I was surprised how much more fun it was having a realistic set-up as a backdrop, and thought I might well hire it another time.

A week after this I was sitting with a date watching a play at the Royal Shakespeare Theatre in Stratford. I wore a nice little white dress and a shawl. From being thrashed over whipping benches with my legs apart to looking demure and cultured, legs together, with Shakespeare – such was my double life. I have to say I was enjoying not only the secrecy but the life itself.

★ ★ ★

Meanwhile a profile caught my attention on the dating site. He appeared on my 'Some Singles Near...', which is a little line of six profiles that the computer has chosen for you according to your respective ages, interests and location. Little did we both know what was to unfold. This one, date no 39, was to become my favourite online date. He had a beard and very broad-looking shoulders. He looked about 50, so I assumed he'd be too young for me, but when I hovered over his photo it said he was 60, came from South Wales and his username was to do with flying.

As I hadn't seen him before, I assumed he was new on the site. This can be advantageous, because newcomers are often more enthusiastic about meeting people who live far away, as they haven't yet experienced the nuisance of trying to maintain a long-distance relationship. It also seems to mean they are keen to meet anyone. On the downside, all the good-looking ones will be contacted by lots of women and you have to wait your turn. It seems to be the women who often make the first move.

I thought I had nothing to lose. I studied his profile a bit further. He was six foot one and had never married; I wondered why. He liked sailing and rugby, and was generally interested in sports. His profile description said the following: 'New here so still thinking what to write without giving the wrong impression. About me. I am regarded I think as reasonably confident by others although maybe not quite so by myself. I am tactile and enjoy showing affection to my partner. Definitely like holding hands when going for a walk. I do look for my partner to be tactile and passionate too. I do not bear grudges. I accept within a relationship there will be differences of opinion. I prefer to be with someone who will say what they mean and not bottle it up. I would say of myself I was relatively easy going but then I would say that wouldn't I. I love the outdoors be it mountains or the sea. Would love to explore all the wonderful places with someone special. Happy doing things by myself if necessary, but find it is even better with someone to share it all with.

'I like meals in and out nice wine, a pub meal with real ale and a roaring fire. If you like some of the same do say hi. Isn't it difficult to write a meaningful introduction without sounding boring!'

I thought two things might be a problem; the distance and the fact that opposite 'Education' he had put 'Some college'. I didn't care if my dates actually had a degree. It's just that it did often seem to mean that they weren't on my wavelength if they hadn't been through the British education system.

I saw that he was online at that moment, so I emailed: 'Hi, You sound nice and you look very nice, and we seem to have the same attitude to life. You might think we are too far from each other though. Brenwyth to Chorton Common is do-able for me, but I know that many people might find it too far. If you like my profile, it would be very nice to hear from you. Best wishes, Anna. PS. By the way, your profile sounds very nice, and honest, and not boring at all.' I sent it off and then realised I'd used the word 'nice' four times.

Within a minute, I saw that he was viewing me. Another minute passed and he sent me an email. A jab of excitement went through me. 'Hi Anna, Thank you very much for your email. It is a shame that we are so far because we do seem to have the same attitude to life. Here's my mobile. I don't mind having a chat some time to see where it goes... Robin.'

Wow. He had given me his mobile. This gorgeous-looking hunk wanted to chat! His spelling was immaculate, I was pleased to notice. Maybe he was well educated after all.

I replied that a chat would be nice, and gave him my mobile number. I explained that my mobile was downstairs on the charger, so here was my landline in case he wanted to chat now. I didn't hear anything, and then suddenly the phone rang. I tried to sound nonchalant, but friendly. A very deep voice with a distinctive Welsh accent said hello back, and we chatted for about an hour very happily. He was very easy to talk to, and was a good listener. He made intelligent remarks in response to what I said, and I almost forgot I didn't know him. In fact I talked more than I normally do on first encounters with men.

We found that we had more in common than the profiles showed. He loved flying and had his PPL (Private Pilot's Licence). He had been paragliding in the Alps (I had done a week's paragliding). We both had an interest in the paranormal, but disliked religion.

After about an hour, he said 'Well I'd better get on with some work. It's been very nice talking to you. If you are ever passing Brenwyth, give me a ring.'

What? Perhaps I'd talked too much. Or perhaps he felt I was too far away after all. But he'd seemed so happy to chat away, so I decided that he must have just found it too embarrassing to ask me for a date straight away on the phone.

'Yeah sure,' I said, trying to sound as if that was absolutely fine, and I didn't think at all that he was completely perfect for a future mate, 'That would be nice.' Nope – I had to go for it. Call it intuition – or plain arrogance. 'Did you want to meet up half way?'

I couldn't believe how forward I was being. I'd always left it to the guy to suggest meeting up during the first chat. To my relief, he said 'Yes, OK. That would be good. I'll look up some pubs which are between us. I'm moving house this week so it'll be no good trying to meet until the end of this week. I'll contact you then.'

So I had got myself a date with the most lovely man on the

dating site. Or had I? I had had one or two men pretend to give me dates by phone or to my face before, out of sheer embarrassment, and then later back out by text. Perhaps Robin had done the same. What else could he say when I suggested actually meeting up?

I didn't hear for a few days, which was fine, since he had said he was moving house. By Thursday, I knew he would have had time for a short chat, but decided I should leave him alone to get on with it. Then I decided I should have realised that he hadn't been interested at all, and that I had forced him into pretending to want to meet up. So I texted him: 'Hi Robin. Let me know if you'd like to chat any time next week.' Back came the reply within a few hours: 'Love to.' What did that mean? When would he 'love to'?

Another week went by and not a sausage. I began to realise I had made a fool of myself, and quite sadly, decided to give it one last shot. It still didn't make sense. But there could be a thousand reasons why he didn't want to meet up.

'Hi Robin. Well a week's gone by and we haven't had that chat. I'm SO clever that I've sussed that you didn't want to. So I will move on. However, I think it's a shame as we had a lot in common and seemed to have the same sense of humour. If you change your mind in the summer, and would still like to meet up, that would be great. And I don't normally talk that much – I blame you for being easy to talk to. :-) – Anna.'

OK, well that was clear. I had given him a way out, and not sounded too downtrodden, or paranoid, or bitter. In fact, having not met him, and having only spoken to him for an hour about a fortnight earlier, the memory of him was beginning to fade anyway.

Within a few minutes, my mobile sounded the arrival of a text.

I remember sitting down on the bed and picking up the mobile and before I'd read the text, thinking that this next text could shape my foreseeable future:

'Well I'm sorry, but I've just had a busy week. I'm in an empty flat with a mattress and pillow and blanket and mug. I've yet to get cutlery and a kettle. :-)'. Phew. Hooray. I had definitely given him a way out, and he hadn't taken it, so he did like me! I replied: 'Oh sorry. That's fine. I will wait for you to be ready to contact me then.'

A week later I hadn't heard a thing. Most peculiar. What did he think dating was all about? Or perhaps he was collecting potential dates without actually going on them. I was beginning to get a little impatient, but realised that he had control. If I 'dumped' him now, I would never meet him and never give him the chance to fall madly in love with me, as he so obviously would do. So I decided to invent a reason for being near Brenwyth.

'Hi Robin. I'm having to come down to Bristol Thursday after next, so if you want to meet up that would be nice. If you haven't got the time, I understand.'

Within a few minutes: 'Sounds like a plan.' Nothing else. I was annoyed and decided to push ahead with a date or get rid of him, as this was becoming ridiculous.

'Do you know of a pub between us?'

'I will look one up.' I knew what that meant – another week's silence probably. 'I will look it up and get back to you.' I said, determined. That seemed to set something off with him. He started texting rapidly after that, telling me about various pubs he knew on the Welsh and English side. So by hook or by crook, we made a date. Hmm – he was probably going to be a bit of handful, this one. I was exhausted and I hadn't even met him.

We eventually agreed on a pub on the Bristol side of the Severn. I arrived 30 minutes early, drove into the car park and spotted his car, but there was no room to park next to him so I had to park the other side of the car park. I got out and, as with the 38 previous times, felt a sense of adventure and excitement about what could be about to unfold as I walked towards his car.

I went over to the back of his car and knocked on the back window. He looked up and smiled and got out of the car. As he came round the car to greet me, I found myself staring at this utterly gorgeous man of six foot one, shoulders a mile wide, chest the size of a football pitch, with glossy black hair and a short dark beard. He was smiling and threw his arms open wide to envelop me in an embrace and place a kiss on my cheek. OMG!

We walked into the pub and asked to be shown to our table, which was in another room. As he let me go through first, I felt his eyes on my bum. He had told me he'd had one previous online date, and although she was nice, she was too overweight for him. I had made sure I was wearing the tightest jeans I could find.

We sat down and we just started talking. As on the phone, he was really easy to talk to, and he also listened well. I learned that he had been to university, but after the first year he had become disillusioned with the electrical engineering course and decided to set up his own company selling and installing garden equipment such as Jacuzzis, marquees and sheds, all over the country. He said he just couldn't work for someone else.

He had had only a handful of girlfriends, and they had nearly all been long-term. He had been with his first girlfriend for about five years, but had split up because she had wanted children and he hadn't. He'd then been with another girl for 19 years, but had never felt the need to marry. For the last three years he had been living with another girl, but for various reasons they had just split up and he was about to move into his own rented flat.

Three hours later we were still chatting quite happily, but as it was the end of the meal we decided to call it a day. We walked outside and he suddenly turned around and gave me a quick kiss on the lips. I returned the kiss as well as I could, but it was over very quickly, and if someone's a foot taller than you it's hard to initiate or continue a kiss unless the other person is in on the plan. But it had been a nice kiss, fleeting as it was. We didn't discuss it, and I felt it was crunch time. Would he ask me for another date? I got the feeling that he found the whole dating issue quite awkward (well, don't we all?).

'Er well, if you are ever passing my town, or I am passing Chorton Common, perhaps we could meet up,' he said. Here we go again, but this time it made even less sense. He had obviously been happy to chat and eat with me for the past three hours and he certainly didn't have to kiss me on the lips.

'Well, wouldn't you like to arrange to meet up? It's not really going to work if we just say we will meet up if we're passing.'

'OK. Send me a text and we can arrange something,' he said, backing off towards his car. Send him a text about what? But I just said 'OK'.

That night I was determined not to contact him. I had done all I could. If he didn't get in touch first, he either didn't like me enough, or he was a wimp. No text appeared that night, but the next morning, while I was getting dressed, I heard the familiar little tune of my mobile, alerting me to a new text. Please let it be him, I pleaded to the air.

It was. 'It was great finally meeting you. I thoroughly enjoyed the evening,' came the message. So I sent a text back: 'Me too. It was lovely.' I was hoping he'd take his cue from me.

An hour later I still hadn't heard anything, so I decided to take the initiative: 'Can you find a plane to fly? I wondered if we could have an unusual second date, and have a flight?'

'I'll see what I can do,' came the reply, not accompanied by the hoped-for 'but in the meantime how about meeting up for another drink or film?'

Sigh. About a week later, no word. So I texted him: 'Hi Robin. It was only a suggestion to have a flight. If that's difficult, I don't mind a normal second date. Otherwise I will forget what you look like. lol.'

'The trouble is, my flying school has just closed down. Leave it with me.' A week later, no word again, so I decided I had had enough. 'Hi Robin. Maybe it's too soon for you to have a second date. I forget that you've only just moved out of your girlfriend's house. I'm happy to leave it there. Perhaps once you've settled down, and if you would like to meet up in the summer, and if I'm not seeing anyone, that would be great.' I sat there deliberating whether I really wanted to send this text. It was cutting off my nose to spite my face. What if he agreed? But then I couldn't really carry on waiting for someone who was going to take two weeks between each date. I'd be 70 before we reached our 10th date. He either wanted to see me regularly or we should call a halt to the whole thing.

My finger hovered near the Send button, and then by mistake it touched the glass – and off it went. I was momentarily horrified, but then decided that it was for the best. I could only wait and see now.

The next day I got a reply, having hardly slept at all that night. 'Hi Anna. Sorry if I've given the impression of not being keen. I'm just so busy. It would be really nice to meet up again.' Phew. But when? For fuck's sake.

'OK. Well I'm free this weekend or next weekend,' I eventually texted, exasperated.

By the Monday after the first weekend I had suggested, I had heard not so much as a teeny, tiny whisper. It was almost funny, if it hadn't been annoying and rude. 'It's just a hunch,' I texted, sarcastically, 'but I think we may have missed last weekend.'

'I had to work in the end,' he replied, with an amazing lack of concern, or follow-up text.

'Well if you can't make next weekend, I will leave it to you to suggest a date.'

'Yes, Ma'am,' was his text, as if he was just beginning to realise that I was peeved. I couldn't send yet another text saying that I was 'happy to leave it and did he want to meet up in the summer,' so I decided I would try and forget about him, and with a heavy heart I returned to the dating site, to try and meet Mr 40.

Two days later I woke up and switched my mobile on as usual, not really expecting anything. A familiar alert, and in my sleepy grogginess and the half-light of the bedroom I thought I saw four words rolling past on the top bar of the mobile, as it displayed a message one quick line at a time. It looked as if it was from Robin, but then I thought I saw the phrases 'character trait' and 'spanking bottoms'. Oh – Robin must have found out about my spankee site, and he doesn't like it. Oh well. So be it. I had become resigned to losing him by then. Then I thought 'ah no. Robin couldn't possibly have recognized me on the spanking web site. I must have misread the name. It must be one of the spankers texting for a session.' So I went into messages.

There was one message unread. It was from Robin. 'Before we have a 2nd date I have to tell you about a character trait of mine. I have always liked spanking bottoms within a relationship. Many people don't like it, but some do. I will understand if you aren't interested, and don't want to take the relationship any further.'

I stared at the mobile, dumbfounded. What were the chances that a date I actually liked would turn out to be a fellow spanker? Then I chuckled. That was one of the reasons he was being so cagey about a second date, I thought. He liked me but didn't want to start anything with me if I didn't like being spanked. I thought of him on the other end of the mobile. For once it was he who was waiting, I hoped on tenterhooks, for my reply.

I waited all of – ooh, a minute – before excitedly replying: 'Guess what. I'm a spankee on an official spankee site! I get spanked by men for money.'

Back came the incredulous reply: 'You like spanking?' I was just about to text back 'No,' savouring his disappointment, with the intention of texting again 'I like BEING spanked', when he rang. He suddenly seemed to have the time to talk to me. 'Well well' he laughed down the phone, 'who'd have thought. That must be a chance in a million.' Everything had changed in a second. We had a huge interest in common. Spankers feel quite a strong connection with each other, in our clandestine, sexy, erotic world, a world we know is often misunderstood by many people. We knew what this could mean, that our sex life could be really erotic and could continue to be enhanced by spanking scenarios, instead of becoming staid like most couples' sex lives.

We chatted and laughed and giggled over the phone for over an hour. He had always had an interest, but only did it within relationships. He wasn't interested in being spanked himself, either. Perfect for me. At one point in the conversation he even said 'If we lived together I would probably spank you every day. And if we went to a party and you spoke out of turn, you would feel a hand on your shoulder and receive a look from me, and you would know what would be in store for you back at home.'

I had to admit it sounded very sexy, even if we were jumping the gun slightly. I said that if we were to have a relationship I would curb my activities with spankers by not permitting any sexual touching by them, but he said he didn't mind, as long as I didn't have sex with them. I assured him I wouldn't, but his reply was an ominous 'Hmmm'. I could see that I would have to convince him of my loyalty by evidence and time.

Then he told me he sometimes used the cane for discipline within a relationship, but only very rarely. Grief! Although I found the idea sexy, I wasn't too sure that I wanted that in reality. That smacked of domestic abuse. What had the poor girls done to deserve such punishments? I *had* to ask. He said he had carried out a caning on a girlfriend who he discovered had had sex with an ex-boyfriend while he was away. She apparently had second thoughts about a similar escapade after the caning. I asked him why he hadn't just got rid of her, after her infidelity, and he answered that it was so difficult to find women who like to be spanked. He no doubt loved her as well, but was considerate enough to omit that part of the story.

On another occasion he had sent a girlfriend round to another man's house to be spanked by him as punishment for being an outrageous flirt at parties. Apparently she would kiss other men in front of him. I asked if he had enjoyed watching her being spanked by another man, and he said he hadn't been there, but he would have found out if she hadn't turned up for the spanking and given her double the punishment. After that, she apparently moderated her behaviour.

But I wasn't interested in that sort of relationship, which seemed a world away from my previous experiences. I wanted a fun, consensual, sexy, erotic relationship based on equality. I couldn't live with the threat of such corporal punishment if I crossed the line in his eyes. I made him promise that he would never use the cane on me for discipline. This wasn't boarding school. After a little persuasion, he promised.

We arranged for him to come to my house. It just seemed sensible to try out our new-found interest in a safe environment. I met him at the motorway service station near my home. We'd agreed that we would both be nervous before meeting again, but that within a few minutes we would be fine.

It took him an hour and a half to drive up from Brenwyth. He got out of his car, got into the passenger seat of my car and gave me a kiss on the lips. My mouth went dry and I found myself stumbling over my words.

Our lunch was a much more relaxed affair than the first. Once you know someone is a spanker, it seems to break the ice. We couldn't wait to go to my house. As soon as we walked in the door, he grabbed me and hauled me over his knee on the sofa. I was wearing a knee-length tight green khaki dress, but he soon had this up over my bottom and wasted no time in starting to spank me. The boundaries between second date and spanker blurred, and very quickly he pulled my knickers down to my knees. It was the first time a normal date had become a spanking session, and it felt very natural. Blue had been a spanker and then become a sort of date, although the dating side had been definitely one-sided (my side). Maybe with Robin, the dating and spanking would work nicely in parallel, one feeding off the other.

'Take this off,' he said, tugging at my dress. And there it was – a slightly dominant personality appearing, as with all the other spankers I'd come across. The dress came off, the knickers were already off, and then he quickly removed my bra, and we went upstairs for what promised to be our first erotic session. He put me over his knee again over the bed and continued spanking me.

'You're taking this well,' he said, 'shall I show you a real spanking?'

'Er – go on then'.

He gave me three very hard smacks in succession, but in fact it was fine. My skin was still quite thick from previous spankings, so I could endure a short, hard volley like that one quite easily.

'If you've got a belt, go and get it,' he ordered. I didn't know if being ordered around by a date was quite what I wanted. He wasn't a paying customer after all. But I guess it went with the territory. A spanker tells a spankee what to do, and that was part of the thrill, so I found a belt of mine and handed it to him. He immediately doubled it up and started thrashing my bottom with it while I was still over his knee. It stung quite a bit, but I was loving it. Spanking and sex all in one.

We got into bed, excited at the thought of our first sexual encounter. But quite soon after we started, Robin's stomach began to rumble and it became apparent that the pub food hadn't agreed with him. He was having problems emptying his bladder, and an erection never materialised. But it was still nice lying naked with this huge man in my bed, and feeling quite at home with him.

After about two hours, he had to leave in order to fulfil a work request for a customer. I felt sure we would meet again. He seemed so keen, but sensibly so, not irritatingly so.

The next day I received a text thanking me for the lunch and saying how much he'd enjoyed the afternoon. As usual there was no mention of meeting up again, but I was now used to this, even if I didn't like it. If this relationship doesn't work out, I said to myself, I'm not going to agree to meet anyone further than 30 minutes away from now on.

By a dreadful quirk of timing, I had planned to be busy for the next four weekends helping my mother leave the family home of 60 years in the West Country and move into a residential home in the Midlands, where I worked and my younger sister lived. (My father had died peacefully six years earlier at the age of 92.) Four weekends to be unavailable after a second date is not conducive to romance. When I told Robin, his half-joking reply was a surprised 'Are you trying to avoid me?' For his part, Robin seemed too busy during the week to meet up. I could see this little relationship going down the pan before it had started.

We texted each other sometimes, but in fact although he initiated some of the conversations, most were about spanking, and no date was mentioned by him. I suggested we could go body-surfing and/or visit a wind-tunnel and/or go for a posh meal. He readily agreed to all three, but never came up with dates to do these activities. I was left wondering when he would ever take the initiative. Maybe the distance between us worried him, but he hadn't mentioned it. I was beginning to think that twice a week would be about what I wanted. I didn't want to see someone every day. I needed my independence and to pursue my own hobbies and see my own friends.

In our first chat about spanking he had mentioned living together, but I had assumed he was just talking out loud. I couldn't see him wanting to move away from Brenwyth on the coast to the landlocked Midlands, and at that point in time I had no intention of moving to Wales. And I didn't want to live with anyone again, if I could help it.

Maybe, just maybe, and I felt I was being charitable here, it was all moving too fast for him. He had just moved out of his girlfriend's house. He was busy working away during the week and sometimes at weekends. I decided to take a step back and see if he texted in his own time. I had become so used to making the first contact in online dating that I'd forgotten that many guys might feel I was trying to move too fast. I actually preferred guys to make the first move, and suggest dates, but as it seems to be left to us girls so often in this new virtual age, I had grown accustomed to my new leading role.

I decided that four weekends on the trot was too many for me to sacrifice. I had made the journey down to the West Country on the two previous weekends to help with packing and farewell drinks for Mum's fellow churchgoers. The next weekend was purely for my mother's neighbours' goodbye party, so I reckoned my two sisters could look after Mum for this one. Don't let yourself resent people, I told myself, by pampering to their needs for an easy life, as I had done on occasions with Pen, like, for example, not insisting on having two embryos inserted.

I checked with Mum. 'Oh yes, that's absolutely fine. We'll manage here with the three of us. You've done enough.' Grace had become very protective of our mother since Dad died and when she heard I wasn't going to be available for one of the four weekends leading up to the move, she didn't hesitate to let me know her opinion. 'That's a bugger, you not being here.' I had long since learned to counter her remonstrations. 'Why?' I asked. As if she had a right anyway! She started to backtrack as usual when challenged.

'Oh – because it's nicer when you're here.'

What rubbish.

'You mean I won't be here to help with the party.'

'That as well.' She gave a little embarrassed laugh.

'I asked Mum and she said it was fine, so it's not a bugger.'

'Er – no,' she conceded, and said no more.

I let Robin know I was free for that weekend. I didn't hear anything for the next week, and then on the Saturday morning, 10 days after the second date, he finally sent a text suggesting we meet for lunch at Symond's Yat, and then go for a walk. I was pleased that it was a normal date, and had nothing to do with spanking. I didn't want to appear too demanding so I replied 'That sounds lovely.' Nothing more.

Up to him now to suggest an exact time and place, which he eventually did. So this third date was now his idea, and he couldn't feel that I was pressurizing him. We met up and had lunch by the river Wye. I started to realise that he was quite a shy bloke when it came to people he didn't know, and relationships. He said he was happy to pay for lunch, and that I could pay next time. Then he suddenly shot me a nervous look: 'If we are saying there's going to be a next time?' he added. I assured him there would be.

We took a canoe and paddled up the river. It was a beautiful day and we chatted and laughed all the way up the river and all the way back down, even when he realised I wasn't doing much paddling.

By the end of the third date, I knew I liked him (even if he was Welsh). He seemed to have a zest for life and new experiences that matched my own. He was an intelligent, calm, quietly-confident individual who maintained that to hold grudges was to harm only yourself. He didn't criticise me, and he didn't say an unkind word about anyone he knew. But given the distance between Robin and me, our respective working hours and time-consuming hobbies (his sailing and my tennis), I considered a relationship fairly unlikely (but not impossible if both of us were prepared to fight for it). For my part, I intended to put the effort and hours in, at least initially. If it didn't work out, meeting him had at least shown me the sort of man I wanted to find.

I realised something else: even though Robin had generously stated that he wouldn't mind my continuing with my spanking exploits, I knew if the right man came along that I would give up being a spankee, except privately for him. I thought it would be unfair to ask any man to put up with a girlfriend being spanked naked and touched by another man. Relationships are hard enough without engendering imagined scenarios with a third party and unnecessary jealousies.

I couldn't help asking him how often he thought a couple should see each other, since it seemed he was happy with once every two or three weeks. He explained that May and June were extremely busy months for the garden equipment business. With the onset of spring, the orders came thick and fast to install equipment for the summer. After that, he would want to see me once or twice a week, even given the distance. He had in fact tried to text me on occasion, but his new flat was located in a depression, and sometimes the texts were returned undelivered. Also, he reminded me, wasn't I the one who had planned to be unavailable for four consecutive weekends?

★ ★ ★

In the three years since Pen died, I've had to do a lot of thinking and reassessing of my life. I like living alone and having my own money, which I can control, without concerns about someone else being irresponsible enough to fritter it away. I hope I never have debts as I did with Pen. Financial worries can ruin your life and your health. I like having my own space and being able to leave a mess in the kitchen if I want to. I don't think I will ever want to live with another man and feel trapped in a relationship that could turn sour.

I've met many new men and enjoyed the huge variety of ideas and stimulating conversation they've brought along the way. I wish online dating could be carried out without rejection on either side, but it's inevitable until you find 'the one'. It's a great fall-back option for people nowadays and fills me with hope. It helped me feel normal again after Pen's death, knowing there were people out there like me searching for their soulmate. If only it had been around when I was 20 – I wouldn't have had to go to so many discos!

The people I've met in my life who have left a lasting

impression are the calm, patient, quietly confident characters who find gentle, respectful ways to express their opinions, rather than becoming bullying, impatient or critical. Successful people often seem to be open and friendly, accepting of other people's differing traits, and never back-stabbing. They listen well, are generous enough to laugh at other people's jokes and don't seek attention or admiration. My goal is to emulate them.

I still have my health and play tennis, badminton, racquetball and table tennis, as well as taking part in ceroc dancing on a regular basis. I have a stable job within a 15-minute commute, and I can work from home three days a week. My mother and younger sister now live within 20 minutes. I have a nice group of friends, and don't feel I need any more, but I guess you can never have too many friends. I like my own company, and I like being with people (nice people).

If Robin doesn't work out and I never meet another man who could potentially be a partner, I would survive. I would rather be alone than with the wrong guy. People continue to meet their 'true love' in their seventies and eighties, so I might just have to wait. I feel at 59 that I have so much more of life to experience in the time remaining, especially now that I have the money and at the moment the freedom to enjoy it. I think the only real failure in life is to be so afraid of failure as to not have a go in the first place, or to give up trying.

I've tried many things and had my fair share of failures, but I've also come through many personal challenges and hope to try out many more. It would be so much more fun if I had someone by my side along the way; someone to hold my hand walking by the sea, to sit by the fire on a cold night with a glass of wine, and to chat about nothing and everything. This is what would bring me happiness and peace, and I will never give up trying to find it.

I've dipped into a strange erotic world, which I've thoroughly enjoyed, albeit with some considerable trepidation on occasion, and where I've met very 'normal', intelligent people who were brave enough to face and indulge their fantasies. But if I met that elusive special man, I would no longer share myself with the spanking world. I would, however, be able to draw on some deliciously erotic and sexy experiences, which I shall never forget.

5567328R00175

Printed in Germany
by Amazon Distribution
GmbH, Leipzig